CHILLING OUT

When people have their livelihoods threatened there's no telling what they'll do...

The body found in the Tamar is that of Dr Adam Goring, the executive behind the imminent closure of the Tamar Transfusion Centre, but who killed him and why did they freeze his body? On the day he disappeared, Goring had taken part in a debate on TV, in which Jessie Pengellis, the centre manager, accused him of corruption. He vowed to have her sacked and sue her for slander – tricky, now that he's dead. When Department of Health Inspector Tom Jones starts poking around the centre, he uncovers a hornets' nest of petty resentments and not so petty hatreds.

CHILLING OUT

CHILLING OUT

by

Andrew Puckett

Magna Large Print Books
Long Preston, North Yorkshire,
BD23 4ND, England.

British Library Cataloguing in Publication Data.

Puckett, Andrew
    Chilling out.

    A catalogue record of this book is
    available from the British Library

    ISBN   0-7505-1741-7

First published in Great Britain 1999
by Constable & Company Ltd.

Copyright © Andrew Puckett 1999

Cover illustration © Alexander Farnsworth by arrangement
with Swift Imagery International Photo Library

Published in Large Print 2001 by arrangement with
Constable & Robinson Ltd.

Magna Large Print is an imprint of Library Magna Books Ltd.

Printed and bound in Great Britain by
T.J. (International) Ltd., Cornwall, PL28 8RW

I would like to acknowledge the help I have had in writing this book, as always, from Carol Puckett. Also thanks are due to Dr Hugh White and John Croxton.

Author's Note

For many years, I worked for the Blood Transfusion Service in Oxford. Tamar Transfusion Centre does not exist and none of the characters portrayed herein are remotely like any I ever worked with or knew.

For Holly and Bryony

1

On a cold Monday morning in January, two boys who should have been at school were standing on the edge of a jetty skimming stones into the River Tamar.

'Wow! D'you see that? Ten!' said one of them, looking triumphantly at his companion. 'Better than borin' ol' history, eh?'

'Yeah,' said the other. He was called Ryan and was already wondering whether perhaps the joys of truancy were overrated. He threw his own stone, which to his surprise seemed to take on a life of its own, skimming away into the tendrils of mist that still ghosted the surface of the flood-tide river.

'Thirt–' he began, then said, 'What's that?' He pointed to where the stone had sunk.

'Dunno,' said the first boy, uninterestedly. Then, in a different tone, 'I reckon it looks like...'

The mists parted for a moment as a stray current took the object and turned it ... and as they watched, a hand sprang up from the muddy, tide-churned water, waved for a moment like some demented Lady of the Lake waiting for a sword, then vanished as quickly as it had appeared. The boys stared open-mouthed, then, at last, looked at each other.

'We oughta tell someone,' said Ryan.

'You can if you want,' said the other boy. 'I'm going to school.'

Thus it was that only Ryan caught the wrath of his father (although the thanks of the police) and learned to choose his friends more carefully in the future.

Two hours later, the body had been taken from the water and was on the bank behind screens. The police surgeon had arrived, declared the man dead and gone again, but not before he'd had something interesting to tell Inspector Bennett.

'This body has been frozen, put in a deep freeze or freezing-room after he died. You'll need the Home Office in on this.'

Forensic Pathology arrived an hour later in the person of Dr Ewan Randall, a short, plump man with greying sandy hair. He knelt down and studied the body from as many angles as he could before saying anything. The body itself was quite rigid, the knees drawn up as though the man had been kneeling, with one arm across his chest and the other, the one the boys had seen waving, outstretched.

'Well, the body's certainly been frozen,' Randall said at last. 'As you can see, it's still completely virgate.' He paused a moment. 'There's no obvious cause of death that I can see and I won't be able to look for one until it's thawed out.'

'How long is that likely to be, doctor?' asked Bennett diffidently – he'd met Randall before. Bennett himself was a man of about fifty with white hair and moustache and a face that always reminded Randall of a ferret.

'Tomorrow at the very earliest,' Randall told him, 'maybe even longer, so I'm afraid you'll have to curb your impatience.' He glanced at the detective, took pity on him and added, 'But we should be able to look through his clothes before then, which might help you with the identification.'

He ordered the Scene of Crime people to photograph the body and its surroundings, and also take samples from the ground and river.

Later that day, after another photographic session in the mortuary, he did go through the man's pockets, but they weren't much help – if there had been a wallet or any other form of identification, it had either been taken or slipped out into the river.

It wasn't until the following day, Tuesday, that Dr Adam Goring, normally resident in Surrey, was reported missing by his wife. He had come down to Tamar the previous Thursday to visit the Blood Transfusion Centre and take part in a TV programme about its impending closure. After that, he

15

was to have flown to America for a conference, which was where his wife had assumed he was until, after two days without contact, she'd phoned his hotel there to be told he'd never arrived.

Bennett showed Dr Goring's description to Randall, who agreed it was very similar to that of the dead man.

'And I think I know the name,' he said. 'Adam Goring isn't he the man who's behind the closure of a lot of the transfusion centres?'

'I'll take your word for that, doctor.'

Bennett had the director of the Tamar centre, Dr George Medlar, brought to the mortuary to see if he could identify the body.

'Yes, that's Adam Goring,' Dr Medlar said at last looking down at the body. He spoke with a distinct northern accent and, as the detective watched him, his angular face seemed to register a range of emotions – first, incredulity, then sadness, suffering and, finally, guilt... He turned suddenly to Bennett.

'You said he was found in the river – did he drown?'

'We don't know how he died yet, sir,' Bennett said noncommittally.

'Has his wife been told?'

'We were waiting on your identification.'

Medlar's eyes swivelled back to the body and he said slowly, 'I know her, and she'll take it badly...'

For a moment, Bennett thought he was offering to tell her himself, then he looked up and continued. 'Could you arrange for some support for her, for a WPC to be there?'

'That'll be done as a matter of course.'

'Good.' He paused. 'D'you need me here any longer, inspector?'

'I'll need a statement from you, sir. At the police station, if you wouldn't mind.'

'Yes, of course.'

As they walked out to the ante-room, something occurred to Bennett. 'Would there by any chance be a freezing-room at your establishment?'

'Yes, there is – why?'

'I'll explain later, sir.' He found his sergeant, Mulholland, told him to go to the transfusion centre and have the freezing-room sealed off, then found Randall and explained what he'd done. Then he went back to Medlar.

The doctor's reactions to Adam Goring's body had aroused Bennett's interest and, although he hadn't intended to start questioning him until they were down at the station, something made him say now, 'You've obviously known Dr Goring a long time, sir?'

17

'Oh yes...' Medlar was trying to speak lightly, but failing. 'Adam and I go back a long, long way – *went* back, I mean – why does everyone make that mistake? Is there somewhere I could wash my hands, please?'

After they'd gone, Randall decided he could start the PM that day, provided he opened up the body to hasten the thawing process, so he and his technicians gowned up and got down to business. *Let's see if we can find out what happened to you before you were dumped in that freezer,* he thought to himself. *And perhaps even why you were dumped there...*

Adam Goring had been an overweight, but otherwise healthy man, and his body showed no signs of external injury, other than some bruising and minor laceration to the hands. His skin was slightly discoloured and there were signs of peripheral frost-bite. There were no internal injuries – other than the tissue damage caused by the freezing – and no sign of disease. There were, in fact, no indications whatsoever of the cause of his death.

2

'So when was the last time you saw him, sir?' Bennett asked. He and Medlar were in an interview room at the police station.

'It would have been on Friday afternoon at about three, I suppose.' Medlar had recovered some of his composure now and was speaking naturally. He was what Bennett thought of as a 'middle man': middle-aged and of middling height and build. He had grey eyes, greying hair and moustache, and his face, Bennett noticed, although naturally rather angular, held the haunted expression of a man under severe stress.

'And that was at the transfusion centre?'

'Yes, in my office.' He'd already explained to Bennett how Goring had come down from London the day before to take part in the TV debate.

'D'you know where he went after that?'

'I assumed he'd gone back to his hotel. He was due to fly to America on Sunday, which is why I was so surprised when...' and he tailed off.

Bennett paused for a moment, then said, 'I believe he was the man behind the closure of your centre, sir?'

Medlar looked up, his grey eyes meeting Bennett's. 'Yes, he was, but how did you know that?'

'Dr Randall recognised the name and told me. So he wouldn't have been a popular man there?'

'No, but–' Medlar gave a half-laugh – 'I'm sure that has no bearing... Surely Adam's death has to be some kind of accident?'

'Perhaps.' Bennett paused again 'When you last saw him, was he upset about anything, depressed?'

'Depressed, no – Adam didn't recognise depression. He was certainly angry.'

Bennett's expression became alert. 'Angry about what, sir?' Medlar, he noticed, was suddenly looking uncomfortable. He pulled a battered pipe out of his pocket and applied a lighter to it, obviously giving himself time to think.

At last he said, 'The television debate he'd taken part in hadn't gone very well from his point of view and he was upset about it.'

'Hadn't gone well in what way, sir?'

Medlar blew smoke. 'He was accused of ... doing something dishonourable.'

'What, exactly?'

'Look, inspector–' he took the pipe out of his mouth – 'I really don't think it's relevant.'

'Perhaps you'd let me be the judge of that,

sir. What was he accused of?'

Medlar's lips pursed, then he shrugged and said, 'Nepotism, I suppose.'

'By whom? Who accused him?'

'My laboratory manager, Jessie Pengellis.'

'And this was live, on local television?'

'It was broadcast nationally.'

'I see.' Bennett paused again. 'You said Dr Goring was angry – in what way was he angry?'

Medlar shrugged. 'Just angry...'

'But how did he express his anger? Did he threaten Miss Pengellis? I'm assuming it's a Miss...?'

'Yes.' Medlar sucked at the pipe, which had gone out, then took some tobacco from his pocket and began filling it. 'He had her suspended, pending an enquiry ... and he told me that after she was sacked, he was going to sue her for slander.'

'Did he mean it?'

'He probably did at the time, although I'm sure he'd have cooled off while he was in America.'

Bennett assumed the pun was unknowing. 'Is that what you really think, sir?'

Another pause, then Medlar shrugged again. 'I don't know.'

'Did Miss Pengellis know what was in store for her?'

'Yes. I had to tell her myself, that after-noon.'

'Was she upset?'

'Of course she was upset, how would you have expected her to be?'

'What time was this?'

'I'm not sure exactly. It wasn't long after Adam left, say about quarter-past, half-past three.'

'D'you know what she did after that, where she went?'

'Not offhand, no. Home, I assumed.'

'Was she upset enough to go and have it out with Dr Goring?'

'I'd very much doubt it,' Medlar said firmly. 'Her main priority was to avoid being sacked, in order to avoid being sued for slander. She knew that.'

'But with Dr Goring dead, she won't be sued now, will she, sir?'

'Inspector,' Medlar said, an edge to his voice, 'I think you might be in danger of jumping to conclusions. I think we should wait until we know exactly how Adam died before engaging in this kind of conjecture.'

Bennett tried to swallow his own irritation. He was more certain than ever that Medlar was trying to stall, cover something up... 'And I think I'd like to know more about how this dispute between them came about, sir.'

3

Thursday, and Jessie was so absorbed in what she was writing that she didn't hear the phone at first. When it did force itself on to her consciousness, she snatched at it and snapped 'Yes?' before remembering herself and saying, 'Sorry, Jessie Pengellis speaking.'

'It's Dr Medlar, Jessie. Would you come along to my office, please?'

'Yes, doctor...' She was about to say more, but a clunk in her ear told her he'd put the phone down.

She replaced her own phone, then slowly took off her reading glasses and put them in their case. What did he want? She and the director, George Medlar, were on first name terms, in private at least, which included the phone – unless he had someone with him...

Who?

She put the file she'd been working on away and looked into the lab office.

'Nina, I'll be with Dr Medlar. If there're any problems, ask Dominic – OK?'

She set off down the corridor past the laboratories: Cross Matching, Plasma Products... *Tomorrow*, she thought, *It has to be about tomorrow*. A bulky, slightly rumpled figure materialised in front of her.

'Jessie, did you see the memo I left for you?' Paul Bannister, head of Donor Grouping.

'Er – not really, Paul, I haven't had the time. I'll deal with it when I get back, OK?'

He didn't move. 'It really is urgent, Jessie, I can't even guarantee to get today's blood banked.'

'I'm sorry,' she said firmly, 'but it'll have to wait.' She smiled, a twist of the lips. 'I've been summoned to the presence. As soon as I get back, OK?'

Still he wouldn't move. Determined not to give way even to the degree of going round him, she said, 'Excuse me,' and he reluctantly stepped back.

Why was it he still had the power to intimidate her? she wondered as she started walking again. She was his boss, wasn't she...? Ah, but that was the trouble, *sod* him! She took a breath, she had a strong feeling she was going to need a cool head for what was coming...

She paused outside the director's suite.

'Who's with him, Annie?' she asked his secretary.

'Dr Goring.' Annie looked meaningfully back at her.

So that was it! No wonder he'd been so formal... So what was it to be? Threats? An appeal to her better self? No point in hanging around... She tapped on the door and pushed it open as Medlar called, 'Come in.'

He was at the conference table rather than behind his desk. Goring was sitting beside him.

'Sit down, Jessie.' He gestured at a chair. 'You know Dr Goring, of course.'

'Of course.' She sat down.

Medlar paused as though not quite sure how to begin, then said, 'It was Dr Goring who requested this meeting, so I'll hand over to him. Adam?'

Goring looked at her without speaking and she found herself comparing the two men, thinking how different they were. Both in their early fifties with that age's stigmata, both conservatively dressed, but Medlar's grey eyes and moustache somehow made him the gentler of the two – in any hard man/soft man scenario, it would always be Goring cast as the former.

His eyes – hard eyes, they were – didn't leave her face and at last he spoke. 'Miss Pengellis, I did indeed suggest this meeting because I hope that, even now, we can find some accommodation.'

They were brown, his eyes, a colour you'd normally associate with softness...

'You see, I don't want the Transfusion Service to lose someone of your obvious talents. We're going to need people like you in the future.'

Soft words from a hard man – soft lies to soften her up?

'So please, can we try and find some position we can agree on?'

'We can certainly try, Dr Goring.'

Another silence, while still he stared. She stared back. *Jowly*, she thought, *ugly as a turnip, but that face has power.*

'I've come down today,' he said, 'because I've decided to accept Western TV's invitation to participate in tomorrow's programme.'

Great! she thought, trying to keep it hidden.

Medlar saw the triumphant flash in her dark eyes and suppressed a smile. *Adam doesn't know what he's taking on,* he thought. *Never underestimate a Cornishman, never mind a Cornishwoman.* Her eyes were as brown as Goring's, but deep rather than hard or soft. She was thirty-three, had springy brown hair and a watchful Celtic face. She wore a dark blue dress with the sleeves buttoned at the wrists.

'However,' Goring continued, 'I'm going to suggest to you that it won't be necessary.' Another pause, then, 'In fact, it can only do both of us harm.'

You speak for yourself...

'So let's try and sort out something between us now, shall we? What can I offer you, how can I help break this deadlock?'

'All I ask for, Dr Goring, is what I've always asked for – a public enquiry.'

His mouth tightened, but he said quietly enough, 'Into what, exactly?'

'Into the proposed reforms of the Transfusion Service. Into whether the closure of this centre, and the four others, is in the public interest.'

'But as you already know, Miss Pengellis, the matter has been exhaustively discussed at ministerial level, and it has been agreed that the reforms are indeed in the public interest. To go over–'

'But you've acted as judge and jury in your own case. There has to be an *independent*–'

'To go over it again,' Goring overrode her, 'would serve no useful purpose. These reforms are going ahead and as a result we will offer the public a better service.'

'Then there's no point in discussing–'

'I want you to be part of this better service, Jessie,' he said, leaning forward. 'Call off your campaign, for your own sake, for all our sakes. Tell Western TV you're not coming, or better still, we could appear together and in agreement. I promise you there'll be a job for you in one of the other centres, a good job, commensurate with your present position.'

'In charge of the stores at Sheffield, perhaps?' Jessie sneered. 'How can there be a position commensurate with what I have here? There're going to be five of us lab managers looking for jobs and I don't see any of the other managers moving aside for us.' She could hear the Cornish burr breaking into her voice now, the rounding of the vowels as it became heated.

'As a matter of fact,' Goring said gently, 'Don Chambers at the East London centre is taking early retirement.'

'But that's one job, between five people...' Why did his voice always sound so calm compared with hers?

'Of course you're not all going to walk straight into managers' jobs,' Goring said. 'But there's nothing to stop you applying for this one. I'm sure Dr Medlar would give you an excellent reference, and I see no reason why you shouldn't...' He tailed off, then continued. 'Anyway, whatever happens, you'll have the same salary as you have now, and the same opportunities for advancement.'

'What about the other thirty lab staff here, Dr Goring? And the drivers, the clerical staff, the donor attendants...?'

'I wasn't aware that they came within your remit–' Goring stopped himself, swallowed. 'As you know, everyone here will be offered either a job in another centre, or a generous redundancy package.'

'But what if they don't want to move to Leeds, or London, or Manchester?'

'Then they'll have to choose between that and the dole,' Goring snapped, losing his temper at last. He swallowed again. 'I don't think there's any point in taking this any further now,' he said. 'Think about it, Miss Pengellis. At the very least, a good job at the same salary. Generous – *very* generous moving expenses. I'll be here for the rest of the day. Think about it, come and talk to me again if you like, but for your own sake, call off this campaign.'

'What if I don't, Dr Goring? Call off my campaign.'

He took a deep breath, then slowly released it. 'Then you will be deemed to have shown yourself of no further use to the Transfusion Service. You'll be made re-dundant.'

'But how–?' she began, then stopped. They, Goring and his cronies, would doubtless prefer the centre to carry on without her for the remaining six months of its existence.

'Will that be all, Dr Goring?' she asked, just this side of rudeness.

'Yes, for the moment.'

'Then I'll get back to my work.' She got up and left, pulling the door closed behind her.

The two men didn't say anything at first. Medlar pulled out his pipe, a battered Edward Peterson, and began filling it.

'D'you still use that thing?' Goring asked,

staring at it.

'Looks like it.'

'I thought this was a No Smoking hospital.'

'Rank hath its privileges,' said Medlar, applying his lighter to the bowl.

Goring flapped at the smoke. 'Well, is she going to back down?'

Medlar puffed away, wondering at the other's obtuseness. When the pipe was going to his satisfaction, he said, 'Listening to her, Adam, what did you think?'

'It didn't sound much like it, I'll agree, but you know her better than me. Perhaps, after reflection...'

'I wouldn't bet on it, Adam – she's a lady of principle, is our Jessica.'

The accents of both men bespoke their northern origins, although Goring's had been softened by his years spent in London.

'Were you really going to help her get the East London job?' Medlar asked.

'That wouldn't be up to me,' Goring said pointedly. Then: 'I'd make sure she was found something.'

'So she wasn't far wrong about the stores in Sheffield?'

'What's wrong with Sheffield?' Goring demanded. 'We both cut our teeth there.'

'You were glad enough to get away, I seem to remember,' Medlar said drily.

'George–' Goring leaned forward –

'choosing where you work is not an option for anyone, let alone a professional.'

'If you say so, Adam.'

'I *do* say so, and there's something else I have to say.' Irritation sharpened his tone. 'It's been suggested at HQ that perhaps you could have done a bit more to keep your staff in order.'

'You mean Jessie and her campaign?' Medlar said, thinking: *Suggested by whom, I wonder?*

'Yes, I do mean Jessie and her campaign,' Goring snapped.

Medlar took his pipe out of his mouth. 'As you know, Adam, I've always believed in keeping my staff on a light rein. I've found, over the years, that it pays.' The words, although not hostile in themselves, were honed with meaning. 'I've warned Jessie that she hasn't made any friends in high places by what she's doing, and where she's overstepped the bounds, I've told her to stop. But don't expect me to threaten my staff for trying to save their jobs.'

'All right, George, I think we understand each other.' Goring held his hands up in conciliation. 'We ought to, after so many years.'

'Indeed,' Medlar said softly.

Back in her office, Jessie sat down, took a few deep breaths, then picked up the phone.

31

'Dommo, it's Jessie – got a few minutes?'

'Sure.'

Dominic Tudor was Jessie's deputy and ran the Microbiology Department. He was with her inside a minute.

'Did you know Goering was here?' she asked as he sat down.

'Annie told me about ten minutes ago. Has he been having a go at you?'

'You could say that.'

Dominic listened while she told him about the meeting. He was a smallish man, albeit a strong one, and at five feet six only a couple of inches taller than her. Everything about him was neat – his shirt and tie, his short dark hair, the small dark beard and moustache that framed his mouth – and Jessie found herself thinking: *It's funny, he isn't bad-looking and I like him, but I could no more fancy him than I could … well, Paul…*

'What I need to know,' she said, 'Is whether everybody's still on board, whether I can rely on their support.'

He thought for a moment before replying. 'Ashley and Verity, yes. Maria and Adrian are wavering and Paul, you can rely on absolutely – to let you down.'

She smiled wanly. 'What about you, Dommo?'

He said carefully, 'You know you've got my support, but would you like some advice?'

'Depends what it is, I suppose.'

He smiled. 'That's the trouble with advice, you're never thanked for it, no matter how well intended.'

'Come on, Dommo, out with it.'

He said slowly, 'I've supported you throughout this, because I've believed in what you were doing, but I'm wondering whether now might be the time for you to stop.'

She gazed at him incredulously. 'You know how long I've been trying to fix up this interview – and to have actually got him to agree to appear on it... I can't stop now.'

'Jessie, even if you win this fight – and that's not a foregone conclusion – the war's already been lost.'

'How can you *say* that–?'

'The reorganisation's gone too far now to stop, even if they wanted to – it's a *fait accompli*.' Dominic was part French and liked to remind people of the fact. 'Even if everything you've said comes true and it's all a total disaster, no one'll thank you. All you'll succeed in doing tomorrow is to make yourself unemployable. It's time you thought about yourself.'

'But it's not about *me*,' she cried. 'Can't you see that? If we can get enough people to complain to their MPs, write to the Health Minister, we can still force them to...'

He was gently shaking his head.

'So I can't rely on your support any more?'

'I didn't say that, I just said you can't win. I'll tell everyone who'll listen that I support you and if they try to sack you, I'll join in any union action–' He broke off. 'You have told the union about this, haven't you?'

'Not yet, and you're right, I must. But thanks, Dommo, that's what I needed to hear, that I've got your support.'

'It's little enough.' He looked slightly embarrassed. 'You're happy about taking Goering on in front of all the TV cameras?'

She nodded. 'Yes, I've got all the facts and figures – and oddly enough, this morning's little fracas was a help.'

'In what way?'

She leaned forward. 'Something that really came over this time – if you put him under pressure, he loses his cool, gets nasty, and it shows.'

'He might not be the same in front of the TV cameras, they might concentrate his mind.'

'We'll see,' she said, 'we'll see. I'm feeling good about it, Dommo.'

He nodded gently, then said, 'I'd better get on.'

As soon as he'd gone, she phoned her union and told them what had happened. They sounded dubious and advised her to do nothing until they got back to her.

Heigh ho, she thought as she put the phone down.

She brought the file back out of the cabinet and opened it. It was all there, everything she needed to beat him. There was a knock on her door and she looked up. Paul.

'Have you seen my memo yet?'

'Er – hang on a moment and I'll look at it now.'

She found it underneath the file.

From: Head of Blood Grouping
To: Laboratory Manager
A potentially dangerous situation is developing in this department due to the shortage of properly trained staff. If this is not remedied, I can no longer accept responsibility for the prompt and accurate grouping of blood.

Pompous bastard! she thought. Of course he was having difficulties with staff, they *all* were – the decent ones were leaving and who the hell wanted to come and work in a place that was due to close in six months?

She said carefully, 'I'm sorry you're having problems, Paul, but it's not easy recruiting staff at the moment. Is there a specific problem?'

His eyes hunted around behind his spectacles, refusing to meet hers. 'I'm two staff down, as you know, and I've had two more off sick since the beginning of the week. The only way I've managed to keep things going is by doing routine work myself. I can't do that and trouble-shoot and do all the admin as well.'

You could if you stayed behind occasionally like the rest of us... 'Have you asked any of the others for help?'

'They all say they're too busy themselves.'

She thought for a moment. Four down was rather a lot.

'I'll see what I can do – OK?'

'If you find me someone, yes,' he said grudgingly.

She had been wondering whether a personal appeal to him might get him on her side, but the implacable expression on his face made her realise it was useless.

As he left the room, a wave of misery swept over her. Were the others feeling the same way? Who *could* she rely on now?

Suddenly, she had to get out, get away... She stripped off her coat, told Nina she was going to lunch, then slipped away along the back corridor so that no one could see her. She slammed the exit plate with her palm in irritation at her cowardice – it rang out like an anvil and she blundered through the sliding doors into the aerial passageway that led to the main hospital. Below her, the city glinted in the winter sunlight and through the haze she could make out the plateau of the moors beyond. Dartmoor ... normally a view that raised her spirits, but not today – today was vinegar in her mouth and every nerve end jangled with the unfairness of it. How had it come to this?

She emerged into the main corridor of the hospital and the hordes – doctors, nurses, porters with patients on trolleys, visitors – they all pressed around her. In desperation, she plunged through a door on her right with crudely shaped pieces of coloured glass instead of a window – and found herself in the hospital chapel.

4

Jessie wasn't religious and never had been, but now she sat down and sucked the silence gratefully into her lungs. Other than the vulgar stained glass in the door, it wasn't an unattractive place in its simple way, she thought. Pale walls, dim lighting, dark wooden cross on a white altar cloth. She leaned back and closed her eyes. How the hell had it all come to this?

What am I going to do? She opened her eyes again and looked up. *And answer came there none. You're on your own, Jessie, so what's new?*

She allowed her body to relax and her mind started drifting back, over the events that had brought her here...

Her wrecked marriage, the hospital lab where she'd worked as a senior until a male colleague was promoted instead of her, and then, against all the odds, the lab manager's job here in the Transfusion Centre. Later, she'd heard on the grapevine that it was George Medlar who'd stood out for her appointment.

And it had worked out. She'd gradually overcome the staff's suspicion and hostility – with the exception of Paul, who'd thought the job his by right – and a sense of purpose had taken hold of the labs, united them ... and then came the bolt. Five of England's fifteen Transfusion Centres to be closed in a reorganisation by the new Blood Division, and one of them Tamar.

No arguments, no debates, or so said the mandarins. But she, Jessie Pengellis, had had different ideas. She'd gathered data showing the drawbacks of the new system, the hardships the region's hospitals would suffer, and started her campaign. She was interviewed by the local papers, on radio and TV. She'd lobbied the local MP, who'd raised the question in the House.

The mandarins had first ignored her, then tried to gag her, and now she was to meet Adam Goring, the architect of the reforms, face to face on a national TV programme. She knew she could beat him, so why had it all turned to ashes?

Was it because Dommo was right, that no matter how many battles she won, the cause was lost? That soon she'd be out on her bum and unemployable? The union obviously thought so too... Her face screwed up as her fingers dug into her thighs and salty water squeezed through her eyelids...

They were *right*.

There was nothing left for her to do but make some sort of obeisance to Turnip Face and then try to rebuild some sort of career somewhere else...

No!

With a jerk, she sat up.

No, they *weren't* right. They outnumbered her, they were more powerful than her, but that didn't make them right.

She found herself remembering something her father had once said to her when she was being bullied at school: 'If you believe you're in the right, then don't give into them, no matter what. Because if you do, it'll stay with you for the rest of your life.'

She blew her nose, got to her feet and made for the door. It opened just before she reached it and the hospital chaplain came in.

He smiled uncertainly. 'Hello.'

'Hello.'

'Can I help you at all?'

'No, thank you.'

Well timed, she thought as she mingled with the throng outside. She went to the League of Friends, had a cheese roll and coffee, and then went back to the centre.

Deliberately, she turned left rather than right, into the main corridor past the labs. The door of the gents' loo opened and George Medlar emerged. There was no one else about.

'Jessie,' he said quietly. 'I'll do my best, but if it gets nasty, I may not be able to help you.'

Before she could reply, Adam Goring came out of the director's suite and walked towards them.

'Well, what did she have to say for herself?' Goring demanded. They were in the lift that went down to the vehicle park underneath the centre.

'Not a lot. I was telling her that if things got bad, there was a limit to how much I could help her.'

'Well, that's no less than the truth. What did she say?'

'You came on the scene before she could say anything.'

Goring grunted. 'If I'd known, I'd have stayed put. So we still don't know what she's going to do?'

'No.'

The lift stopped, the doors slid open and they stepped into the half-world of the underground park. The centre's trucks and vans peered at them through the gloom as they walked to Medlar's car. He pointed his key, the locks clicked and they got in.

'Well, let's hope she sees sense,' Goring said as they emerged into the sunshine. 'I've got a feeling she will when she realises what she stands to lose.'

'I wouldn't bank on it, Adam.'

'We'll see. It'll be her funeral if she doesn't.'

Medlar gave a non-committal grunt and they drove in silence for a while. They were lunching with the General Manager of the Regional Health Authority.

'Good of you and Sarah to have me over for dinner tonight,' Goring said suddenly. 'I hope it's not putting you out.'

'Not at all.' *Of course it's putting us out, you moron...* Medlar had been astonished, then dismayed when Goring had accepted the routine and insincerely put invitation. 'Sarah will be delighted to see you again.'

'And I her.' He studied Medlar's face. 'How is she at the moment?'

'Pretty well, considering,' he said, not wanting to talk about it. 'Here we are.' He drew into a space and pulled on the handbrake.

Shit! The file she normally kept locked away was grinning up at her from her desk ... how long had she been gone? An hour? *You're getting paranoid, Jessie,* she told herself as she put it away and slammed the cabinet drawer.

The thought of going round the department heads trying to rally support appealed to her not at all. No, the best approach would be to get them together in her room and all agree on something, no matter how loose.

She rang round and, with varying degrees of enthusiasm, they agreed. All that is except Adrian Hodges, who ran the Issue Department. He was too busy. Adrian was always too busy for anything, especially meetings, but usually managed to turn up just after they'd started.

Dominic was the first to arrive and carefully moved his chair next to hers – he always did that, she noticed, presumably to underline the fact that he was her deputy.

Next came Ashley Miles ('Wotcher, Jessie...') a fair-haired, fresh-faced extrovert of about thirty who ran the Reagents Lab. Closely following were Paul, Verity Blane from Plasma Products, and Maria N'Kanu, who was in charge of Cross Matching.

When they'd all found seats, Jessie said, 'We may as well start now, Adrian said he'd come when he could.'

'Which I wager'll be in exactly...' Ashley made a show of consulting his watch. '...two minutes from now.' There were one or two chuckles, but no takers.

'I'll get the minor matter out of the way first,' Jessie continued. 'Are any of you fully staffed this week?'

'Chance'd be a fine thing,' muttered Verity.

'I am,' Maria said. Her voice was soft, slightly husky.

'Can you lend someone to Paul? He's four down and having problems.'

'For how long?' Maria asked. 'Next week might be difficult for me.'

'Let's say this afternoon and tomorrow – we'll worry about next week next week. OK, Paul?'

'Yes. Thanks, Maria.' He made it plain that his gratitude was for her alone.

'Let's move on to the main business...' The door opened and a thickset man of about forty with greying hair came in.

'Sorry I'm late.'

'OK, Adrian. Find a seat.'

Ashley was looking ostentatiously at his watch and some of the others tried to smother grins. Adrian looked round resentfully. 'What's so damn funny?' he demanded.

'Nothing, Adrian,' Jessie soothed. When he'd sat down, she continued, 'I think you all know about the Western TV programme tomorrow – well, there's been a development. Dr Goring from the Blood Division now says he wants to take part in it.'

There was a buzz as people reacted in different ways. 'Is that good or bad?' Ashley asked.

'I saw him arriving,' Verity said. 'I'd assumed he'd come to stick electrodes on to you.'

'He did, in a manner of speaking...' Jessie told them what had happened, but leaving out the threat of redundancy.

'So what are you going to do?' Verity asked.

'I want to go ahead with it, more than ever.' She looked round at them. 'But I have to be able to say that I have the full support of all of you.'

'Goes without saying, doesn't it?' Ashley again, and there was a murmur of agreement. 'Unless there's something you haven't told us.'

'I don't think so, but this would be make or break, so I must be able to present us as a united front.'

'Then there's no question,' said Verity with a shrug. 'You have our full and unconditional support.' There were nods and more murmurs of agreement.

'Thank you,' Jessie said. She'd intended leaving it there, but then Dominic spoke up.

'There's something Jessie's left out.'

She looked askance at him.

'There's every chance that they're going to try and sack her after tomorrow and I think we need to pledge her–'

'Dommo, this isn't the time–' she began as Verity said,

'Is that true, Jessie?'

She hesitated. 'I don't know. It's a possibility, but–'

'What did you mean just now?' Verity asked Dominic. 'The union? Industrial action?'

Dominic nodded. 'That's exactly what I meant.'

'Well, I have no problem with that,' Verity said, looking round.

'Nor me,' said Ashley.

'Well, I *do* have a problem with it,' Paul said, biting off the words. 'It's all right for Verity, who's got private means, or Ashley, with no kids, but I've got four. I want to get another job after the centre closes, and I'm–'

'But that's the whole point,' said Jessie, trying to regain the initiative. 'If we can prevent closure, then you won't have to look for another job.'

'But the centre *is* going to close,' Paul said. 'I wish it wasn't, but it is, and we all know it. Of course I support what you've been trying to do, but I'm not taking industrial action.'

'Nor me,' said Adrian.

'Well, I will, if it comes to it,' said Dominic. 'Who'll join me?'

Verity and Ashley raised their fingers.

'Maria?' Dominic looked at her.

'I – I need to think about it. Of course I appreciate what you've done for us, Jessie, but I don't know about industrial action. Wouldn't it turn the public against us, make things worse?'

'Well, I don't think it's going to come to that,' Jessie said firmly. 'All I'm asking for at the moment is your support for tomorrow.'

Paul pressed his lips together. 'All right,' he said, 'you've got that. And now, if you don't mind, I have work to do.'

As he got up to go, there was a knock on the door and Steve Tanner, Dominic's deputy, put his head in.

'Sorry to interrupt, but I thought I ought to tell Dominic that the minus thirty door is jamming.'

'All right, I'll come and have a look,' Dominic said, standing up. He was the centre's Safety Officer.

'Dommo,' Jessie called after him, 'I want to see you when you've done that.'

'OK.' He raised a hand without looking round.

The meeting broke up and people filed out. Verity moved over to her. 'A wordlet?'

Jessie nodded curtly. 'All right.'

'Are you mad at him?' Verity asked when she'd shut the door.

'Dommo? Yes. I am rather.'

'Well, he shouldn't have homed in the way he did, but isn't it possible he has a point?'

'That was not why I called the meeting.'

'I know that.' She hesitated. 'What did Goering actually say to you?'

Jessie realised that she wanted to tell Verity about it. 'Sit down,' she said.

'So it's back off or else?' Verity said when she'd finished. 'You won't, of course.'

Jessie shook her head. 'That's why I called the meeting – to try and cobble together some sort of united front.'

'You wouldn't have *had* to do any cobbling if it wasn't for Paul. Slimy scrote,' she growled. 'Who'd give him a job, anyway?'

She had straight honey hair, blue eyes and a classic profile and Jessie thought she was almost beautiful; she found herself wondering again why she wasn't attached... *But for all I know, she is.*

At most times, and with most people, Verity Blane surrounded herself with an invisible barrier, and yet at other times, Jessie felt there was an unspoken bond between them.

Verity said thoughtfully, 'You know, in some ways it might not be such a bad thing if they did try to sack you–'

'Oh, thanks.'

'No, listen... Some sort of industrial action might be just what we need now, to raise our profile and concentrate minds.'

Bit of a firebrand, aren't you, despite the cut-glass accent. 'I don't know, Verity, it only needs one newspaper or TV report about us putting patients' lives at risk and we'd be finished... Maria's right, it's best avoided if possible.'

'You may not have a choice, Jessie.'

'Let's wait and see, shall we?'

Verity looked for a moment as though she wanted to continue the argument, then shrugged and smiled. 'OK...' She paused. 'How does George stand in all this?'

'Oh, studied neutrality.'

'Has it ever occurred to you that he's using you, making the bullets for you to fire?'

'He's got troubles of his own, Verity. He's worried sick about Sarah, and how he's—'

'Very laudable, I'm sure, but don't you think he's being just a teeny weeny bit hypocritical there?'

Jessie looked back at her. 'I didn't hear that,' she said. Then, 'You don't like him much, do you?'

'Oh, he's all right. It's just that I don't think he should be leaving the defence of this place to you.' She sighed, got to her feet. 'I've said enough, so I'll leave you in peace. But if I can be of any help...'

'Thanks, Verity.'

She touched Jessie's shoulder, then gently squeezed it. 'Nil Carborundum, eh?'

Verity walked thoughtfully back towards her own lab, then, on impulse, continued down the corridor and round the corner to the Microbiology suite. She pushed the door open and went into the main lab.

There was nobody there, no sound, save the whisper of the ventilators that kept the suite under negative pressure because of the hazardous material stored in the adjoining containment lab.

Bad, she thought, to leave a department unattended – there should always be someone to answer the phone...

As though on cue, the phone in Dominic's office at the other end of the main lab began ringing. She hesitated, then realised that there *was* someone there, working in the containment lab, but they were gowned up and unable to come out. She crossed the room and picked up the phone.

'Microbiology Lab.'

'Is Mr Tudor there, please?' The voice seemed vaguely familiar.

'Not just at the moment, I'm afraid. Can I–? Wait, he's just come in.' She held out the receiver to Dominic, who took it.

'Hello? Er ... no, not at the moment... All right, yes.' He banged the phone down rather pettishly and turned to Verity. 'Can I help you at all, or is this just a social visit?'

'No, it isn't,' she said irritably. 'I just came to tell you that I found myself in agreement with you for once. If we don't do something positive, Jessie is going to lose her job as well as her campaign for the centre.'

'By positive, I assume you mean some sort of industrial action?'

'Well, you were the one who suggested it.'

'But we're in a minority, aren't we?'

'Well, there's you, me, Ashley...'

'And Paul and Adrian and Maria against.'

She snorted. 'Since when did Paul and Adrian count for anything?'

'Do they not have votes,' he asked sonorously, paraphrasing Shylock, 'as we do...?'

'Oh, for God's sake,' she snapped, 'whose side are you on – other than your own?' Not for the first time, she had to physically suppress the urge to slap him.

'On Jessie's, believe it or not,' he said. The door opened and Steve, his deputy, came back in. 'Talking of whom, she wanted to see me, didn't she?' He walked off, leaving her staring after him.

'Well, you weren't going to tell them, were you?' he said defiantly a couple of minutes later.

'No, I wasn't,' Jessie said, 'because I didn't want them to know, not yet, anyway. All you succeeded in doing–'

'Jessie, Goering is going to try and sack you. You have to know who's going to stick up for you.'

'All you've succeeded in doing is driving a wedge between them when I wanted them united. There's no way–'

'They never were united, Paul was always going to let you down.'

'Not necessarily ... and all that talk of industrial action, you even succeeded in driving Maria away.'

They stared at each other a moment, then Dominic dropped his eyes.

'I'm sorry, Jessie, I just thought it would help to–'

'But you *didn't* think, that's the trouble.'

'I thought it was time they knew what it's costing you.'

Jessie let out a sigh. 'All right, Dominic, I'm sure you meant well ... just don't do it again, OK?'

'I just wanted to say I'm sorry if it seemed like I was letting you down.' Maria N'Kanu sat uncomfortably, twisting her fingers, rather like a naughty child, Jessie thought.

There *was* something childlike about Maria, a simplicity that was usually refreshing for its honesty, but now, faced with moral dilemmas, it was somehow pathetic.

'It's OK, Maria – I know how you feel

about industrial action. I wouldn't do it myself, except as a last resort.'

'Is it going to come to that? Are they really going to try and sack you?'

'I don't know, I hope not. It is a possibility, though.'

'You see, I'm on call this weekend, so it would be me who'd–'

'It's not going to happen that quickly,' Jessie said with a smile, 'so you can stop worrying.'

'Well, that's something...' Her face relaxed a little.

I don't think I've ever seen her wearing make-up, Jessie thought, looking at her. *Inclination or upbringing?* Maria's father was a Kenyan diplomat, long-time resident in Britain, and had sent his daughter to an expensive, although somewhat old-fashioned school...

'Is there any other way I can help you?' Jessie asked without quite knowing why.

'I don't think so, thanks. You know how it is.'

'Yes, I think I do, Maria.'

Her face in repose wasn't beautiful, or even pretty; its attractiveness lay in its strength.

'If they really do try and sack you, Jessie,' she said quietly but with intensity, 'I won't let you down.'

5

He turned as the rattle of the taxi died away and stared for a moment at the outline of the old farmhouse before starting up the drive. The farmer and his fields were long gone and it was, Goring thought, just the sort of place where he'd have expected George and Sarah to end up. He reached the porch and gripped the bell handle.

He'd had a busy evening already. A visitor had called at his hotel room and stayed for half an hour's urgent talk, then he'd phoned his office in London before bathing and dressing.

Footsteps, then Medlar pulled the heavy door open.

'Come in, Adam, let me have your coat.' He hung it up. 'No trouble in finding us, then?'

'The taxi driver didn't have any. I might have.'

Medlar smiled. 'Come on through and say hello to Sarah.' He led the way into a comfortable living-room.

'Hello, Sarah,' Goring said softly. His voice was trembling slightly, he noticed.

'Adam, how good to see you.'

He bent over the steel framework of the

wheelchair and kissed her flaccid cheek.

'Sit down,' she said, 'by the fire. It's a bitter night, isn't it?'

'It is,' he agreed. *What can I say to her?* he agonised. *I can't say "How are you?" or "You look well"*...

'A drink, Adam?' Medlar asked.

'Whisky and soda, please, George.'

'Of course, we're spoiled down here,' Sarah said as her husband went over to the sideboard. 'This is the first really cold snap we've had. How's Audrey?'

'Well, thank you. She asked to be remembered to you.'

'And I, her.' Sarah paused. 'And Richard and Fiona?'

It was as though she had divined his difficulty and was making it easy for him, he thought, as he told her what his children were doing.

Sarah Medlar had still been a beautiful woman at fifty, but then, ironically on her birthday, the first symptoms of multiple sclerosis had manifested themselves. It's a disease that can sometimes be merciful, slow-developing with remissions, but not in Sarah's case. After just eighteen months, she was wheelchair-bound, her useless body bloated with drugs. She still had mobility of her head and one arm.

I'd have still recognised her, Goring told himself...

'Adam?' Medlar handed him his drink, then carefully placed Sarah's in her hand.

She raised it. 'Good health,' she said.

Her eyes, he thought, as they sparkled ironically at him, *I'd have recognised those eyes*.

'What are Hugh and James doing now?' he asked.

'Hugh's still at RADA and James started medical school last autumn.'

'You must be proud of them.'

'I think I'll wait a few more years before committing myself to *that*,' she said, her eyes still twinkling. 'One should never underestimate the capacity of one's children to let one down.'

He chuckled; he should have remembered her acerbic wit.

'Dr Medlar?' a soft voice called. 'It's all ready.'

Goring looked round to see a soberly dressed woman of about forty in the doorway.

'Thanks, Mary. We're eating in the kitchen,' he said to Goring. 'We find it easier.'

He released the brake on the wheelchair and gently manoeuvred Sarah across the room.

The Medlars had retained as much of the character of the farmhouse kitchen as was practical. The stone floor was uncarpeted and the heavy table had just a plain white cloth. A row of pots hung from a massive beam.

'Oak?' asked Goring, pointing to it.

'More likely to be elm,' Medlar answered as he locked the wheelchair into place. 'It was a little more readily available in those days.'

He carved the meat, which was venison, dispensed vegetables, poured wine as he and Sarah kept a light flow of conversation going. He cut Sarah's food into pieces and put it on the platform in front of her so that with her one good hand she could feed herself. They talked of children, past colleagues, past friendships.

I shouldn't have come, Goring thought to himself. *But I couldn't have stayed away.*

Sarah looked up, smiled at him as though reading his thoughts. 'I hope you're not going to be too hard on poor Jessie tomorrow, Adam,' she said.

Goring smiled back. 'I think perhaps you ought to put that to her,' he replied. 'I've a feeling that poor Jessie is more than able to look after herself.'

'Such a waste,' she said.

'Yes, it is,' he agreed. 'Is there any chance she may yet accept my offer?' he asked Medlar.

'I very much doubt it.'

'Then it is, as you say, a waste.'

'It's a great pity,' Sarah said slowly, looking at him, 'that there wasn't some other way of implementing the necessary improvements to the service. All those people losing their jobs, all those skills going to nothing.'

It suddenly became a matter of supreme importance for Goring to justify himself in her eyes.

'But they needn't go to nothing,' he said.

'I'm listening, Adam.'

'I won't bore you with the practical arguments since I'm sure you already know them,' he said, 'but I'll give you a philosophical one.' He drank some wine as he gathered his thoughts.

'I think we make a fundamental mistake in our society when we refer to our work as our occupation rather than our livelihood. Our culture became great because every individual was prepared to do whatever and to go wherever necessary in order to thrive. The hunters followed the herds. The Celts came to Britain and the Irish went to America. We go where we can best earn our livelihoods.

'But now, we expect society not only to find us work, *fulfilling* work, but to find it whatever place may take our fancy. Our culture is in terminal decline because of our self-indulgence—'

'Oh come, Adam, that's rather sweeping isn't it?'

'I don't believe it is. I moved away from my home to better myself, as did George. It's what keeps you alive. These people expect to be paid for vegetating... Life's about moving forward, doing what has to be done, not indulging ourselves. Can't you see that?'

She said gently, 'I can *hear* you, Adam.'

He suddenly grinned broadly. 'I'm sorry, Sarah. Perhaps *I* was indulging myself, rather. Can I have some more of that wine, please?'

Sarah said insistently. 'But you won't be too hard on her, will you?'

'No,' he said. 'I'll confine myself to facts.'

They finished eating. 'We'll go back in the living-room, shall we?' Medlar said.

She looks tired, Goring thought. *I really must go soon.*

They had brandy by the fire. The phone went and Medlar got up to answer it.

Goring looked at her. They were sitting close together.

'How are you really, Sarah?' he heard himself saying. 'You know what I mean.'

The fire danced in her eyes. 'I've no regrets, Adam,' she said. 'None.'

'I'm glad,' he said softly as Medlar came back in.

Shortly afterwards, as the taxi pulled away from the old farmhouse, he realised that he'd probably never see her again. He also realised that he was still in love with her.

On the other side of the city, Jessie came to a decision: *I don't want him in my house any more.*

The object of her disdain was seated a few feet from her, absorbed in the TV. His name was Craig Scratchley and he was a lab orderly at the centre. Tall, tow-headed, blue-eyed, he was in his early twenties and had shared her hearth and bed for the last two months.

Ego, she thought. I *was pandering to my ego having him here.*

His parents were subsistence farmers on the edge of Dartmoor and taking the lab orderly job had been his way of trying to escape. He'd asked her for a dance at a social; she'd been amused at first, but then, as the wine and the disco beat set her body alight, genuinely attracted. *Why not?* she'd thought to herself.

She hadn't had a man since the break-up of her marriage, eighteen months earlier, Craig had been animal magic in bed and she'd persuaded herself she could control him...

'What's this about you gettin' the boot, then?' had been his greeting when she'd come in that evening. His accent wasn't as broad as that of his parents (she'd met them once, which was enough) but was still pretty strong.

'Where did you hear that?'

'It's goin' round the centre. Is it true?'

'No, it isn't,' she said, 'although they might try and make me redundant.' She told him about Goring's offer.

'Sounds to me like you could've had him by the shorties if you'd played your cards right,' he said.

'And how would I have played my cards right?'

'Tell him you'd drop the programme if he promised you a better job, in writing.'

'It's a bit late for that,' she said.

'I bet if you rung him now, he'd bite your hand off.'

'Still a bit late to stop the programme.'

He grinned at her. 'S'all right, make him promise you *on the telly*. No way he could wriggle out of it then.'

She gave a short laugh. 'Craig, I *want* to do the programme. I want to stop the centre closing.'

He shook his head, rather patronisingly, she thought. 'No way you're going to do that.'

'How do you know?' Something in his eyes made her go on. 'Who've you been talking to?'

He hesitated, shrugged. 'John Chambers.'

Paul's deputy... 'I wish you wouldn't talk to people like him behind my back.' She paused. 'What did he say?'

'That you can't win.' He looked her in the eye. 'That you're on an ego trip.'

'Oh, he did, did he? We'll see about that.'

'Jessie,' he said, 'nobody's gonna pull you out of the soft 'n smelly 'cept you.'

'We'll see,' she repeated. *But what if he's right?*

A score of tiny irritations had pricked at her as she'd prepared a meal for them, watched him troughing it, cleared it away afterwards, watched him watching TV.

He's good for nothing. And God, wouldn't it be nice to have my house to myself again... The prospect of him remaining there suddenly became intolerable. *I'll break it to him this weekend.*

In bed, thoughts of the coming interview kept her awake. Had she covered everything? Would she remember it all? She thought so, but...

But. She'd have to get up, make herself a drink.

A hand stole under her night-dress... *No*, she thought, and was about to push it away when his fingers lightly touched her nipple and she shivered.

His fingers gently stroked her thighs and she turned to him...

He is good for one thing, she thought later as she drifted into sleep, *but I still don't want him in my house.*

Medlar had got Sarah into her night-clothes, washed her face, cleaned her teeth and hoisted her into bed.

'Comfy?' he asked after he'd tucked the duvet round her.

'Yes, thank you.'

They slept in a downstairs room now. It was equipped with the electric hoist, remote control phone, TV and radio, and a purpose-built bookcase she could reach during the day.

'I love you, George,' she said as he got in beside her. 'I don't deserve you.'

'Love you too,' he said. 'I don't deserve you either.' *Only I mean it,* he thought. He closed his eyes and tried to swallow the lump in his throat as he waited for her breathing to become even, then he slipped out of bed and out of the room. Her eyes opened as he pulled the door shut.

In the living-room, he poured himself some whisky, sat down and sipped as he thought. After he'd poured the second glass, he filled and lit his pipe.

In his hotel room, Adam Goring was also drinking whisky as he thought about what his visitor had told him.

6

She lit another cigarette and drew heavily on it as she leaned against the balustrade on the top storey of the car-park. The pale lemon sun glinted on the windows of the high-rise blocks, flashed from the waves in the sound, etched the outline of the moorland plateau.

God, I love this place. Beautiful it ain't, but I love it.

Tamar itself wasn't beautiful. Badly bombed, even more badly redeveloped, the city sprawled, unlovely, around the river for which it was named. But where to the north it ended, Dartmoor began, and to the south, the sea...

This is stupid, Jessie thought, stubbing the cigarette and stuffing her frozen hands into her pockets as she walked over to the lifts.

The TV studio was on the ground floor. She rang, gave her name into the intercom grille and the door clicked open. Traci-the-receptionist was waiting for her and showed her to Suzee's office.

'Jessie, hi, come and sit down. Coffee?'

'I'd kill for one.'

Suzee relayed the order to the waiting

Traci and asked for another for herself.

'Well, you're nice and early,' she said after the door had closed.

'I've been up top for the last twenty minutes trying to calm down.'

'Nervous?'

'You could say that. I even started smoking again.'

'Thought I could smell it.' Suzee grinned. 'If it's any consolation, this is my first big national interview, so my adrenalin level's up a bit.'

'It doesn't look it.'

'I'm paid for it not to.' Suzee Price-Taylor had a magpie's nest of red hair, a palette of make-up, a clinging scarlet dress and still looked cooler than Cool Britannia.

'Listen,' she said, leaning forward, 'I'm going to give you first shout and I won't let him cut in on you, but don't go on for too long or you'll lose the impact. After that, I'm going to have to be seen to be neutral.'

'Fair enough.'

'I'll only cut in if it gets nasty ... but it's not likely, to, is it?'

Jessie took a breath. 'He does have a reputation for having a short fuse.'

'Well, try not to light it, Jessie, for my sake, eh? Rows might be fun for the viewers, but they leave a bad taste. And more to the point, my boss won't like it,' she added.

'OK.'

The intercom on her desk buzzed. 'Dr Goring has arrived,' Traci-the-receptionist intoned.

'Show him in, Traci – oh, and offer him a coffee and bring it in with ours, please.'

Jessie impulsively held up crossed fingers, then tried to let her hands relax on her lap. She hadn't known what to wear and had eventually settled on a dark jacket and skirt.

There was a knock and the door opened.

'Dr Goring,' said Traci, and they both stood up.

'Hello,' Goring said, smiling as he shook Suzee's hand. Her bracelets jangled.

'Do sit down, Dr Goring. Has Traci offered you coffee?'

'She has, thank you.'

Traci withdrew as Goring sat. He was dressed in a sober blue suit.

'Hello, Jessie,' he said.

'Dr Goring.' *He's smiling a lot this morning,* she thought sourly, thinking of Hamlet.

Traci returned with the coffee and Suzee explained to them how she was going to conduct the interview. Jessie's guts twisted and she craved more nicotine.

'Well, it's quarter to,' Suzee said, looking up at the clock, 'so I'd better get you along to make-up.'

'Make-up?' queried Goring.

'For the cameras,' Suzee told him. 'Believe

me, doctor, you'd look dreadful without it. Pale and shiny.'

'Well, I'd better submit myself in good grace then,' Goring said. 'So long as you'll promise not to tell my wife,' he added with a chuckle.

I bet he already knew about the make-up, Jessie thought as he chatted easily with Suzee along the corridor. *What's he been taking?*

In the make-up room, he gallantly waved her to the chair first. Her heart was swelling in her throat; her bladder just swelling. She made excuses, found the loo, remembered just in time not to sink her head into her hands and smudge the makeup.

Whatever possessed me to agree to this...? Agree with it? You connived *at it, you stupid cow.*

She washed her hands, took several deep breaths and made her way back. They were waiting for her in the studio.

'Here, Jessie,' Suzee said, indicating a chair opposite Goring. 'Are you OK?'

'I'm fine, thanks.'

They tested their microphones, then the cameramen checked their angles. A red light came on overhead.

'One minute,' said Suzee.

They waited in silence. Jessie gripped her knees, glanced up to meet Goring's eyes, which immediately flickered away.

The light went out. 'Ten seconds,' whispered Suzee.

'Action,' said the cameraman.

Suzee lifted her head and smiled at the camera. 'Good morning and welcome to *Western View*, not only to our regular viewers, but also to viewers in the rest of the country. Joining me this morning are Ms Jessie Pengellis, who is the Scientific Services Manager of Tamar Transfusion Centre, and Dr Adam Goring from the Blood Division...'

How does she do it? wondered Jessie, watching her as she outlined the scenario.

'Ms Pengellis,' she said, turning to Jessie, 'you've been conducting a vigorous campaign against the closure. Why is it so important we have our own centre here in Tamar?'

'It's important,' Jessie began, hearing the quaver in her voice, '*vitally* important, because without it the hospitals in this area will suffer a worse blood service. Put quite simply, this means that patients will die.'

As she felt Goring stir in his seat, some of the nervousness fell from her and she continued:

'At the moment, we recruit and organise all our donors, and they appreciate the personal service we give them. Which is why they go on donating.' She smiled. 'It's harder actually keeping donors than recruiting them. We send out the teams who take the blood at the local sessions, we test and type it in our own laboratories, then process and store it ready for issue to our local hospitals.

'If we close, all of this will go. Everything will be done from the East Dorset centre in Poole, more than a hundred miles away. How can they possibly offer the service from that distance that we provide here?'

She felt her confidence strengthen as she explained how they cross matched and supplied blood for patients with rare types; how, if they closed, the hospital would have to send a sample of the patient's blood to Poole, then wait for them to send the right blood back. 'It's delays like this that cost *lives*.'

She paused, hurried on: 'We've been told that the closure of our centre is to save money – but how *can* it when the donor teams will have to travel so far, and all blood has to be issued from Poole? Transport costs will soar. Donors will become disillusioned with a faceless organisation too distant to appreciate their needs. They will stop donating and there will be a general short-age of blood – this has already happened in the areas where other centres have closed ... and by the time the Department of Health realises what a terrible mistake it has made, it will be too late to repair the damage.'

There was a pause, a hush, then Suzee said in a sober voice. 'Thank you, Ms Pengellis. Dr Goring—' she turned to him – 'by any standards, it's a horrifying scenario that Ms Pengellis has painted for us. It does rather sound as though you're making a mistake.'

'It would indeed be horrifying if that were the case,' he said, 'but we in the Blood Division are in the business of saving lives, not putting them at risk. And that is what our reorganisation is going to do – save lives.'

He spoke quietly and with authority, the slight northern accent giving his voice a homely, trustworthy feel. Patients, he told them, were already dying because of the shortage of rare types and they were installing a new and powerful computer system that would link all the centres and provide a national database of donors and blood stocks.

'Suppose a patient here in Tamar needs blood of a rare type and there isn't any ... the computer at East Dorset will be able to show that there's some in Manchester, and it can be brought down, flown down if necessary.'

'Why can't the system be installed here?' Jessie cut in.

'A computer system as powerful as this is expensive, very expensive, and the only way we can afford it is to rationalise the service.'

Suzee quickly came in: 'What about the other point Ms Pengellis made, Dr Goring? The people who make blood transfusion possible – the donors. Can they really expect the same level of attention from East Dorset?'

'Certainly they can – in fact, it'll improve. The new computer system will ensure that they're informed, well in advance, of where and when they should donate.'

'That hasn't happened in the South Midlands,' Jessie said. 'It's chaos up there.'

'There were some problems to start with,' Goring admitted candidly, 'but there always are when you go over to a new system – you know that,' he added with a friendly smile. 'It's settled down now and is working well.'

'That's not what I've heard.'

'Then we must have different sources of information,' Goring told her, still smiling.

'There's one matter neither of you have mentioned yet,' Suzee interposed neatly, 'and that is the staff who are losing their jobs.'

'Indeed,' said Jessie quickly. 'Thirty of us are being made redundant here, thirty trained scientists, and that's just the laboratories – three hundred staff are being made redundant nationally–'

'As you well know,' Goring cut in, 'there are plentiful job opportunities in the other transfusion centres–'

'But not for all of us. We have to apply for these jobs, compete for them, and hard luck if you get left out. A nice repayment for all the years of loyal service we've put in–'

'Loyal service?' Goring said incredulously. 'You talk about loyal service when you're planning to take all the staff out on strike? Who's endangering the patients now?'

'Whatever d'you mean? We're not planning anything of the kind–'

'Oh? Do you deny then that you called a department heads meeting yesterday for the purpose of discussing strike action?'

'But it wasn't ... and we decided not to go on strike,' Jessie said weakly, too shaken to think out a better reply.

'Good of you,' Goring said as he leaned back, satisfied with the point he'd scored.

'Is it true though,' Suzee said quickly, trying to gain Jessie some breathing space, 'that as many as three hundred staff are to lose their jobs nationally?'

'It's nothing like as bad as that, as Miss Pengellis well knows,' Goring said easily ...Oh, there might be some early retirement for those who wanted it, he told the camera, perhaps even a very few redundancies, but they would all be treated very generously...

By now, Jessie had recovered herself enough to fire some more questions at him, but he seemed to have an easy, natural answer for every point she made.

Transport? Well, the present system was very costly, he had the figures to prove it, and they were contracting it out to make it more efficient...

Blood shortages? Well, that came down to good housekeeping on the part of the hospital blood banks, and to be frank, some of them were less than desirable...

He was so bloody *plausible,* and he hadn't shown the least sign of losing his rag, not once – it was as though he'd known in advance everything she was going to say. She realised that she was beginning to sound shrill, even unreasonable; she sensed that Suzee was about to bring it to a close.

I've lost it, she thought desolately.

I've only one card left to play ... and it was an explosive, dangerous card, could easily destroy them both. *But what have I got to lose?*

'There is one other thing we haven't mentioned, Dr Goring...'

Suzee's look told her that it was the last thing and would have to be pretty quick.

'And that's the choice of those centres to close.'

'We chose those whose areas were most easily covered by other centres. Tamar seemed to slot naturally into East Dorset's area.'

72

'Why couldn't East Dorset slot into Tamar's area?'

'Because East Dorset centre is larger, has better facilities and better communications.'

'Surely a matter of opinion...'

'A matter of fact.'

'Were those the only reasons?'

He shrugged. 'Of course.'

'I suggest that there may be another.' Goring became suddenly alert, his eyes narrowed as he watched her.

'A research directorship is being created at East Dorset, and your son-in-law, Dr Mike Derby, who is a consultant in Poole, is the heir apparent.'

Goring froze, they all did, but he turned white under his make-up. 'How did you–? How *dare you* make such–?'

'I think perhaps–' Suzee began.

'How did I know? I only found out last week, by chance. It's certainly been kept under wraps, hasn't it? And it certainly explains–'

'That is the most outrageous, *infamous* suggestion–'

'I think perhaps–' Suzee tried again.

'But *true,*' Jessie said.

Goring's face was less turnip, more giant plum now.

'I came here in good faith to discuss the future of the Transfusion Service and I find I've been set up for this *slander,* these *lies–*'

'I think we'll leave it there,' Suzee almost shouted. 'Thank you both so much for a ... such a lively and stimulating debate.'

'I want her fired.'

'You've already told her she's being made redundant. Isn't that enough?'

'She has to be fired, George,' Goring said a little more calmly. 'You simply cannot allow staff to make that sort of allegation in public.'

Medlar drew in a breath. 'But won't it make you look rather vindictive, Adam? Not to say ... vulnerable. To the accusation she made.'

'And after she's fired, I shall sue her for slander.'

It was two hours later and they were in Medlar's office.

'Adam, I'm sorry but I have to ask you this – was there any truth in what she said?'

It was Goring's turn to draw breath. 'It's true that there's a research post being created at East Dorset. It's also true that Mike has his eye on it, but he only told me that *after* the decision had been made to close Tamar.'

'*Was* it your decision as to which centres shut?'

'It was a *collective* decision, you know how we work. And it was obvious that Tamar close rather than East Dorset, for all the obvious reasons.'

'Because it's bigger and has better ... connections.'

Goring's eyes flicked up sharply. 'Was that intended to be a *double entendre*, George?'

'Good heavens, no.'

'Then don't you agree that the choice was obvious?'

Medlar sighed. 'I suppose so.'

'And didn't that come over in the interview?' Goring pressed.

'It was a masterly performance, Adam, if a little skewed now and again.'

'No more than the rubbish she was coming out with. And those two were obviously in cahoots.'

Medlar continued mildly, 'It was so masterly, Adam, that you might almost have known what she was going to say, not to mention the business of the so-called strike meeting.'

'Now you are being ridiculous,' Goring said, but wouldn't meet Medlar's eyes.

'The fact is, Adam, that I can't sack her for what she said on the telly.'

'Then find another reason,' Goring snapped.

'I don't think there is one to find.'

'No? Let me tell you something, George – this centre's a maggots' nest of corruption.'

'So you *do* have a spy here,' Medlar said lightly. He took out his pipe and began filling it, knowing that Goring found it irritating.

'Let's just say that one of your staff's a little more public-spirited than the rest.'

'Then get him, or her, to do your dirty work for you.' He applied his lighter to the bowl.

'Oh, I shall. But wouldn't *you* like to know some of the things this public-spirited soul has been telling me?'

'I can't think of anything I'd like less.' Medlar blew smoke.

'Nevertheless, George,' Goring said, staring at him intently, 'I think that you *should* know...'

'He *knew* Dommo, he knew what I was going to say.'

'That's ridiculous,' Dominic said impatiently. He looked preoccupied and obviously had troubles of his own. 'How could he have known?'

'Somebody told him, that's how.'

'Aren't you being just a little paranoid, Jessie?'

'No, I am *not* – he knew about the meeting we had yesterday, and he knew what I was going to say.' She told him how she'd left her file on her desk...

Earlier, after a cooler than cool adieu from Suzee, Jessie had gone home to lick her wounds. She'd wept for a while as reaction set in, then told herself to stop being a vapouring female and driven back to the centre. She'd thought about phoning her union, then called Dominic instead.

'Not like you to leave things lying around,' he said now.

'Put it down to stress,' she said. 'But someone could have easily photocopied them in that time.'

'D'you have anyone in mind?'

'Oh, Paul or Adrian, I suppose.'

'Isn't it possible that Goering had thought everything out and was ready for you?'

'Were you watching?'

He nodded. 'I've never seen the rest room so crowded.'

Jessie winced. 'Didn't it seem to you as though he knew exactly what was coming?'

'Well, he certainly wasn't ready for your *pièce de résistance*. Is it true? About his son-in-law?'

She nodded.

'How d'you know?'

She hesitated. 'Someone at East Dorset told me – I can't tell you who.'

He smiled wryly at some thought of his own as she continued: 'Goring should have declared an interest and not been on the committee that decided which centres were to close.'

Dominic said softly, 'They'd almost certainly have come to the same decision.'

'Maybe, maybe not – it still makes him look bad.'

'Yes, it does, and he's not going to forgive you for that.'

'He wasn't going to forgive me anyway.'

You still made a mistake, his eyes told her.

The phone rang and she picked it up.

'The boss wants to see me,' she said, putting it down.

'Best of luck,' he said quietly.

7

Five o'clock and the centre was nearly deserted. Not long since, it would have been hustling with life and purpose as the returning blood was sorted and centrifuged, and the plasma separated for Factor VIII extraction, but the spectre of CJD and the imminent closure had squashed all that like a thumb on a fly. Most of the staff left at four on Friday now.

In his office, George Medlar stood up, took his coat from his peg and switched out the lights. At the door, something made him stop and look back at the windows. He put the coat down on the armchair and went over to them, pulling up the venetian blinds.

Tamar lay beneath him in the dark: the

threaded beads of the main roads, the high-rise office blocks like starship computers, even the odd anachronistic glowing church tower, and the whole coalesced into a shimmering golden haze above the city that faded into the velvet night.

God, I'm a coward, he thought.

Jessie's body language as she'd come in earlier had been of defeat, and yet somehow defiant at the same time.

'Whatever possessed you, Jessie?' he'd asked quietly.

'Desperation, I suppose,' she'd said at last. 'I had nothing to lose. He knew about the meeting I'd held, he knew everything I was going to say and had an answer ready.'

'You were doing better than you think.' He paused. 'Is it true, what you said about his son-in-law?'

She didn't reply. 'You know you can trust me,' he said.

She did, even more than Dominic, so she told him.

'Yes,' he said when she'd finished, 'that does sound like Adam. But you could never prove it, and going back to what you said just now, I'm afraid you do have something to lose...' He told her that she'd been formally suspended and she nodded. Obviously, she'd been expecting it.

'I'm afraid that's not all. He wants your blood, Jessie.'

'Well, he won't get anyone else's, not here in Tamar,' she said with a wry smile, and after a moment he unwillingly smiled back.

'Probably not.' His face became serious again. 'He wants you fired. Not just made redundant, but sacked, which would mean no settlement, and no money. And after that, he says he's going to sue you, for slander.'

Her face went still as she absorbed it all. 'Can I be sacked, for what I said?' she asked.

'I don't know. You'd better check with your union. But he's determined to find some way of doing it – he even told *me* to find a way...' He tailed off, then continued slowly, 'I may as well tell you, he did indicate he has some kind of informant here.'

Jessie stared at him. 'Did he say who?'

He told her exactly what Goring had said. 'The thing is, Jessie, if he does have someone like that here, they'd be in the best position to give you away. Is there anything, any skeleton hidden away...?'

'I ... don't think so.'

He pursed his lips. 'Then there's a chance it may blow over. He's going to America on Sunday, which'll give him a chance to cool off. They'll still make you redundant, though, whatever happens.'

'So it's really over?' she said in a small voice.

'I'm afraid so.'

'You know, George, I really thought we had a chance. I thought that if we built up enough public pressure...'

'You gave it your best, but I'm afraid their minds weren't for changing.'

She pressed her lips together. 'You did warn me.'

'Jessie,' he said, 'there is something I'd like to tell you, if you'll promise to keep it to yourself.'

'You know that.'

'You know that in our trade nothing ever gets said directly, it's all hints, innuendo, nothing on the record – but if you don't pick up those hints, then God help you...' His voice trembled with anger.

'I don't know how much longer Sarah has to live,' he continued quietly, 'but while she's alive, I want to give her the best. That costs money.' He gave a short laugh. 'You probably think that as a medical director, I have plenty, but you'd be surprised how quickly it goes.'

'I don't think I would.'

'Anyway, in six months, I'll be out of a job as well and whatever handshake I get is very much up to the gnomes of Blood Division. D'you see what I'm saying?'

'If you'd rocked the boat, campaigned with me, they'd have slashed your settlement.'

'Those are your words, but ... yes. A couple of years ago, it wouldn't have mattered so much, but now...'

'Bastards,' she said without expression.

'That's why I've played the poltroon, cheering you from the wings, but not doing much. I really did think you might have a chance at first.'

'Thanks for telling me, George, I appreciate it.'

'What d'you think you'll do? You know I'll help you any way I can.'

They'd talked for a while longer, then she'd thanked him again and got up to go.

Now, something made him turn from the window to see a figure silhouetted in the doorway.

'Maria?'

'Can I come in?'

'Please.'

She came over and stood about a yard away from him.

'You're working late,' he said.

'I'm on call this weekend.'

After a pause, he said, 'I'm going to miss this.' He nodded at the city lights below.

'It makes Tamar seem more important than it really is,' she said.

'Yes.'

'You can hardly see any stars.'

'No. Light pollution, I suppose. But think about it.' He glanced at her. 'It would only take one person in a power station some-where to pull a switch and the whole lot would go out. You'd see the stars then. Have you ever seen the stars free of light?' *Why am I gabbling like this?*

'Yes, in Africa.'

'Ah, Africa...'

'In Africa, the stars can actually light your way, even when there's no moon.'

'Twinkle twinkle little star. Maybe that's how it should be.'

'Yes.'

After a short silence, she said, 'Was it bad today?'

'About as bad as it could be.' He turned to her. 'Did you see the interview?'

'Yes.'

'Adam wants her blood.' He smiled as he thought of Jessie's comment, then told her what had happened.

'Where is he now?' she asked when he'd finished.

'Back in his hotel, I expect.'

'So it's all up with Jessie?' she said after a pause.

'I'm afraid so, one way or another. Her priority now is to somehow avoid being actually fired.'

'She's already been in touch with the union.' She told him about the meeting.

'I hate to say this,' he said when she'd finished, 'but Paul's right. Those who do take industrial action will be cutting their own throats. It won't change any minds and it'll be remembered when it comes to handing out new jobs. Adam isn't the only vindictive bastard at HQ.'

'It's all so bloody unfair,' she said. 'Especially on Jessie. I felt like a rat not supporting her, siding with people like Paul...'

Her eyes were as bright as the stars with tears. Without thinking, he put his arm around her. She buried her face in his chest, gripped him fiercely, and when she looked up, he kissed her eyes, her cheeks, her mouth... Their tongues met as they desperately tried to off-load the charge swirling around them...

'I'm sorry, I'm sorry, I'm *sorry*,' she said, breaking off. 'I didn't plan it, I just had to find out...'

'It's all right,' he soothed, stroking the soft cloud of her hair. 'It was going to happen again sooner or later...' He kissed her again and she responded, slowly, deliberately, purposefully.

He kissed her neck, her throat, fumbled with buttons and catches, then he was kissing her small, dark breasts as she arched her head back and pulled him into her...

'Sweet Christ I want you,' he muttered and she looked back at him, not saying anything, her face glowing in the light from the city. He went quickly over to the door, shut and locked it.

Adam Goring was at his hotel, talking to his wife on the phone. 'It's taking longer than I thought,' he said. 'I might not make it back tomorrow.'

'Oh, Adam, you promised you'd come back before going to America ... what's keeping you?'

'Damage limitation,' he said. 'I've been working out a statement with HQ to refute the things *Ms* Pengellis said.'

'Couldn't you do that from here?'

'I think there may be some evidence down here I can use. I'm going out shortly to have a look. It really is important, I don't want Mike's chances compromised.'

'No,' she agreed. 'It would break Fiona's heart. Do whatever you have to, Adam...'

Dominic Tudor was squirming on his seat in the dining-room.

'Food not to your liking?' his father-in-law enquired silkily.

'I'm just not particularly hungry,' he said neutrally. Dominic detested Jane's father beyond expression. He turned to her mother: 'I was taken out to lunch today by a rep who's interested in the research I'm doing. Not something I could really turn down at the moment...'

'Of course not, dear. Do stop nagging, Bill.'

'Just don't like to see good food wasted, that's all.'

Dominic sat waiting while the rest of them ate their puddings, wondering whether it was all worth it, then at a little after seven, excused himself.

'Off out then?' Bill wanted to know.

'Yes – why?'

'Just wondered what was taking you from your loved ones.'

'I'm going to see a man about a job. See you later, love.' He kissed Jane's cheek and left.

He was, in fact, due to meet Ashley at eight, something they'd arranged earlier.

Paul Bannister was also at home, and also squirming, but in his case it was due to the quarrelling and screaming of his four children. And to guilt.

He looked at his watch. 'I'm off, then,' he said, getting up from the table.

'D'you have to go now?' his wife said tiredly. 'I could do with a hand with these kids...'

'I'm sorry, but I told Adrian seven thirty and I don't like keeping people waiting.'

'All right,' she said resignedly.

Adrian Hodges was at the door before his

mother said, 'Going out, Adrian?'

'Just to the centre for something I forgot. Won't be long.'

'Thought you'd have seen enough of that place,' his father said.

'George, where have you *been?*' Sarah wailed from her chair.

'I did say I might be late.' He gingerly pecked her cheek, hoping that none of Maria lingered for her to smell.

'But it's nearly half-past eight...'

'I've been on the phone to HQ,' he temporised, 'trying to clear up some of the debris from this morning. Did you see the interview?'

'Naturally I did.'

'Adam wasn't best pleased and wants Jessie's head on a spike.'

'And doubtless wants you to help him put it there.' She sighed. 'Still, it was rather silly of her, wasn't it?'

'Yes.'

After a pause, she said, 'Now you're here, George, would you mind, please...?' Her eyes told him what she wanted.

Strange how she still can't say it out loud, he thought, a lump forming in his throat. He opened a drawer and took out tobacco and hashish...

Jessie had gone home at four to be

87

enveloped by the low growl of the TV as she opened the front door.

'Hello,' she called. *Echo answers,* she thought.

She stuck her head through the living-room door. 'I said, Hello.'

'Oh, hello.' Craig's head didn't move.

She continued along the passage to the kitchen. A mug squatted on the table, ringed with a puddle of cold tea. She found a cloth and wiped up the mess. Filled the kettle, switched it on, then picked up a used tea-bag from the work surface and threw it into the bin. The stain it left there resisted her attempts to remove it.

'If you're making more tea,' his voice called from the living-room, 'I could do with a refill.'

'Oh you could, could you?' she muttered through clenched teeth. *Tomorrow, Jessie, leave it till tomorrow...*

The kettle boiled, she made tea for them both, sat down with her own and lit a cigarette. A minute later, Craig appeared in the doorway.

'Tea ready yet?'

She pointed to his mug on the work surface.

'Smoking again? Thought you'd given it up.'

'I've had a bad day.'

He grunted, not unsympathetically. 'Yeah.

I saw you on the telly this morning. Boss mad at you?'

'You could say that.'

He looked at her closely. 'Did he give you the sack?'

'I don't know yet.' She stubbed her cigarette and told him about being suspended.

'Well, I told you, didn't I? You should've screwed him for a better job while you had the chance.'

'Yes, Craig, you did tell me that.' She flipped open the pack, took another cigarette and lit it.

'So what're you gonna do?'

As he flapped theatrically at her cigarette smoke, all the frustrations welled up from deep inside her in a livid red pulse that roared in her ears.

'I'll tell you what I'm going to do for starters, Craig.' Her voice, she realised, was shaking, as was her whole body. 'I'm throwing you out, as of now.'

He grinned uncertainly. 'Yeah, all right...'

'I mean it. Craig. I'm telling you to leave my house.'

He looked at her, realised she was serious. 'You can't do that.'

'I can, Craig, and I am. You've got–'

'OK,' he interrupted. 'I'm sorry about what I said about your fags. I apologise, OK?'

She shook her head. 'Sorry, Craig, but no. I don't want you in my house any more.'

'I said I'm sorry,' he shouted. 'What more d'you want?'

'Nothing. Just you out of my house.'

There was a long silence, or at least it seemed long to Jessie, then he took a breath and shrugged. 'OK, I'll clear out tomorrow.'

'No, Craig – tonight. It's not as if you haven't got anywhere to go–'

Without warning, he jumped forward and pushed her so that she and her chair fell backwards on to the floor, banging her head. 'Stuck-up bitch,' he shouted. 'Think you can treat people like shit 'cos–' He took two rapid strides, stood over her, raised his foot and she thought, *He's going to kill me*... 'Just 'cos you think you're God's fucken gift...' Spittle flecked down on to her face.

'I'm *glad* they've sacked you, I'm really glad, I hope they give you fuck all, *nothin'.*' Now he spat deliberately, and as a gob of it hit her eye she realised he wasn't going to kill her after all. She twisted round, got to her feet and faced him. There was a faint look of surprise on his face, whether at her or himself she didn't know. She found a handkerchief and wiped her eye.

'I'm going out, for an hour. When I come back, I want you gone.'

'An' if I don't?'

'Then I call the police.'

He looked back at her with impotent hatred. 'An hour isn't long enough.'

'Two then. You haven't got that much stuff here.'

Another look came over him and she said, 'I've still got some of your money in my account, remember? So I wouldn't trash the place if I were you.'

She saw that she'd read him correctly, picked up her bag from the table and walked out. She heard him spitting again, but whether it hit her or not she didn't know.

'An' good fucken riddance,' floated after her as she pulled the door shut.

She felt her legs shaking as she walked to her car, unlocked it and climbed in. She knew reaction would hit her any minute, but she had to get away.

A horn blasted, brakes screamed as she pulled out.

'Watch where you're goin', stupid cow,' a voice shouted, female.

She raised a hand in apology, waited until the car had gone, then very cautiously started off again. She knew she shouldn't be driving, that she'd have to stop soon, that she'd left her fags on the kitchen table...

Singh's shop, just ahead. She looked very carefully into her mirror, signalled and pulled into the parking area.

Can't cry yet. She wiped her eyes with a tissue, looked in the mirror and patted down her hair, then got out and walked into the shop.

Old Singh was sitting at the end of the aisle with his grey beard and turban, as usual. He gave her a gap-toothed grin and waved, also as usual. She walked up to the counter and asked for some cigarettes. Young Singh looked at her a little strangely as she paid for them.

'You all right, miss?'

'I'm fine, thanks.'

As she turned to go, another voice said, 'Jessie?'

She turned to see Verity, holding a bottle of wine. 'Are you all right, Jessie?'

'Not really, no.'

'Hang on while I pay for this...'

Young Singh said quietly, 'Good thing you were here, I think, miss,' as he gave her the change.

Jessie burst into tears the moment they were outside.

8

Verity helped her into her car, a newish BMW, then climbed in herself.

'I'm s-sorry,' Jessie managed.

'It doesn't matter.' Verity put her arms

round her, waited until the worst gusts had passed, then said, 'What's happened, Jessie? Is it work?'

'N-no...' In hesitant sentences, she told her about Craig.

'And now you're afraid to go back? I'll come with you.'

Jessie sniffed. 'It isn't that, I don't want to go back yet anyway. It's just *everything...*'

'Sure. You'd better come home with me for a bit. Can you drive, d'you think?'

Jessie nodded. 'I'm OK now. But I don't want to put you to any bother.'

'It's no bother.' She hesitated. 'If you *can* drive, I suggest we go now – I'm fed up with all these people staring.'

Jessie nodded again, vigorously, and a minute later, followed the BMW out. Verity's home was a little under a mile away, a smallish detached house that wasn't quite a cottage, set in its own grounds. It was older than the surrounding property, Edwardian, Jessie thought, just the sort of individual place she'd have expected Verity to own.

'Your car's fine there,' Verity called, producing keys from her bag.

Jessie followed her in, carefully wiping her feet on the mat. The ornately tiled hallway shone and the whole place smelt of polish.

'Let me have your coat.' Verity took it, hung it on a peg. 'Come and sit down.' She led the way into a light, airy sitting-room, delicately furnished. Two large, rather nondescript plants grew in pots either side of the french window. Jessie sank into the sofa.

'What would you like – whisky, gin, vodka?'

'Vodka, please.'

'Tonic?'

'Please.'

'I'll join you.' She poured the drinks and brought them over. 'Feeling any better?'

'A bit, thanks. This should help.' She took a mouthful.

'I meant what I said earlier, I'll come back with you if you like.'

'That's sweet of you, Verity, but I'll know if he's still there by whether his van's there.' She took some more drink. 'I suppose it's the mess I'm worried about.'

'Has he ever been violent before?'

Jessie shook her head. 'But then again, I've never chucked him out before.'

Verity grinned and after a moment, Jessie smiled back.

'I'll tell you what,' Verity said, 'I was going to make a risotto this evening – I'll do that now and we'll decide how to handle things afterwards.'

'No, Verity, I feel bad enough as it is–'

'Good, that's settled then. You stay here and finish your drink while I get on with it.'

'Thanks...'

'My pleasure.' She finished her own drink and stood up. 'Help yourself to another if you want.'

'Can I give you a hand?'

'No thanks, probably quicker on my own.'

Jessie noticed an ashtray on the occasional table. 'I wouldn't normally even ask, but would you mind if I smoked?'

'Sure – that's what the ashtray's for.'

'I'd actually managed to give up, you know, but these last few days...'

'Sure. I'll go and cook.' With another smile, Verity left her.

On an empty stomach, the drink had already gone to her head, giving her a not unpleasant sense of surreality. Better not overdo it, though... She stripped the cellophane from the pack and lit up. Her fingers were still trembling and she wondered what she'd have done if she hadn't run into Verity. She looked round the room. The pictures on the walls seemed to be originals and the glass cabinet was certainly antique. The bookshelves were filled and she'd have normally got up for a look, but felt too lazy.

She stubbed her cigarette. Strange how Verity was so open and helpful at work and yet so private – she'd not heard of anyone else being invited to her house...

What the hell was she going to do about

going back to her own home? *Better take up her offer, I suppose.*

And if he was still there, go to the police... Thinking about him made her shudder and she picked up her drink and finished it. She resisted the temptation to pour herself another and lit up again instead.

Would he really have hurt me, killed me? She didn't think so. When it came down to it, all he'd done was to push her over and spit at her ... *although, God knows, that was enough.*

Verity appeared. 'It's ready. Come on through.'

She followed her into the kitchen. Verity took off the apron she'd been wearing and hung it up – she really did have the most magnificent figure, Jessie thought.

'Over there. Jessie.'

The table and chairs were dark against the pastel yellow walls. Risotto steamed gently on plates.

'Wine?'

'Please.'

Verity took the bottle from the cooler and poured. It was Chardonnay.

'And this is why you went to Singh's?'

'Yes.' She looked up. 'Just as well I did, isn't it? D'you not have family in Tamar, Jessie?'

'They're all down in Truro. I'm the only one who's gone to foreign parts.'

Verity smiled. 'Let's eat.'

Jessie hadn't thought she'd be able to eat much, but once she started, realised she'd never tasted so delicious a risotto in her life. She said so.

'It's the herbs I use,' Verity said. With hardly a pause, she continued: 'I saw you on TV this morning. I thought you did very well.'

'It seems like weeks ago ... and I don't think I did well at all. It was a mistake to bring in his son-in-law.'

'I thought it was inspired – it brought out his nastier side and made him look as guilty as hell. Is it true?'

'Yes, but I can't tell you how I know.'

Verity smiled again and shrugged. Jessie continued: 'I felt I had to do something – he'd been in control up till then. He seemed to know everything I was going to say, he even knew about our meeting and twisted it round.'

'D'you think he really *did* know what you were going to say, then?'

Jessie told her how she'd left her file on her desk the day before and what Medlar had said to her earlier.

Verity thoughtfully drank some wine, refilled their glasses. 'If it wasn't for George confirming it, I'd have found it hard to believe.'

'Dommo said I was being paranoid.'

Verity gave a small, but unladylike snort.

'Well, there's one gentleman I wouldn't trust.'

Jessie grinned at her. 'I know you don't like him, but I've always found him trustworthy.'

Verity hesitated, then shrugged again. 'You must speak as you find.'

'Has he ever let *you* down?' Jessie asked, curious.

'I can't say that he has,' she said slowly, 'it's just that he's so damn pleased with himself all the time, so *smug*...' She grinned back at Jessie. 'I know, I shouldn't let that influence me.' She took another mouthful of wine.

'The worst thing,' Jessie said, 'is knowing that Goring's actually searching for evidence to sack me – it's like having a price put on your head.'

'Are there any skid marks for him to find?'

Jessie shook her head. 'Not that I know of.'

Verity said slowly, 'Then maybe I should find one for him...'

'What d'you–?'

'I mean a false one. Get him to accuse you of something utterly ridiculous. He'd make the most awful fool of himself, which might get you off the hook.'

'It's a lovely idea, Verity, but I can't imagine what.'

'Let me think about it...'

After they'd finished everything, they returned to the sitting-room.

'Brandy?' Verity was over by the sideboard.

'Better not, not if I'm going to be driving home.'

'You could always stay here tonight – in fact, I think it would be better if you did.' She had taken a small wooden box from a drawer and now brought it back with her drink. 'Still worried he's smashed the place up?'

'I suppose I am...' She took a cigarette from her pack.

'That's the least of it.' She grinned. 'Better that than you.'

'I suppose so.'

There was a pause, then Verity said suddenly, 'I can understand you having a fling with him, Jessie, but what on earth made you take him into your house? You don't have to answer that...'

'A combination of libido and bravado, I suppose,' Jessie said slowly. 'What are you doing?'

'Rolling a stogie.'

'I didn't know you smoked.'

'I do sometimes, here at home.'

Although Verity didn't press her, Jessie felt that she had to go on talking, to relieve the pressure inside her. 'You know I was married before I came to the centre?'

'Yes.' Verity lit the rolled cigarette with a

small, gold lighter.

'Well, it was a bad marriage, a mistake. It completely undermined me. I suppose, with Craig, I wanted to show that I'm my own person now.'

'Show whom?'

'Everybody. Myself mostly, I suppose.' She turned. 'Is that what I think it is?'

'I expect so. Like some?'

'Not just now, thanks.' She looked round at the potted plants – the tiny elliptical leaves were obvious now that she could smell the bittersweet smoke.

'I use the dried leaves,' Verity said. 'How long were you married?'

'Three years, although it seemed a lot longer.'

'No children?'

'Only my husband – there wasn't room for any more.'

Verity smiled. 'You'd have liked children?'

'Ye-es...' She drew the word out as the use of the past tense hit her.

'He was an emotional parasite,' Verity said.

It was a statement, not a question, Jessie noticed, and nor was it the platitude she'd half expected about there being plenty of time. She said, 'Yes, he was, and I didn't realise it for ... oh, years ... I think I will have one after all, Verity.'

'What was his job?' Verity asked as she teased a line of tobacco along the paper and mixed in the dried leaves.

'Lab manager, like I am – *was*, that is.' She smiled wryly. 'He was my boss.' She took the proffered reefer, lit it. 'Everyone thought he was so *wonderful*, that I was *lucky*.' She inhaled a lungful of the bittersweetness.

'How did he undermine you?'

'Oh, socially, professionally, even domestically...'

'Sexually?'

'Yes, that most of all.'

'In what way?'

She took another thoughtful drag of the reefer. 'He destroyed the pleasure of sex for me,' she said at last.

'How?'

'I'm not sure ... he blamed me when it wasn't good, said I wasn't trying, and I didn't realise for ages that it was *him*, not me.' Another lungful. 'The thing is, he *looked* so sexy, all the girls in the lab doted on him and he had this way of flirting with them that had them all drooling in their knickers – sorry, sorry – I'm going on too much.'

'No, you're not,' Verity said urgently. 'Someone should have listened to you years ago.'

'When we were engaged, it was so good, the sex that is, but after we were married ... it just wasn't the same ... it was as though he wasn't really there.'

'Could it have been *you* who wasn't there, Jessie?'

'*Me?*'

'Please, I'm not taking his side ... what I'm getting at is that maybe before you were married, you had an image, an *ideal* of him and that afterwards he just didn't come up to it. As a person, that is.'

'But it was so good before we were married...'

'Because you loved the *ideal* you had of him. That's what made the sex good.'

'You're saying it's all in the mind?'

'Well, isn't it?'

'I – I don't know...' She stubbed out the reefer. Verity handed her another and she lit it without thinking. 'You know, when I got this job,' she said, going off tangentially, 'it was the best thing that ever happened to me.' She drew deeply on the fresh reefer.

'After I left him, I found a senior job, up in Bristol. They wanted me for it, told me there was a Three post coming up, more or less told me it was mine. But then, when it did come up,' she said slowly, 'they brought in someone else.'

'Did they ever tell you why?'

Jessie shook her head. 'Not really. They said he just pipped me at the post – what a vapid expression that is!' She sighed. 'There was nothing in writing, so there was nothing I could do about it.'

'Could your husband have had anything to do with it?' Verity asked after a pause. 'You did say he was a lab manager ... he'd have been pretty influential.'

Jessie swallowed. 'I've tried not to think about that. I didn't want to believe anyone could be that spiteful.'

'But you left him, Jessie. Capital offence.'

'Anyway,' Jessie hurried on, not wanting to think about it now, either, 'after that, I applied for pretty well every job going.' She gave a tiny laugh, a snicker. 'I couldn't believe it when I got this one.'

'Neither could I.'

'Oh thanks, Verity!'

'No, listen... I was expecting some po-faced stiff to get it, Paul being the worst possible case. I was over the moon when it was you, but I *was* surprised.' She paused. 'Why d'you think you did get it?'

'I dunno.' She inhaled another lungful. 'I s'pose it was because George and I just clicked. He showed me round the centre before I applied and asked me what I'd do if I got it. I had nothing to lose so I told him. Then I realised from his expression that I'd said all the right things, that I really was in with a chance.' She smiled at the memory. 'I know I shouldn't say this, but it was wonderful, the best feeling in the world when they told me it was mine.'

'Why shouldn't you say–?'

'To be able to wave two fingers at those bastards, to tell them exactly what I thought of them.'

'Did you?'

'No.'

'I thought not.'

'No need to.' She gave a cat-like smile. 'I smiled at them and said nice things and they smiled back and said nice things to me, and they hated every minute of it. It was *great!*' She let out a huge sigh. 'But they who laugh last, eh? And I had such *plans*, it was going to be the best run place in the...' Her face suddenly crumpled and she let out a sob. 'What the hell am I going to do, Verity?' She began to cry, then took a breath, swallowed. 'I'm sorry, I...'

'No, let it come,' Verity said, moving swiftly over to her. She took her in her arms and held her. Jessie sobbed, feeling the wetness of her tears against Verity's cotton jumper.

After a while, she stopped crying and Verity's fingers began gently massaging her, first her back, then her shoulders, her neck, and she felt more relaxed than she could remember.

'Thank you,' she breathed, 'thank you, thank you...'

Verity whispered, 'There now...'

Jessie thought, *I could die now and be happy.*

'There now...' Verity whispered, her mouth against her ear, then her neck, her cheek, her own mouth and it was so natural, her lips were clean, soft, sweet ... the tips of their tongues met, circled, set up a tingling wave of electrons that surged softly back through her face, neck, body ...

She couldn't remember when last another person had made her feel so good.

At last, Verity drew back and Jessie realised she was trembling all over, from the very top of her head, through her loins to the tips of her toes.

Verity whispered, 'I think we'd better go upstairs...'

9

Dr Ewan Randall kicked himself – hard, on the ankle.

The PM hadn't established any cause of death. He'd briefly considered electrocution, but there were no burns, so he'd then had samples taken to send to the Poisons Unit at Guy's. He'd been on the point of leaving it at that when one of his technicians spoke up.

'Can I suggest something, doctor?'

'Well?'

'Couldn't he have frozen to death?'

Of course he could.

He said carefully. 'You might have a point there, Simon – it would explain the pancreatitis we found, wouldn't it?' *Not to mention the frostbite and discoloration...* 'So what else, what other sign of hypothermia should we be looking for?'

'The stomach lining for erosions?'

'Very good.'

And there they were – not many, and very small, but erosions in the lining of the stomach.

'Well done, Simon. It's not definitive of course, but in the absence of anything else... I think we'll still send those samples to Guy's though, just in case.'

And he kicked himself – surreptitiously, but quite hard.

Then he phoned Bennett, who'd finished interviewing Medlar and was planning his strategy for when he knew how Goring had died.

'*Frozen* to death?'

'Yes. Obvious really. Should've occurred to me earlier.'

'The freezing-room at the Transfusion Centre?'

'Could be. Just as well you had it sealed off.'

'Could it have been an accident?'

'I've no way of knowing that,' Randall said. Then, 'If it was an accident, why was he dumped in the river?'

Bennett swallowed. 'I take it you still can't give me a time of death?'

'He's been *frozen*, man.' His irritation came through at last. 'It could have been any time since he was last seen.'

Bennett thoughtfully put the phone down, then picked it up again. 'Sergeant, could you come up here, please?'

Yes, Mulholland confirmed, the freezing-room had been sealed off, but he didn't know whether the forensic team were there yet.

'I think we'd better go and have a look for ourselves,' said Bennett. 'Not inside,' he said, seeing the look on Mulholland's face, 'just the general layout.'

Bennett was sure he'd found the 'murder weapon' as soon as he saw the notice about the faulty handle on the door of the minus thirty room – and when Verity Blane, whose department was next to it, admitted she'd found 'a bit of a mess' there on Monday morning, he was convinced.

'How would you describe this mess?'

Verity shrugged. 'Bottles where they shouldn't have been – one was broken and had been pushed under the bottom shelf.'

'You didn't think it worth reporting?'

'I assumed it was some mucky slob who couldn't be bothered to clear up.'

'Where were you on Friday night?' Mulholland asked her.

She looked over at him. 'At home.'

'Any witnesses to that?'

'Yes, as a matter of fact – a friend stayed with me overnight.' She gave them Jessie's name, which Bennett noted with interest.

He then commandeered the library to use as an interview room and sent a car to collect Jessie.

While he was waiting, he got Medlar to show him the centre's card key security system. As they walked back, Medlar said, 'Are you absolutely certain that Adam ... met his death here, inspector?'

'We're waiting on Forensic for proof, but I'm as certain as I can be, yes.'

'Surely, some sort of accident is still the most likely explanation?'

'An accident is always possible, of course, sir,' Bennett said, trying to keep his voice level. 'But it would leave a few things unexplained, wouldn't it?' How, for instance, would Dr Goring have got into the centre without anyone knowing? He hadn't got a card key, had he? Which suggested that he'd come in with someone who had...

'However, let's suppose for a moment that he *did* get in by himself, and for reasons only known to himself, went to the freezing-room.'

Having seen the warning notice on the door, would he really have then gone in and pulled it shut behind him? With respect, Bennett didn't think so.

'And if it was an accident, sir, why was the body later removed and put in the river?'

Medlar had no answer for that.

Bennett studied Jessie very carefully as she was brought in. She seemed shocked when he told her about Goring's death, but something left him unconvinced that it was news to her.

'Could you tell me where you were on Friday night, Miss Pengellis?'

'Yes, I was at a friend's house...' She told him about the scene with Craig, meeting Verity and staying with her that night. They dispatched a man to Craig's parents' farm, where a truculent Craig confirmed her story. He'd given in his notice on Monday and hadn't bothered turning up for work since.

'It doesn't necessarily let her off, sir,' Sergeant Mulholland said a couple of hours later.

'No?' Bennett demanded. 'Perhaps you'd like to tell me how it doesn't.'

'Well, for a start, sir, just because no one saw Goring after seven on Friday doesn't mean he wasn't still alive. He could have been killed on the Saturday.'

****ing stroll on, Bennett thought – he was an old-fashioned man who avoided F-word, even in his thoughts. 'Sergeant, let's look at what we know so far: Goring phoned his wife at around seven and told her he had a possible source of evidence against Pengellis – let's call them X – and was going out. That must be what brought him to the centre. Nobody saw or heard him after that and his bed wasn't slept in that night. That's good enough for me.'

They'd questioned the hotel staff, and also Audrey Goring, who'd been driven down by her son. She'd told them about her husband's last phone call.

Mulholland pressed his lips together. 'All right, sir. But assuming it was Friday, how do we know Blane's telling the truth about Pengellis staying with her that night?'

How indeed? They had Verity in again.

'She was with me from about five until about ten the next morning,' Verity insisted.

'And she was with you all that time?'

'Yes.'

'Are you sure about that? You wouldn't have known if she'd got up and gone out during the night.'

'I think I would, inspector, since we were in the same bed.'

Mulholland said coolly, refusing to be put off, 'There is another possibility, Miss Blane–'

'It's Ms.'

'Another possibility, *Ms* Blane: that Miss Pengellis did leave earlier and that you are

... protecting her.'

Verity said with equal coolness, 'Are you calling me a liar, sergeant?'

Mulholland didn't reply, just looked at her.

'Well, are you?' she demanded.

'As I said, I'm putting another possibility to you.'

'Well, it's a pretty stupid one.' And more to the point, unprovable, her eyes seemed to add.

They questioned Jessie again.

'No. I didn't like him, inspector,' she agreed. 'Nobody here did.'

'But you were the only person he was trying to sack, weren't you? You had more reason to hate him than anyone else here – especially since he'd said he was going to sue you afterwards.'

She said tiredly, 'Even supposing I'd wanted to kill him, what could have possibly persuaded Dr Goring to come to the centre – to the freezing-room – with, of all people, *me?*'

It was a good question and Bennett put it to Medlar.

'Nothing would have persuaded him, inspector. He loathed her.'

Bennett looked at Medlar, decided that perhaps it was time to expose him to a little heat.

'What about your own movements on

Friday, doctor? You told us earlier you were here until about eight – are there any witnesses to that?'

Medlar hesitated, looked away for a moment, then back to Bennett. 'Inspector, can I speak to you in strict confidence?'

'We're often asked that question, sir, and we always do our best. But we can't make promises.'

'It only comes out if absolutely necessary – isn't that the phrase?'

'That's right, sir.'

Medlar swallowed. 'Well, as a matter of fact, there is a witness...' He told him about Sarah's illness and his relationship with Maria. 'I really don't want it to get back to my wife, inspector. It would hurt her terribly.'

You should have thought of that earlier, shouldn't you? thought Bennett unsympathetically. 'Until what time were you here with Miss N'Kanu, doctor?'

'As I told you earlier, it was about eight. I got home at half-past.'

'So you were in your office with Miss N'Kanu from between five and five thirty until about eight, sir?'

'Yes.'

Maria was summoned. She was extremely self-conscious and stumbled over her words, but confirmed Medlar's story.

'But who's to say *they* haven't cooked it up

112

between them?' Bennett demanded of Mulholland when they were alone.

'She was pretty embarrassed, sir. They both were.'

'Yes, but embarrassed about *what?*'

Over the next few days, they systematically questioned all the staff. Nearly all of them could be eliminated and they concentrated on Dominic, Paul, Adrian and Ashley.

Dominic had been the first to realise the dangerous state of the door handle of the freezing-room.

'After I'd been told about it, I went and had a look, then stuck the notice on the door and put in an urgent request for it to be repaired. As you can see,' he added, 'the hospital engineers don't regard us as a high priority any more.'

His own movements on Friday night? He'd left home at a little after seven to go for a drink with Ashley Miles.

'So you were with him from about seven till eleven?'

'No, I was with him from about eight.'

'So what were you doing between seven and eight?'

He explained about his father-in-law. 'I had to get out of the house and decided to go to the library.'

'Would anyone there be able to confirm that?'

Dominic shrugged. 'They might remember me. I took out some books, so they'll have that on computer.'

'So after that, you drove to the – er – Red Lion and met Mr Miles at eight? What did you talk about until eleven?'

'Mostly what the hell we're going to do about getting new jobs.'

'Had a bit to drink, did you?'

'Four pints of shandy in three hours, inspector. I don't believe in drink-driving.'

'Four shandies is still two pints of beer.'

'Over three hours, inspector.'

'All right, all right. Did you go straight home afterwards?'

'I did. My wife was still up. You can check all this if you like.'

'I shall, sir.' Dominic had succeeded in getting up Bennett's nose.

Paul came in looking uncomfortable and, like Medlar before him, asked for diplomatic immunity. Also like Medlar, he was told they'd do their best. He hesitated as his eyes went from Bennett to Mulholland and back.

'I was with a prostitute,' he said at last.

'Her name, sir? I assume it *is* a her?'

'Sherree. I don't know her second name.'

Mulholland said, 'Barum Road, would that be, sir?'

Paul blinked. 'How did you know?'

'We know most of what goes on around

114

here, sir. What time exactly were you with her?'

'Roughly between seven thirty and eight thirty.'

'And she'll be able to confirm that, will she?'

'I should hope so,' Paul muttered. 'She charges me enough.'

Adrian lived with his elderly parents and had spent Friday evening with them, although he had come briefly back to the centre to collect a book at a little before seven.

'Did you see anyone while you were here at the centre, sir?'

'Only Arthur Selwick, the orderly.'

'No one else?'

'No.'

Ashley confirmed that he'd met Dominic at about eight and that they'd stayed in the pub until about eleven.

'What time did you leave home, sir?' asked Mulholland.

'About seven thirty.'

'And it took you until eight to get to the Red Lion?'

'No. I stopped for petrol on the way.'

'Whereabouts would that have been, sir?'

'At the supermarket off Tavvy Road.'

'From your house to the Red Lion shouldn't take more than ten minutes. Add another five for the petrol and that still leaves fifteen minutes unaccounted for.'

'I knew I had the time to spare,' Ashley told them, 'so I checked my oil and water and tyres while I was about it.'

There was no way of either proving or disproving this, and no immediate reason to disbelieve him.

They checked all the statements relating to the Friday insofar as they could and they all matched. Sherree confirmed that Paul had been with her at the time he'd said. Dominic's wife confirmed his departure from and arrival home, as Ashley's did his. The library confirmed that Dominic had been in and even produced a computer print-out of the books he'd chosen. Adrian's parents confirmed his story.

They questioned the orderly, Arthur Selwick, who swore that he'd seen nobody that night except Adrian, but they also discovered that he was slightly deaf...

They then looked at who'd been into the centre during the rest of the weekend. Jessie had come in on Saturday afternoon and spent a couple of hours clearing her desk. Maria had been called in at three forty-five on Sunday for an urgent cross match and had left at a little after seven.

Bennett was a great believer in Motive, and thus Jessie was still his prime suspect. He had her brought down to the station where he gave her 'the works'. She broke down and cried at one stage, but they couldn't shake her story. It was the same with Verity, except that she fought back with more venom.

'This is sexual harassment, inspector, and I am going to sue you for it.'

'I think you might find that difficult, Ms Blane. The reason this interview is being recorded, and that WPC Collins is here, is to ensure that harassment doesn't occur.'

'You're all the same,' sneered Verity. 'I shouldn't expect justice from any of you lot.'

Harassment or no, she couldn't be shaken in her story.

By Thursday, Bennett knew there was going to be no quick answer, so he decided to go to his superintendent before his superintendent could come to him.

'With at least six suspects and virtually no help from Forensic, sir, I wonder if HOLMES might help us here.'

Superintendent Lewis regarded him with something akin to pity. 'I'm glad you've had the honesty to come to me, Vic.' He paused. 'I don't know about HOLMES, but as it happens, I have been approached by the Blood Division. They're very embarrassed about the corruption aspects of this case and want it sorted as quickly as possible. It seems they have an investigator there who's had experience in this kind of thing–'

Oh no... Bennett had a horrible pre-
monition.

'—and they want to send him down. His
name's—'

'Jones,' supplied Bennett. *The bastard.*

'You remember him, then?'

'I'm not likely to forget, sir. I didn't find
him the easiest of men to get along with,
sir—'

'He sorted it out though, didn't he?'

'Not before there were three more corpses
lying around the place, sir.'

Not to mention a few cases of hurt pride,
thought Lewis. 'Well, I've already told them
yes, Vic, so you'll have to try and make your
peace with him.'

10

It was just as Sheila had said, she thought as
they were shown into the room, they were a
double act: one of them bald, moustachioed
and urbane in a dark suit; the other in a
leather jacket, younger, harder and somehow – there was no other word for it –
meaner.

'Thank you for coming so quickly,' she
said, walking round from her desk to greet
them. 'Would you like some coffee?'

'Please,' said Marcus for both of them.

Lady Margaret, Chairman of the Blood Division, nodded to the receptionist, who silently withdrew.

'Please sit down.' She indicated some leather armchairs a little way from her desk, waited until they'd sat before seating herself opposite them.

'As I told you over the phone, Mr Evans, the matter I wish to discuss with you – with both of you – is delicate.'

'As are many of the matters we deal with,' Marcus said. 'As I believe I mentioned to you.'

She nodded. 'Indeed.' She paused, continued: 'Were you aware of the death of my colleague, Dr Adam Goring, at Tamar last weekend?'

'I read about it in the paper,' Tom said. *With a certain morbid fascination*, he didn't add. 'I thought the police had arrested someone.'

'The someone in question was helping them with their enquiries. She's now been released.'

'Oh,' Tom said.

'Yes. Which brings us to why you are here–'

There was a light knock on the door and the receptionist returned with what looked like a silver tray.

'On the coffee table, please, Emma,' Lady

Margaret told her. The tray was deposited between them and Emma departed as discreetly as she had arrived. 'I'll be mother, shall I?'

A less motherly person than Lady Margaret Tom could scarcely imagine. Immaculately permed grey hair (with not a trace of blue) crowned her long, appropriately equine face (she owned a racing stable) and she was dressed in a severe white blouse and tweed skirt. The coffee was delicious.

'Did your newspaper say why Dr Goring was in Tamar?' she asked Tom.

'To take part in a TV programme about the Transfusion Service, I believe.' He knew perfectly well.

'Yes. It was ill advised and I told him so, but he was always obstinate. He was convinced he could scotch a problem we had – and still have – there once and for all. I think at this stage I'd better give you some of the background...'

She told them how the Blood Division had been instructed by the previous government to make the Blood Service more efficient and, at the same time, cut £10 million from its £135 million budget.

'A tall order, as you can imagine,' she said, 'but that's what we're paid for.'

The only way it could be done, she explained, was to close five of the fifteen centres and use the money saved to buy in a computer system that would link the remaining ten.

'Initially, there was a lot of resistance to this, but we'd overcome most of it. Except in one place – Tamar...'

She told them how Jessie had organised her campaign and become a major thorn in their corporate flesh, culminating in the live TV debate.

'I warned Adam that no good would come of it, but he insisted on accepting their invitation.' She sighed, told them about Jessie's allegation of nepotism at the end of the programme.

'He lost his temper, which made him look guilty – his temper was always his Achilles' heel. I telephoned him, told him that I'd told him so, and he said he was going to put it right before going to America. The next thing I heard he was dead.'

'Are the details as reported in the papers correct?' Tom asked.

'That he was locked into a freezer in the Tamar centre and froze to death, yes...'

Marcus glanced quickly at Tom as she said this, but Tom's face was inscrutable – he'd once been trapped in the same freezer and had been lucky to escape.

'You'll have to ask the police about the rest,' Lady Margaret said. Her voice was quavering slightly and they realised that she

121

was human after all, that she'd been genuinely fond of him.

'Would you like some more coffee?' she said. Her voice was under control now, although her eyes were bright. Marcus declined and Tom accepted.

The police were confident of finding the killer, she told them, but had warned her not to expect an early arrest.

'Our problem is that while this uncertainty drags on, we can't lay the allegation of nepotism to rest. It's been very damaging – we've already had one of the other centres due to close claim that it's being done simply to pay off old scores. I'd like you to go down to Tamar and sort it out for us as quickly as possible.' She looked from one to the other of them. 'Please.'

'From what you say,' Marcus said, 'the allegation is more important to you than the murder.'

She compressed her lips before speaking. 'So far as the Blood Division's concerned, the murder is a matter for the police – officially. But since they may well be linked, it could mean, in effect, that you're looking for the killer as well.'

'I'd have thought you could have checked the allegation for yourselves. To an extent, anyway.'

'And so we have, to an extent. Mike Derby, Adam's son-in-law, freely admits he'd have liked the research director's job, but says he didn't discuss it with Adam until after the closure was announced. Charles Coldman, the director at East Dorset, says he didn't discuss it with Adam at any time. That, of course, does not solve our problem.'

'Was it Dr Goring who actually chose which centres were to close?'

'In effect, yes. In theory, it was a joint decision, but as Medical Executive, Adam clearly knew more than the rest of us and we took his advice. I have to say that he made a perfectly good case for the closure of Tamar,' she added.

'What do you think, Lady Margaret?' Marcus asked. 'Could he have been ... influenced in his decision?'

'I really wouldn't have thought so.' She hesitated. 'Adam Goring could be a hard, sometimes even a ruthless man, but I find it very difficult to believe that he was actually corrupt.'

'You realise that, whatever we discover, it may well be impossible to actually prove anything either way?'

Yes, she did realise that, she told them, but Sheila Castleton had been happy with their efforts. 'I can only ask that you try.'

'And if we do find he was corrupt?'

'I'll take that risk.'

Marcus nodded slowly. 'Anything you'd

like to ask, Tom?'

As Tom turned to her, the leather of the armchair made a slight farting noise. 'Er – have you spoken to the police about our involvement, Lady Margaret?' He wondered why it was that although both he and Marcus spoke with London accents, his always seemed to sound the more vulgar in his ears.

'Yes. I know the Chief Constable of Devon quite well, and he's perfectly agreeable.'

'Good,' Tom said, thinking, *But what about the Indians?*

Lady Margaret was smiling a tight little smile. 'He's not aware yet, of course, of your – how did Sheila put it? – your rather bracing style of interview, your propensity for puncturing egos...'

Marcus's lips compressed as Tom said, 'Are you saying, Lady Margaret, that I should modify my–?'

'No, I'm not, Mr Jones. Sheila said that you got results where the police had failed, and that's what I'm interested in – results.'

Tom nodded his thanks, then allowed his gaze to drift over the room as Marcus and Lady Margaret settled administrative details ... rosewood desk, thick carpet, real oil paintings, Irvine wallpaper ... then Marcus was assuring her they would keep in touch and they stood to go. Downstairs, they shrugged into overcoats and a footman opened the door for them.

'How the other half work, eh?' Tom observed as they crossed the small formal garden to the cast iron railings dividing it from the street.

'Mm,' Marcus said non-committally as they started up Whitehall. 'Your reputation seems to have gone before you.'

'How d'you mean?'

'Your bracing style of interview.'

'Oh, that.'

Marcus smiled, then said more seriously, 'How d'you feel about going back to Tamar?'

'It's not Tamar as such that bothers me.'

'The centre? Its memories?'

Tom nodded. 'Yes, those ... but mostly its contents.'

'Ah.'

Tom's younger brother Frank, now dead from AIDS, had been a haemophiliac and when they were boys, Tom had often been blamed when Frank had a bleed. The beatings his father meted out had resulted in a lifelong phobia of the sight of blood that he'd never quite managed to overcome...

Marcus touched his shoulder. 'You'll be all right. You told me it gets a bit better every time, didn't you?'

'Yeah.' *Except that I was lying...*

The plane trees stood bare and etched against the pale blue sky and a brisk east wind hustled them along the pavement. Marcus turned to him again: 'Has Holly said anything to you about the reorganisation, all the transfusion centres closing?' Tom's wife Holly worked in a hospital lab.

'Yes. It's caused a lot of problems already.'

'What sort of problems?'

'Shortages of blood and delays in getting it to the hospitals. There's been a decrease in the number of donors too, but that's only part of it – the new computer system Lady M. mentioned apparently isn't all it was cracked up to be. The irony is,' he continued after a pause, 'that they'll probably end up having to spend a lot more than the ten mill they've saved to sort it all out.'

Marcus nodded. 'It's what usually happens when you fix something that ain't broke.'

They reached their own building and went up to Marcus's office.

'You know what this is really all about, don't you?' he said.

Tom waited.

'It's politics. Our New Masters have spotted the chance of slinging some more ordure at the Old Lot and Lady M. is to be the target.'

'And she's seen it coming and wants me to catch it for her,' Tom said gloomily. He looked up suddenly. 'If that's true, Marcus, if it's political, then we shouldn't have anything to do with it, should we?'

Marcus thought about it. 'No, it's OK,' he said, 'because we're not actually doing it for her. There's a real possibility of high-level corruption here and that's what you'll be looking for. Nice try, though,' he added after a pause.

11

Holly's parents still lived near Tamar and when Tom told her about the job, she insisted they stay with them.

'They haven't seen Hal for ages,' she said. 'And think of the money you'll save.'

'The department'll save,' Tom grumbled, 'not me.' He got on well enough with Kath and Henry Jordan, his in-laws, but he'd always felt that the maxim of guests being like fish (they go off after a couple of days) worked both ways – besides which, they didn't like the smell of his cheroots. Which was why now, on Sunday morning, as he passed through the gates of Sticklepath, the Jordan smallholding, and pointed the Cooper at Tamar, he told himself to think of it as another incentive to get the job done quickly. They'd driven down on Saturday and Bennett had agreed to meet him today.

Tom had felt almost as apprehensive as

Bennett when he'd heard that he was in charge of the case, the same who'd been so irritated by his contribution a few years earlier, and he wondered how many other ghosts would be putting in an appearance this time round.

He was shown into Bennett's office almost straight away.

'Have a seat, Mr Jones.' Bennett indicated the chair in front of his desk.

Tom sat. 'It's been a long time, inspector.'

'Indeed it has,' Bennett said cursorily, obviously not wanting to dwell on it. He hadn't offered to shake hands, either.

Tom mentally shrugged – if that was the way he wanted it... He studied the other's face, wondering whether he'd have recognised Bennett if they'd met in the street. Probably not, he thought, his hair and moustache were both nearly white now, and the skin more heavily lined ... although, as he looked, the strongly musteline flavour of his face seemed familiar. *Strange, people say I'm like a stoat, maybe it's something detectives have in common...*

'Shall we get started?' Bennett broke in on his thoughts. He had a distinct, though not unpleasant, Devon accent.

'Fine.'

'I'll take you through what we've done so far, then we'll go to the centre for you to have a look at the SOC.'

128

He described the discovery of the body, Randall's efforts to ascertain the cause of death and how he, Bennett, had realised as soon as he'd seen the freezing-room with its faulty door that Goring must have died there.

'No chance it was an accident?' Tom asked.

'I'd have thought you, of all people, would have realised the odds against that,' Bennett said in his first direct reference to Tom's earlier involvement. 'No one going in there on their own would shut the door under any circumstances, let alone when there was a notice on it warning that the handle wasn't working.'

'No,' Tom agreed.

'And the fuse for the siren had been dislodged, so he couldn't raise the alarm once he was in there.'

'So you think it was premeditated?'

'I'll come to that in a minute.' He told Tom how he'd interviewed all the staff and come to the conclusion that Jessie had the strongest motive... 'Find the motive and you've nearly always got your killer, alibi or no alibi.'

'Goring had her suspended, you said?'

'He was going to have her sacked, Mr Jones, and after that, he was going to sue her. Look, why don't you judge for yourself while I get some tea for us.' He opened a drawer and took out a video cassette. 'This is the TV interview where she accused him of rigging the closure.'

He switched on the monitor, gave it a few seconds to warm up, then pushed in the cassette. 'D'you take sugar?'

Tom hesitated – he loathed police tea. 'Would you mind if I had coffee?'

'It'll have to be instant.'

'That's fine.'

Bennett left the room as Cool Suzee was introducing Goring and Jessie. Tom studied them, glad to have the opportunity to put a living face to the dead victim, since one of his own beliefs was that murder victims often carry the seeds of their destruction within them.

Bennett came back half-way through and they watched in silence as the interview built up to its crescendo.

'See what I mean?'

'Well, they didn't like each other much, did they?'

'Not a lot, no. Want to see it again?'

'I think I will, if you don't mind.'

Bennett obviously hadn't been expecting this, but he rewound the video and pressed the start button. Tom studied it intently, making notes, asking to go back once or twice.

Bennett stirred his tea. As the video finished, he said, 'Immediately after that,

Goring had her suspended and then told the director that she was to be fired come what may. Even told him to find the evidence to help him do it.'

'But did she know the full extent to which he was gunning for her?'

'Oh yes, Dr Medlar told her that afternoon. Dr Goring was a powerful man and it was a foregone conclusion that he'd get his way. She'd have been ruined.'

'So why haven't you arrested her?'

Bennett sighed. 'Because she's got an alibi for the time he was killed.' He told Tom about Jessie's domestic spat with Craig and her spending the night with Verity.

'Couldn't they both be involved?' Tom asked.

'That's possible, of course, but so long as they stick to their story, difficult to prove.'

'Another thing,' Tom said, 'how could *she* of all people have persuaded Goring to walk into a freezer?'

'I don't know,' Bennett admitted.

'And why use such an esoteric method of killing him?'

He hesitated. 'I had wondered about the fact that with the body frozen, the actual time of death would be next to impossible to work out.'

'But I can't see how that would help her... I mean, wouldn't she want to make it look as though it had been done at a time for which she had an alibi?'

'Yes, and it was almost certainly done on Friday night.'

'*Almost* certainly?'

Bennett told him about their enquiries at the hotel. 'For practical purposes we can assume he was killed then.'

'So why was the body dumped in the river?'

'I can only assume that the killer realised it hadn't been discovered and did it to confuse us.'

'But think about it – moving a frozen body without being seen, it's a hell of risk to take... Were any of the staff in over the weekend?'

Bennett told him about Jessie and Maria.

Tom thought for a moment. 'Whoever shut him in the freezer did it without being seen, and the same could apply when they took him out. So it doesn't necessarily have to be one of those two.'

'Not necessarily, no,' agreed Bennett.

He took Tom through every stage of his investigation and gave him copies of all the relevant statements.

'He can't have enjoyed telling you about that,' Tom observed, on learning of Medlar's indiscretion.

'Any more than he'll enjoy telling you, I imagine,' Bennett said with the ghost of a smile.

'No.' Tom looked down the list of names.

'Don't any of these others have a possible motive – anything?'

'Not really, no. Goring was widely disliked, but not so much as to be worth killing for.' He continued slowly, 'The only one would be Medlar, if Goring had somehow found out about his affair with Miss N'Kanu. But since he volunteered the information, I didn't think so.'

'No,' Tom said thoughtfully. He looked up. 'So was it premeditated, d'you think?'

Bennett hesitated. 'If I was planning to kill someone, that wouldn't be the way I'd do it. There are so many variables – I could so easily be seen going into the centre with Goring, leaving without him for that matter... Look, why don't we go up there now and you'll see what I mean?'

They went in separate cars.

Tom had more or less resigned himself to the fact that he would never completely conquer his haemophobia, the quaking, gut-liquefying terror of the sight, even the proximity of blood. *It isn't as though I haven't tried,* he told himself as he stopped the car and gazed up at the Great White Elephant On The Hill. *It's just that...* It was just that every time he had to face it anew, it felt like starting all over again.

Tamar Hospital was one of the last of the mega-hospitals planned in the sixties and stood unabashed and defiant, like a fortress, its white tiled façades glinting in the winter sunshine. Tom didn't like it now any more than he had those years ago on his first major job for Marcus, but there was no doubt it had completely changed his life. It was where he'd taken his first steps towards facing his phobia instead of hiding it, and it had led to his reconciliation with his brother. It was where he'd met Holly.

He sighed, restarted the car and drove up. Bennett was waiting for him outside the main entrance.

'What kept you?'

'Got lost. Sorry.' *Lost in the past...*

Bennett grunted, walked over to the door and pressed the intercom button. It squawked back at him almost immediately.

'Yes-can-I-help-you?'

He identified himself; about half a minute later, the door opened and they were admitted by a disgruntled Arthur – he was having to work extra because of Craig's desertion.

'Mr Tudor wants to see you,' he told Bennett.

'Oh, he does, does he?' Bennett muttered.

They followed Arthur along the wide corridor. The smells were the same and Tom swallowed and gritted his teeth. There had been changes, he noticed. Blood Issue, Cross Matching and the manager's office seemed to have been swapped around –

were there any more?

Dominic looked up from the desk. 'Hello, inspector. I didn't realise you were coming in today.'

'And I didn't realise you'd be here, sir.' He paused. 'This is Mr Jones from the Department of Health. He'll be assisting us and I'm showing him the scene of crime.'

'That's all right, inspector,' he said, graciously acceding to Bennett's non-request. He got up, held out his hand to Tom. 'Dominic Tudor, acting lab manager.' His smile was for Tom alone. 'Is that your Mini Cooper outside?'

'Yes,' said Tom.

'Looks in beautiful condition. You don't see so many about now.'

'Not so many,' agreed Tom.

'If you're coming in tomorrow, you'll have to leave it in one of the car-parks – we need the space out there for loading. The underground one would be the best.'

'OK.'

'Well, let me know if you need me for anything.'

Tom told him he would and Bennett took him along to the freezing-room corridor.

'Arrogant little tick,' he said when they were out of earshot.

'You don't like him?'

'No, I don't.'

'Is he in the frame at all?'

'I don't think so.' Bennett sounded regretful. 'He's the one with the library books.'

He pushed open another door and they were outside the freezing-room. A notice was stuck to the heavy insulating door:

DANGER. Faulty release handle.
Do not enter without supervision.

'No mistake about that,' said Tom.

'No,' said Bennett. 'That's the fuse box for the lights and siren,' he said, pointing.

Tom went over. After looking at it for a moment, he pulled out the screw, slid aside the holding clip and pulled off the cover to reveal the fuses.

'Careful,' said Bennett.

Tom looked up. 'The screw was loose – if I can do that, so can anyone.'

'But we don't know whether it just happened to be loose at the time, do we? Or whether it was doctored beforehand.'

He twisted the light switch and a red bulb glowed, then he pulled the door open. Tom felt the cold air washing round his feet as the whine of the fans inside died away and a veil of mist formed in the doorway where cold and warm air met. Bennett showed him the handle.

'Normally, if you push it from inside, the door opens.' He pushed it. 'Now, it's jammed.'

'Intentionally?'

'The engineers say not. D'you want to go in?'

'I'd better have a look.'

They stepped through the curtain of mist. Inside, the air was crystal and the light sparkled and flashed from the thick coating of ice on the walls and shelving. Icicles hung from the coolant radiators at either end and the hairs froze in Tom's nostrils as he breathed in.

'Forensic didn't need to thaw it out, then?' His voice hung thick, like smoke.

'No, they thought they'd have a better chance of finding evidence by leaving it frozen. They were right. There were particles of Goring's shoes and trousers on the floor here–' he pointed – 'and they found traces of skin and blood on the door and on the pull cord for the siren, here.'

Of course they would, thought Tom, *where he'd have bashed and scrabbled and screamed and yanked at the cord in blind panic until the cold finally...* He could feel the cold himself now, nibbling stealthily at his neck and ankles, and for a few parsecs he was back eight years, trapped in there alone and in the dark... *Until it gnawed through to his bones and he knew it was the end. Tom* had known what it was to give up hope.

'Seen enough?'

'Yes.' He followed him out into what

already felt like a tropical rain forest. Bennett slammed the door and turned off the light.

Tom forced himself to think. 'We come back to where we started – was it premeditated?'

Bennett took a breath and released it. 'As I said earlier, it's such a risky way of killing someone. I know that orderly's a bit deaf, but he might easily have come out of his room at that moment. He might even have gone to the freezer for some reason and found Goring there before he died – none of them likely, but all quite possible.'

'So you think it was spontaneous?'

Bennett shrugged elaborately. 'That's just as difficult to see. Why were they here, why hadn't they made themselves known to the orderly? If they came in for X to show Goring some evidence against Pengellis, what could have triggered X to kill him?'

'There are other ways in, aren't there?' Tom said after a pause. 'Besides the way we came in.'

'I'll show you.'

He took Tom down the main corridor and left past Medlar's office. 'That door leads to the main hospital, as I'm sure you remember.'

Tom nodded and Bennett walked swiftly on past Microbiology to reception. 'This is where it's changed. You can still get in through there–' he pointed to the reception office – 'but there's a lift and staircase here now that take you down to the underground park where they keep their trucks and vans. If Goring and X parked there, then came up in the lift and went down *here*–' he led Tom into the back corridor – 'they'd have been able to get through without much risk of being seen.'

He pushed open a door on the left and they walked through the wash-up area to the Products Lab.

'Presto.' Bennett pulled open another door. 'Here's the freezer.'

'D'you think that's what happened?'

'It fits the facts. We know Goring was expecting to be shown some evidence – the question is, by whom?'

'Bit of a fazer, innit?' Tom said after a pause.

'And I wish you joy of it,' Bennett said.

The two men reluctantly smiled at each other, as though aware suddenly that they were on the same side.

'So what's your first move?' Bennett asked.

'Dr Randall, I think, in case he's had any third or fourth thoughts, and then Miss Pengellis, since she comes so highly recommended. D'you have her address?'

'Sure. D'you want her phone number as well?'

'No, I think I'll let it be a surprise for her.'

After Bennett had left, Tom went up to the hospital library where he could concentrate on the statements without distractions, make notes and formulate a few questions.

None of the main players really had a watertight alibi, he thought; with the exception of Paul, they were all provided by each other, their spouses, or both. Jessie and Verity ... Medlar and Maria ... Dominic and Ashley.

After an hour or so, his brain felt saturated and he decided to go back to Sticklepath. They'd kept some Sunday lunch for him which he ate by himself in the kitchen, then he, Holly and Hal donned wellies and took Henry's dog for a walk round the fields. Hal was fascinated by the sheep nosing round the feeding cages and had to be physically restrained from investigating the horns on the ram that was calmly appraising them with his disconcerting devil's eyes.

'It's not so bad being here,' Holly said quietly. 'Is it?'

Tom smiled. 'I suppose not,' he said.

12

Dr Randall seemed to be regretting the impulsive generosity that had led him to grant Tom an audience. 'Mr Jones? Come in, sit down. How can I help? I'm rather busy at the moment – I have to go soon.'

Hello, I must be going, thought Tom. Fortunately, he'd already worked out his questions, and the smell of the Path Lab rendered him as anxious to leave as Randall.

'I know you can't be exact, doctor, but I'd be glad of anything you can tell me about the timings.'

'How d'you mean, timings?'

'Inspector Bennett thinks that Dr Goring was locked into the freezer on Friday evening. What do you think? And if so, when was the body taken out – Saturday or Sunday?'

Randall spoke a little more slowly. 'As you've observed, it's impossible to give definitive answers, since the study of heat loss and gain in the human body is an inexact science.' He took a breath. 'He was last seen on Friday evening and nothing I found suggested he went into the freezer any later than that.'

'But he could have?'

'Have could have, yes,' he agreed. 'The events following that are even more difficult to predict – how quickly the temperature of the body fell would depend on how long he remained alive...'

'How long would you think?'

Randall looked away for a moment, then back at Tom. 'I understand that Dr Goring wasn't a popular man, but I wouldn't wish that death on anyone. He would have remained conscious for at least twenty minutes, probably longer, judging by the cuts and bruises to the hands, but not much over forty minutes because of the chill factor – you know what I mean by that?'

Tom nodded.

'Well, the fans in that freezing-room blasting out air at minus thirty degrees chill someone very quickly.'

'What about clothing, or layers of fat?'

'He was well built, but had no overcoat, just a light jacket – it wasn't particularly cold on Friday evening. With the chill factor I've described, I think he would have been unconscious after about thirty minutes – mercifully – and dead about an hour after that. Body temperature would have fallen quite rapidly after death, the rate slowing as it approached minus thirty.'

'So when do you think he was taken out?'

'I don't know, Mr Jones.' He paused again.

'The human body is a very poor conductor of heat, especially immersed in cold water, so the temperature would have risen much more slowly than it fell in the freezer. The body was still rigid when I first examined it, so I would guess, and I must emphasise that it really is only a guess, that it was taken out on Sunday. Does that answer your question?'

'It does, thank you.'

'I could never swear to any of this in court, it's only what I think.' He looked at his watch. 'Was there anything else?'

Tom hesitated. 'Doctor, someone, somehow, got him into that freezer without being seen and left him to die. They then took the risk of coming back later, taking the body out and dumping it in the river. Inspector Bennett thinks it was done to confuse the police, but–'

'Not difficult in his case.'

Tom smiled dutifully. 'Can you think of any reason for it?'

'Not really, although it's not my job, of course. But Bennett's idea of it being done to confuse the time of death won't wash. If the body had been found in the freezer on Monday, *I* wouldn't have known when he'd gone in. It could have been Friday or Saturday, maybe even Sunday, so where's the advantage of moving it?' He considered a moment. 'The only thing I can think of is that it was an attempt to confuse the *manner* of his death – they probably thought the body would thaw and hoped we'd think he drowned.'

'One last thing, doctor.' Tom could see that his patience was very nearly exhausted. 'Moving a frozen body is going to be difficult in any circumstances, but *how* difficult would depend on its posture – d'you see what I mean?'

Randall nodded. 'It would have been difficult, but not impossible, in the posture in which I found it.' The look of near pity touched his face again as he described it. 'You see, I think the instinct of a person dying in those circumstances would be to curl up, adopt a foetal position – partly of course to reduce heat loss, but maybe also something more primitive ... his arm probably became outstretched as he lost consciousness.' His eyes flicked back to Tom. 'I hope you catch him, Mr Jones. I hope he's put away for a very long time.'

'*He*, doctor?'

'I'm incorrigibly sexist – of course it could have been a woman. And now, you really will have to excuse me.'

As Tom walked back to his car, he thought about the living image of Goring he'd seen on the video, about what Randall had said about his death. He was right, nobody deserved to die like that, and he wondered whether the killer had known what he (or *she*) was subjecting his (or *her*) victim to. He shook his head as though to clear it, unlocked the car and got in.

Jessie's house was in a back street terrace, the middle one of the block with the date, 1907, high on the wall between the top windows. There was no answer to the bell, but this may have been due to the electric drill he could hear going somewhere inside. He waited until it stopped, then tried again. After about half a minute, the door opened against a chain.

'Yes?' said a voice.

He could make out a pair of eyes behind the crack. He explained who he was and passed his identification through.

'I think I will phone this number and check,' the voice said.

'That's what it's there for,' Tom said equably.

He looked around while he waited. A trellis separated the front garden from its neighbour; it looked tidy now and was probably very pretty in the summer. Although the house was small, the doorway was attractively arched and the whole property well cared for.

The chain rattled again and the door opened.

'Come in, Mr Jones.'

'Thank you.'

As his eyes adjusted, he saw a slight, almost boyish figure in blue dungarees. Dark brown hair framed a thin, attractive face with high cheekbones and button brown eyes. Dust and wood shavings clung to her and, as though reading his mind, she said, 'I've been doing some DIY, since I'll probably have to sell this place soon.'

She showed him into the living-room. 'Would you like a coffee?'

'Please.'

'Milk and sugar?'

'Just milk, please.'

She went out and he looked round. The room was tidy, but lived in and comfortable. There were books on the shelves and the small TV was pushed back in a corner. She came back with mugs of coffee.

'Thanks – that was quick.'

'The kettle hadn't long boiled.' She sat down opposite him.

Tom sipped the coffee, waiting for her to ask how she could help him or some such.

She didn't, so after a pause, he began. 'The Blood Division is very embarrassed about what's happened down here...'

'I'm not surprised.'

'They want it resolved quickly, which is why they've sent me.'

'Have the police given up on it, then?'

'The police never give up as such, but they don't see themselves getting a quick answer in this case. Also, they're not so concerned with the allegations you made about Dr Goring as are the Blood Division. About the reasons for the closure of the Tamar centre.'

'I see.'

There was another silence while they appraised each other under the guise of drinking coffee. *She's tough,* he thought, *but a killer...?*

Again as though reading his mind, she said, 'I didn't kill Dr Goring. I know Inspector Bennett thinks I did, but I didn't.' She held his eyes. 'And if you've been sent here by the Blood Division, by Lady Margaret, I'm just wondering what it's in *your* interest to think.'

'How d'you mean?'

'I'd have thought it obvious. The best scenario for Lady M. would be that the allegation was groundless, that I made it up out of spite, and that when Dr Goring had me justifiably punished, I killed him–'

Tom couldn't remember such cynicism ever being ascribed to him before. 'Try and regard me as a simple seeker after truth,' he said.

'Ah, but "what is truth, said jesting Pilate"... You see, I've had time to catch up on my reading. What if the "truth" you found was not to Lady M.'s liking?'

'Then she'd have to listen anyway.'

Her eyes widened. 'An honest apparatchik – my word!'

Tom smiled. 'This isn't really getting us anywhere, is it?'

'No? I was rather enjoying it.' She took a cigarette packet from the front pouch of her dungarees, extracted one and offered the pack to him.

'Not at the moment, thanks.'

She found a lighter, applied the flame. 'Then ask me your questions.'

'I've seen a video of the TV interview you had with Dr Goring. Was the allegation you made true?'

She blew smoke. 'I believe so, yes.'

'What's your source?'

She hesitated. 'Someone at the East Dorset centre.'

'Who?'

'I can't tell you that. I gave my word.'

'I have to know if I'm going to check it. I can promise you it wouldn't go any further. And it would be to your advantage,' he added.

'How do I know I can trust you?'

'Ultimately, I suppose, you don't. But I wouldn't last very long in my job if I habitually broke my word.'

She nodded slowly. 'All right. It was Diana Small. She's in charge of the Reagents Lab at Poole.'

Tom noted it down. 'How does she know?'

'She overheard Dr Goring and Dr Goldman talking about it.'

'So why did she tell you? I mean, isn't it to her advantage if Tamar shuts rather than East Dorset?'

'She's honest. She doesn't like corruption.'

'I wonder how she felt about you letting it out so dramatically.'

'She was very annoyed about it. I hadn't planned to let it out like that.' She continued quickly, 'You say you've seen the interview – what did you think, did anything strike you about it?'

'Other than the revelation at the end, you mean?'

She nodded.

Tom thought a moment. 'Only that you were pretty evenly matched.'

'But who did you think came out on top?'

'I suppose Dr Goring did – because he had a convincing answer for all the points you made.'

'Exactly!' she said. 'Thank you, Mr Jones. That's why I made the allegation.'

'To get back at him any way you could?'

'No, because it was the only thing left that wasn't scripted, so to speak. I spent weeks collating all that data, and yet he had an immediate answer for every single point I made. There's only one way that could have happened...' She explained how she'd left her file on her desk, how it could so easily have been taken and photocopied, and how he'd even known about the staff meeting she'd held.

'That was the clincher, and that's why I did it. I had to hit him with something he wasn't ready for, and that was the only thing I could think of.'

'Well, you were right there,' Tom agreed. 'He certainly wasn't expecting it.'

'No, and it showed him up for what he was – a blustering, lying bully– *Sorry!*' she said. 'I know you shouldn't speak ill of the dead...'

'Bullying liar or not, he's certainly that,' observed Tom.

'Yes, but I didn't do it.' Again, she looked directly into his eyes.

'So you're saying he had a spy here?'

'Yes.'

'Who?'

'I don't know.' Seeing the sceptical look on his face, she continued, 'Dr Medlar told me that Dr Goring had admitted it to him.'

'Didn't he say who it was?'

'No.'

'Did you know about the freezing-room door, that it was jamming?'

She blinked at the abrupt change of subject. 'We all did,' she said, and told him how Steve Tanner had come into the meeting to tell Dominic.

Who exactly had been there, he wanted to

know; she told him and he noted down the names.

'All right,' he said, 'so what were you doing that night?'

'Which night?'

'Friday night. The night Dr Goring was killed.'

'I'm sure you already know all that from the inspector.'

'I'd like to hear it from you.'

She shrugged. 'Very well,' and she told him about Craig and how she'd fled from her own house.

'Weren't you frightened?'

'I was bloody terrified.'

'Why didn't you go to the police?'

'I didn't want the hassle, I just wanted him out.'

'OK.' He made a note to talk to Craig himself. 'Then what happened?'

She described how she'd met Verity and gone back with her to her house; the meal, the wine, although not the hashish. 'I was worried about Craig, whether he'd trash my place, whether he'd still be here, so I ended up spending the night there.'

'Sharing a bed?'

'Yes,' she said matter-of-factly.

'What time would you say you arrived at her house?'

She made a mouth. 'A little after five, I suppose.'

'And you had a meal, some wine and went to bed together – what time would that have been?'

'I wasn't exactly watching the clock at the time... I'd say sometime after eight.'

'Quite early.'

'If you say so.'

'And you stayed there until ten the next morning?'

'That's right.'

Tom looked at her and she looked steadily back at him. *Bennett's right,* he thought, *she is lying...*

He decided to push her.

'So, I suppose you could say you discovered something about yourself that night?'

'How d'you mean?'

'About your sexuality – you could say that you discovered your ... true self that night.'

'"What is truth?"' she repeated after a pause.

'What indeed?'

'You're right, I suppose I did discover something about myself that night.'

'Didn't it surprise you? I mean, you had been living with Craig, a man, for the last two months. Had you had a normal sexual relationship with him?'

'What's normal?'

Tom didn't say anything, and after a moment she continued: 'Yes, I suppose it did surprise me.'

'So you could say, in a manner of speaking, that you were seduced by Miss Blane?'

'Yes, I suppose you could, in a manner of speaking.' Her voice was still light, but her face was beginning to flush.

'What did you do in bed?'

'I beg your pardon?'

'What did you do when you got into bed with Miss Blane?'

'What do you *think* we did?' Her voice was forced now and the flush covered her cheekbones, making them stand out more than ever.

'I've no idea, I don't know about these things... Strapadictomy? Steely Dan Three for all I know...' He realised he'd gone too far as soon as the words were out, wondered fleetingly whether she'd ever read *The Naked Lunch*...

She had. She leapt to her feet, her face crimson, her voice choking. 'I think you'd better go...' and Tom realised he'd escaped being slapped by a whisker.

'All right,' he said, standing up slowly, making sure he kept out of range. 'I'll see myself out.'

At the door, he said, 'I'll almost certainly need to speak to you again.'

She didn't move, but her eyes glowed as red as her face. 'Do I have any choice?'

'You can refuse, of course, but I'm not

sure it would be in your interest.'

'Get out.'

He pulled the front door shut behind him, walked to his car and drove off.

I wonder if she'll complain ... she'd have grounds. Tom hadn't meant to push his luck that far, but he felt fairly sure she wouldn't complain. *Because she is lying, about something.*

The ready answers, the prepared story, the too frank stares when she wanted to look sincere...

And she should have simply told me to MYOB when I got intimate.

He'd talk to Craig, and Verity of course, although she'd certainly be forewarned. He took a breath and drove to the centre.

13

He sat waiting in reception, thinking, telling himself: *It's not so bad as the first time I was here and there's no reason I should actually have to see any...* He badly wanted a cheroot.

A secretary arrived and took him to the directorial suite.

'Mr Jones, Dr Medlar.'

'Come in, Mr Jones.' Medlar got up from behind his desk as the secretary pulled the door shut and shook Tom's hand. His grip was neither slack nor too hearty.

'Do sit down.' He indicated a seat and resumed his own behind his desk. 'I can't pretend your visit's a pleasure, although I do appreciate its necessity. Where do you want to start?'

Tom could detect the nervousness behind the firm, no-nonsense approach; he'd expected it and given some thought to his approach. 'Has Lady Margaret explained to you why she's asked me to come here?'

'Yes. It seems she's as much worried about the corruption aspects as she is about poor Adam's death.'

'I believe you'd known Dr Goring for some time?'

'Yes, we were old friends.'

'Close friends?'

Medlar hesitated. 'It was the friendship of colleagues who'd ... shared a lot of experiences.' He smiled as he said this, a small smile that nevertheless softened his rather angular face. 'I wouldn't say we were really close.'

'How long had you known him?'

'Oh, it must have been nearly twenty-five years.'

'That long?'

'Yes. We met at the Sheffield centre in the mid-seventies when we were doing our post-grad fellowships, and afterwards, we were both employed there.'

'Sheffield's your home?'

'No. I came from York originally.'

Yes, thought Tom, his accent was harder, more distinct than Goring's had been on the video, rather like his face. And yet it was Goring who had indisputably packed the punch.

He said with a smile, 'You seemed a little ... equivocal about your relationship with Dr Goring just now.'

'Did I? Well, I suppose you could say that there was a – a certain rivalry between us one way and another in those days.'

'In what ways?'

'Well, we were both taken on as registrars, but we knew that the deputy directorship would be coming up before long. We both applied, and Adam got it.'

'Why was that, d'you think?'

'Basically, because he wanted it more than me.'

'Did you resent it?'

'No – I was never as ambitious as he. Besides which, he left after three years to become director of the West London centre and I took over from him.'

'He was always a high-flyer, then?'

'Oh, very much so.'

'So it was really only a matter of time before he moved on?'

Again Medlar hesitated. 'Yes, although he

did have other reasons for wanting to leave at the time. His fiancée broke off their engagement and married me.'

The words themselves were neutral, but Tom thought that, even now, he could detect an ancient satisfaction behind them. He was wondering why he'd told him when Medlar added with a shrug, 'If you hadn't heard it from me, you'd have heard it from someone else.'

'So you're suggesting that despite all his success, it was he who resented you?'

'I think he probably did at the time, yes. We certainly didn't see each other for a while after that. But he was, as you observed yourself, very ambitious. Even then, together with two or three of the other most influential directors, he was planning the formation of the Blood Division.'

Tom allowed a small silence, then said, 'What made *you* move down here, Dr Medlar?'

He told Tom how he'd been happy enough as deputy director at Sheffield, but that some twelve years later the director had retired. He'd applied, but not been successful.

'Why did it happen that time, d'you think?' Tom probed.

'Selection panels are there to select, and this one was more impressed with another candidate.'

157

He was taking every question with an almost studied equanimity, Tom thought. Time to increase the pressure a little, perhaps...

'You said just now that Dr Goring was influential, one of the most influential directors, you said ... could that have had anything to do with your – er – non-selection, d'you think?'

'Oh, I shouldn't think so,' Medlar said easily. 'I can't imagine he'd bear a grudge that long.'

Too easily...? 'But you know what that sort of man says to himself when he does you a bad turn, don't you? That it's for the good of the service, nothing to do with personal feelings.'

Medlar shrugged again. 'Maybe so, but it was Adam who was more or less instrumental in getting me the post here. Dr Falkenham was retired, as you know–'

So he knows about my involvement ...

'–and Adam came down as interim director for six months to clear up the mess. It was a sort of precursor to his becoming Transfusion Co-ordinator, I think. Anyway, he afterwards suggested to me that I might like the job. To be honest with you, I bit his hand off. I didn't get on with the new director at Sheffield and it was a relief to get away.'

'Didn't that feel a bit like picking up the

crumbs from under his table?'

Medlar went still. 'No,' he said. 'No, Mr Jones, it didn't feel like that.'

Tom knew he was pushing him, but wanted to know how far his equanimity would stretch. 'I mean, that was the second time you'd taken his ... his place after he'd moved on to better things.'

'Have you never heard of cutting off your own nose to spite your face? There are some things more important than pride.'

'In six months, of course, your job here will cease to exist.'

He stared at Tom. 'Are you seriously trying to suggest that Adam knew nearly eight years ago that Tamar was going to close? Besides–' he forced a smile – 'it's in some ways to my advantage. You see, my wife has developed multiple sclerosis and I shall welcome the chance to be able to spend more time with her.'

He's getting that in now, Tom thought, *before the other business comes up...* Time for a switch. 'You were the one who said he was influential, Dr Medlar. Is there any truth in Miss Pengellis' allegation that he used that influence to close Tamar rather than East Dorset in order to help his son-in-law?'

Medlar's eyes flickered as he absorbed the change. 'It was most unwise of Jessie to suggest that so publicly – it's almost certainly cost her her career.'

'But is there any truth in it?'

'I find it very difficult to believe that someone in Adam's position would do such a thing,' he said carefully. 'And it has to be said that, on paper at least, it does make more sense to close Tamar.'

'Why is that?'

'East Dorset is a larger centre with better communications.'

'So you're broadly in favour of the closure, for logistical as well as personal reasons?'

'That's not what I said, or meant, Mr Jones. I'd rather no centres shut.'

'Even although it's to your advantage, as you told me just now?'

'I said that in answer to your ridiculous theory that Adam knew when he suggested I come here that it would close.' His words were clipped now, his face pale. 'And I have to say that I don't much care for your attitude. Am I some kind of suspect? The police were a good deal more polite than you.'

Tom smiled. 'I'm sorry for that, but as I'm sure you're aware, Dr Medlar, this is a very complex business and–'

'Don't patronise me.'

'Lady Margaret is very worried about the effect this alleged corruption may have on the Blood Division, which is why–'

'The only thing Lady Margaret's worried about is her own backside, so you needn't try and intimidate me by invoking her name.' His anger was under control now. 'I'd suggest that the best people to ask about the alleged corruption are those it most concerns. Have you spoken to the director at East Dorset, or Dr Goring's son-in-law?'

'Not yet, although I'll be seeing them on Wednesday. Miss Pengellis made another curious assertion,' Tom hurried on, 'that Dr Goring had some sort of spy here who told him everything she planned to say on television. Is that possible d'you think? He certainly did seem very well prepared.'

Medlar sighed, his equanimity back in place. 'I wouldn't have believed it, except for one thing...' He told Tom how Goring had admitted it to him.

'Did he say who it was?'

'No.'

'Who would you think?'

'I haven't the least idea.'

Tom said, 'Miss Pengellis seemed to think that Dr Goring was given a copy of her file the day before the interview. Would it really have been possible for him to have found all the answers he needed in such a short time?'

'I see what you mean...' Medlar said slowly. 'Although in a matter like this, he'd have had people working at Blood Division through the evening.'

'Inspector Bennett told me that Dr Goring had actually instructed you to find evidence against Miss Pengellis?'

Medlar smiled grimly. 'It was an instruction I had no intention of complying with.'

'Were you surprised he was going to such lengths to have her sacked?'

'Not really, no – Adam could be vindictive. And she had undermined his credibility, in his eyes, anyway.'

'Did he mean it about suing her for slander?'

'I think he did at the time.'

'D'you think she killed him?'

Medlar's eyes flickered again. 'I find that, too, very difficult to believe.'

'All right,' Tom said. 'I'd like to come now to your own movements that evening–' he judged the time was right – 'when you were here with Miss N'Kanu.'

'Doesn't the statement I made to Inspector Bennett cover that?'

'Yes, but since it was possibly around that time that Dr Goring was locked into the freezer, I'd like to hear about it from you myself.'

'Very well.' He drew out his tobacco pouch and pipe and began filling it. 'The inspector assured me it would go no further – do I have a similar assurance from you?'

Tom nodded. 'Yes.'

'Very well,' he said again, and applied his lighter to his pipe. The smell of the smoke reminded Tom of his own craving for nicotine, but this wasn't the time for any suggestion of chumminess.

'I was here in my office working until a little after five, I suppose. I was about to go home when Miss N'Kanu came in, wanting to talk to me. We stayed here until about eight, then we left.'

'Here in this office?'

'Yes.'

'Were you expecting her?'

'No.'

'Did anyone see either of you?'

'No. Nearly everyone had gone home at four. Besides ... I locked the door.'

Tom said quietly, 'Did you have sex with her?'

Medlar's eyes went over his shoulder to the door. He lowered his voice but said levelly enough, 'I can't see what possible concern that is of yours.'

'Then I'll put it another way – was your relationship with her platonic or erotic?'

'Oh, for God's sake...' He leaned forward, spoke quietly but intensely. 'Yes, we made love.'

'I assume it wasn't the first time?'

He swallowed. 'You assume correctly.'

'How long has–?'

'It started three months ago. We went to a conference in Birmingham and had dinner together one night. We'd always got on, been attracted to each other, I suppose, and the

163

wine, the distance from home did the rest.'

'How often–?'

'I don't expect you to believe this, Mr Jones, and I frankly don't care, but I love my wife. Making love with her has been impossible now for well over a year and ... the flesh is weak. However, that Friday evening was only the fourth time. I had told her previously that we must stop, but as I said, the flesh is weak... Is that what you wanted to hear?' Throughout his speech, he'd spoken in the same low, intense voice, his eyes fast on Tom's face. His pipe had gone out.

'I'm not concerned with your morals, Dr Medlar, I'm just trying to find out what happened that night. She came here at a little after five?'

'Yes.'

'You were here until about eight, then you both left?'

'Yes.'

'Together?'

'No, separately. She left about five minutes before me.'

'You went straight home?'

'Yes. The police have been into all this.'

'Did you see or hear anyone else in the centre?'

'No, but I wouldn't anyway. My car is in the underground park just beneath us, so I walked down the corridor and took the lift.'

'Did you see anyone in the car-park?'

'No.'

Tom took a breath and said, 'Well, thank you for being so frank with me, Dr Medlar – it can't have been easy for you. I don't see why it need go any further and I certainly wouldn't want to upset your wife.'

Medlar studied Tom. 'To tell you the truth,' he said, 'I've been wondering whether it might not be best to make a clean breast of it to her.'

'That's something only you can judge,' Tom said, thinking, *Was that for my benefit?* He took a breath. 'One last thing. Miss Pengellis could be said to have a clear motive for killing Dr Goring – are there any others you know of with a motive, anything?'

'I suppose we all could be said to have a motive,' Medlar said slowly. 'We are all losing our jobs.'

'But that's going to affect some of you more than others, surely?' Tom persisted.

Medlar appeared to give this some thought. 'Paul – Paul Bannister, that is – and Adrian Hodges might find it difficult getting other jobs... I do know that Verity Blane is very settled here although, of course, none of them actually *wants* to move... Dominic Tudor has a research programme going that he may well have to drop... That's all I can think of at the moment.'

Tom noted them down, then told him he'd need to interview the rest of the senior staff and asked if there was a suitable room he could use. Medlar suggested the deputy director's room, which was just along the corridor, and showed him.

It was as Tom remembered, small, almost poky, with an inspiring view of the hospital stores opposite. 'It'll be fine,' he said.

He didn't know what it was, but something – the smell, the colour of the walls, the way his voice echoed from them – brought on a flashback and for a microsecond he could hear, feel Donald Chalgrove giving him advice about Frank, his brother. It was so real that it brought a lump to his throat.

He turned to Medlar. 'I'm sorry about your wife,' he said impulsively. 'Is she coping?'

'Yes.' Medlar looked surprised, but not offended. 'She copes remarkably well. I think loneliness is probably her worst problem, which is why I won't be sorry to retire early. I'll take you to Dominic Tudor now – he's acting lab manager and he'll help arrange your interviews.'

14

Dominic put the phone down and turned to Tom. 'I expect you caught the gist of that – she's in the middle of a difficult cross match and can't get away.'

Tom compressed his lips in irritation; Verity and Maria were the two people he most wanted to see, since they provided the alibis for Jessie and Medlar, but Verity had gone out (and he could hazard a guess where) and now Maria was unavailable.

'How long d'you think she'll be?'

Dominic shrugged. 'Maybe half an hour, maybe longer.' He paused. 'D'you want to see one of the others while you're waiting?'

'All right. How about you?'

Dominic smiled, shrugged again. 'If you like. It'll have to be in here, though – in case anyone needs me.' They were in Jessie's office.

Tom explained how he was looking into Jessie's allegation as much as Goring's death. 'Although the two may well be linked.'

'Only if it was Jessie who killed him, surely?'

Tom smiled at his quickness. 'I suppose

that's right, but she does have the most clearly defined motive. Wouldn't you say?'

'I wouldn't know.'

'He had her suspended, he was going to have her sacked and then he was going to sue her. Can you think of anyone with a better motive?'

'Not offhand, no, but isn't that your job?'

'Are you saying you don't think she did it?'

'I wasn't saying anything.' He paused. 'I will say this, though – I find it extremely difficult to imagine her doing it.'

'Why?'

'Because she simply isn't the type. Besides, she's got an alibi, hasn't she?'

'What do you think about that?' Tom asked.

'About what?'

'Her alibi. The fact that she spent the night with Verity Blane.'

'What is there to think about it?' He looked straight back at Tom.

'OK.' Tom said wearily. 'Your non-judgemental correctness is taken as read. Now, were you or were you not surprised by it?'

Dominic thought for a moment. 'Not entirely in Verity's case,' he said at last. 'I was in Jessie's, though.'

'Why not in Verity's case?'

'As an old-fashioned MCP, I'd wondered about a good-looking woman who never had anything to do with men.'

'Do you believe in their relationship, that it actually occurred?'

'If they say it did, then I assume it did.'

'All right,' Tom said, aware that he wasn't going to get any further with this. 'You were Jessie's deputy – did she ever say anything to you about Dr Goring's motives for closing Tamar?' Although Tom could hardly be said to be on Christian name terms with Jessie, it was easier than to go on saying 'Miss Pengellis'.

'The nepotism, you mean?' Dominic shook his head. 'I was watching her on the TV when she came out with it. It was as much of a shock to me as anyone.'

'How long have you worked here?'

'Nearly eight years, now.'

'So you'd have known Dr Goring when he was interim director here?'

'Yes, although "known" is probably too strong a word. I was only basic grade then, very much the bottom of the heap.'

'Did you like him?'

'As a person, I neither liked nor disliked him. I hated what he was doing.'

'Are you talking about then or now?'

'Now. When he was interim director, he did some hard but necessary things. What he was doing this time is costing us all our jobs.'

Tom said, 'But in your case, it's costing a bit more, isn't it?'

Dominic blinked. 'How d'you mean?'

'Your research. Dr Medlar told me you had a research programme going.'

'Oh, that – I wondered what on earth you were getting at for a moment. Yes, I'll be sorry, but I dare say I'll find somewhere else to do it.'

'What were you doing that Friday night?'

'What Friday...? Oh, I see – I went out for a drink with a colleague here, Ashley Miles.'

'Yes, but I believe you told Inspector Bennett that you went out some time earlier than you met your colleague.'

'I left home at about seven and met Ashley at eight. But if you've been speaking to Inspector Bennett, you'll know what I was doing.'

'I'd like to hear it from you.'

'All right.' He told Tom about his relationship with his father-in-law. 'He was being particularly obnoxious that evening, so I went to the local library for an hour to get away from him–'

'You spent the whole hour there?'

'Yes. Well, about thirty or forty minutes, I suppose, what with getting there and then getting to the pub.' He told Tom how he and Ashley had stayed at the pub until closing time. It all tallied with the statement he'd given Bennett, even down to the barman remembering them.

'Who else would have known about the

faulty door on the freezing-room?' Tom asked, changing tack again. *'I do not like thee, Dr Fell, the reason why I cannot tell...'* He didn't know why he didn't like Dominic – perhaps, as Bennett had suggested, it was something to do with his overall aura of bantam cockiness.

'All the department heads, for a start,' Dominic told him, explaining how Steve Tanner had interrupted Jessie's meeting, how as Safety Officer he'd examined the door, left a notice on it and put in a requisition for it to be repaired. 'But anyone who saw the notice would have known,' he added.

'Who would be the most likely to see it?'

'Anyone. All the departments use the freezer at some time or another.'

'Who uses it most?'

'I suppose Plasma Products do,' he said slowly. 'That's why it's where it is.'

'One other thing,' Tom said and told him about Jessie's theory of Goring having a spy in the centre. 'What d'you think about that?'

'I think it sucks. I like Jessie, but she was getting a bit paranoid towards the end.'

'Dr Medlar told me this morning that Dr Goring admitted it to him.'

'Really?' For the first time, he'd actually surprised Dominic with something. 'Well, I suppose in that case there must have been...

Did he say who it was?'

'No. I was wondering if you had any idea.'

'None whatever.'

'Does anyone here have any reason to dislike Jessie?'

Dominic pushed out his lower lip. 'Well, I suppose you could say there are two, but I really can't see either of them...'

'Who are they?'

He hesitated. 'Paul Bannister and Adrian Hodges,' he said at last.

'Why? Why did they dislike her?'

'Jealousy in Paul's case, he thinks he should have had her job. As for Adrian ... because she's a clever, independent female and because he's Adrian.'

That figures, Tom thought as he noted the names down.

Dominic looked at his watch. 'If you've finished with me, I usually go to lunch now. So if you wouldn't mind...'

'Not at all.' Tom closed his notebook. 'In fact, if *you* don't mind, I'll come with you.'

Dominic looked momentarily taken aback. 'I'm only going to the canteen,' he said. 'It's nothing special.'

'That's all right.'

He shrugged. 'OK then.' He hung up his white coat, transferred his bleep to his jacket and told his secretary next door where he was going. 'This way,' he said to Tom.

They walked down the main corridor.

'What will you do when the centre closes?' Tom asked.

'Not sure yet. I'll find something.'

They walked past Medlar's office, out of the centre and into the glass passage joining it with the main hospital, the one that Tom had always thought of as the Space Corridor, because of its panoramic view across the city and to Dartmoor.

He said, 'I'd have thought someone like you would've already had something planned.'

Dominic shot him a look. 'How d'you mean, someone like me?'

It was Tom's turn to shrug. 'I had the impression you were ambitious, what with your research and everything.'

'Well, until recently, I suppose I was hoping that the centre could be saved.'

'Jessie's campaign, you mean?'

'Yes.'

'You really thought it had a chance?'

'Yes, I did, Jessie's a brilliant organiser and she really had the gimboids at HQ worried – that's why Goring came down here, to deliver what he thought would be the *coup de grâce*.'

They reached the canteen and Dominic held the door open for him.

'And got murdered instead,' Tom said.

'You're still assuming the two are connected.'

'Not necessarily,' Tom said, looking round

173

the canteen. It hadn't changed much in eight years, he thought, and the food wasn't anything like as bad as Dominic had implied. Tom had roast beef while Dominic had a cheese omelette. Tom paid.

'What's your research about?' he asked as they sat down.

'You have a couple of hours to spare?'

Tom smiled. 'Briefly, then.'

Dominic explained how his normal job was running the Microbiology Department, screening blood for infectious disease such as hepatitis and HIV. 'You know about CJD, I imagine? Creutzfelt Jakob Disease and its so-called New Variant.'

He looked over at Tom's plate. 'Don't worry, I'm not about to tell you you're going to catch it from that.'

Tom swallowed a mouthful. 'I never thought I was. Why so-called?'

'Well, that's the *raison d'être* of my research. Everyone's assumed that scrapie in sheep, Mad Cow Disease and conventional CJD are all caused by the same thing, a prion that's passed from sheep to cows to humans. D'you know what a prion is?'

'I've heard of them, but that's about all.'

'I'll have to give you a bit of the background.' He took a mouthful of omelette. 'Scrapie's a brain disease of sheep – a sort of Mad Cow Sheep Disease, if you like. It's been around for a long time, although no one knew what caused it. Anyway, back in the seventies, someone at the Min of Ag had the brilliant idea of saving money by feeding rendered sheep offal to cattle as a source of protein – a quite unnatural practice as well as a revolting one.

'Well, after a few years, the cattle began developing a disease rather like scrapie, and it became known as Mad Cow Disease.' He shrugged his shoulders again in his curiously Gallic manner. 'So who cares about a few mad cows, so long as they don't do us any harm?'

'But they did, didn't they?' said Tom.

'It certainly seemed that way,' agreed Dominic. 'People began to get Mad Person Disease, which itself seemed very similar to Creutzfelt Jakob Disease, and those who like to think of themselves as experts began drawing all sorts of hasty conclusions.'

He frowned as he developed his theme. 'CJD's been around for a long time as well. It's a degenerative disease of the brain that kills about eighteen months after the first symptoms appear.'

'What are the symptoms?'

'Tremors, incoordination, dementia and finally death. Very nasty. Areas of the brain seem to simply dissolve away without any recognisable cause. CJD itself is remarkably similar to a disease called *kuru*, which used to affect the natives of certain tribes in New Guinea.'

'Used to?' queried Tom.

'Yes. It died out when the Australian Colonial Administration took over and banned cannibalism. They used to eat the brains of their dead relatives as a mark of respect, and then developed *kuru*. There was even a story suggesting that it all started when a Russian missionary with CJD went to New Guinea early this century and was eaten for his pains.' He grinned, slightly maliciously, Tom thought. 'Haven't put you off your food, have I?'

'It's all right,' Tom said, pushing his half-finished roast beef away. 'Do go on.'

'Well, the theory is that these diseases, *all* these diseases, are caused by a prion. It's a protein particle that replicates like a virus, but doesn't have any DNA or RNA. That's why prions are so difficult to kill, as well as to detect. It's also why we've been banned from using our own plasma products in this country and are having to buy them at enormous expense from abroad.' He leaned forward. 'The fact is, though,' he said slowly, 'that no one's ever actually demonstrated a prion, or even seen one for that matter.'

'Are you suggesting they don't exist?'

'No, I'm not suggesting that, there is some evidence for them. But what if these particular diseases, Mad Cow Disease and

176

New Variant CJD, are completely different from the others, aren't caused by a prion at all?'

'That's pretty revolutionary, isn't it?'

'It sure is, and it would have pretty far-reaching implications. *Financial* implications. Did you know that the Transfusion Service was about to spend £70 million a year on taking all the white cells out of donated blood? On the off-chance they contain prions that might be transmitted by transfusion.'

'I'd heard something about it. So what d'you think causes New Variant CJD?'

'There are several theories – organophospates, for one.'

'Is that what you think?'

Dominic shook his head. 'No, I don't. There's another theory recently put forward, that it's caused by a bacterium called *Acinetobacter*. It's a bug that's commonly found in soil and water.'

'I've never heard of it.'

'There's no reason why you should – it doesn't cause human infection as a rule.'

'But you think it causes CJD?'

'I think it's possible.' He grinned again as he finished his meal and pushed his own plate aside. 'But more to the point, much more to the point, Professor Blom of London University thinks so. His theory is that certain genetically susceptible people overreact to *Acinetobacter* when they meet it and make very fierce antibodies to it. These antibodies then confuse *Acinetobacter* with their own brain tissue and destroy it – a sort of autoimmune disease.'

'You're getting a bit deep for me now.'

'Well, I did warn you. Anyway, through Dr Medlar, I contacted Prof Blom and we've set up a study – looking for *Acinetobacter* antibodies in donor blood to try and establish the incidence.'

'Found any?'

'A few. I'm not sure yet of their significance, though.'

Tom looked at him with a little more respect. 'Well, it sounds as though it's pretty important research to me. Surely some other centre would be interested in it?'

'I'm certainly hoping so, although most people still accept the prion theory. Besides, every centre has its own pet projects. It's possible someone might be interested, but I'm not banking on it.'

'If we stick together, it'll be OK,' Verity repeated, putting her hands on Jessie's shoulders.

'No, Verity.' Jessie shrugged them off and turned away. 'He's too bloody clever. I *want* to do it this way.'

'Is it Craig that's bothering you? I can help you with Craig.'

'It's not just Craig.'

'What, then?'

'I'll tell you, Verity,' she said, turning back to her. 'Jones was right about one thing – you *seduced* me, and in more ways than one.'

'I seduced you because you wanted to be seduced, Jessie,' Verity said levelly.

'Oh yeah?' she stormed, losing her temper at last. 'With God knows how much dope swilling round inside me? And as for the other business ... and letting everyone know – you had *no right*.'

'I did it for the best.'

'Whose best? Certainly not mine. You got me into this mess – now you can get me out of it.'

Verity realised it was no use, that whatever they'd had was probably dead and there was nothing she could do about it. 'All right,' she said, trying to swallow the bitterness that rose like bile in her throat. 'I'll do as you ask. Can I use your phone? I'll call Steph now and arrange it...'

As she drove back to the centre, she felt a rage well up from deep inside her and boil over. *The bastard, if it wasn't for him ... the bastard.*

At home, Medlar gently placed the reefer between his wife's lips and lit it for her. *Now would be a good time, tell her now...* 'Sarah?'

'Mm?' She exhaled gratefully.

'The DOH have sent down an investigator to look into Adam's death.'

She looked at him. 'Aren't the police supposed to be doing that?'

'I think it's finally dawned on Mad Maggie that this affair could be the end of her. I think she's hoping this chap'll show that Adam was as pure as the driven – fat chance.'

'That's a bit hard isn't it, George? Shouldn't speak ill of et cetera.'

'No, I suppose not...' It was too late now, the chance had gone. 'No, you're right, dear.'

'Has he spoken to you, this investigator?'

'Yes, this morning.'

'What's he like?'

'Pretty ruthless, which I suppose is what you'd expect from an emissary of Lady M. For all that, I don't know what more he can do than the police.'

15

She came in slowly, her dark eyes meeting Tom's for only an instant. He was standing.

'Miss N'Kanu?'

She nodded. 'Yes.' She was wearing a red skirt and white blouse.

'My name's Jones and I'm from the Department of Health. Please sit down.' He smiled as he spoke, but she didn't respond.

They sat. Tom at the desk with his back to the window. 'It's Maria, isn't it? Can I call you Maria?'

'Yes.'

His first impression was of a plainness, even heaviness of feature, then he realised it was because she wore no make-up or jewellery that he could see. Her hair was a simple dark cloud covering the top of her head.

'D'you know why I'm here, Maria?'

She cleared her throat. 'I thought it was to look into the death of Dr Goring.'

'Well, yes – that and the allegations that were made about him. Did you see the TV interview with him and Jessie?'

'Yes.' She half smiled. 'I think most of the centre was crammed into the rest room that morning – it's where the television is.' Even though it was only a half-smile, it lifted her face, making it pretty for a moment.

Had she known Dr Goring at all? he asked her. No.

Had she met him, even briefly, had she spoken to him at all? No.

'D'you think it's true, what Jessie said about him?'

'That he was closing Tamar to help his son-in-law, you mean? I've no way of knowing.'

'Don't you have an opinion?'

'How could I?' As I told you, I didn't know him or anything about him.'

This was a little disingenuous, Tom thought, given her relationship with Medlar.

'Did you agree with what Jessie was trying to do here?'

'Keep the centre open, you mean? Of course I did – she was trying to save our jobs.' Her voice and speech were precise, unaccented, uninflected.

Had she been at the meeting Jessie called the day before the TV interview, the Thursday? Could she remember who was there?

Yes, and yes: her list was identical with Jessie's.

'Where were you at lunch time that day?'

'The Thursday, you mean?' She paused. She always seemed to answer one question with another, he thought, presumably giving herself room to think. 'At lunch, I imagine,' she said.

'Where d'you go for lunch?'

'Sometimes to the canteen, sometimes I buy a roll and have it in the staff room.'

'Which was it that day?' His questions were all in the same soft voice, but following immediately from each other to keep up the pressure.

'The staff room, I think.'

'Did you go to Jessie's office at all?'

'I ... don't think so, no.'

'You see, Jessie thinks that someone photocopied all her notes while she was out, and gave them to Dr Goring.'

'Well, it wasn't me,' she said flatly.

'Who d'you think it was?'

'I've no idea.'

'Perhaps Jessie imagined it.'

'Perhaps she did. I've no way of knowing.'

'The next day, when you stayed here late with Dr Medlar, what time did you leave?'

'I...' The change of direction flustered her slightly ...'at just before eight.'

'How did you know it was just before eight?'

She looked away, swallowed, then looked back at him. 'Because he said we should leave five minutes apart and I looked at the clock on the wall as I left.'

'You were there in his office a long time – I make it nearly three hours.'

'We had a lot to talk about.'

'How long have you been seeing him?'

'Since it began, you mean? We haven't actually *seen* that much of each other. About three months, I suppose.'

'Have you ever met his wife?'

Her eyes snapped back to his. 'Are you trying to make me feel ashamed or something? Dirty?' Her voice was as quiet as his, but steel sharp. 'I'm not proud of what's happened, but I won't accept any moralising from you, Mr Jones.'

'You're not under any obligation to answer.' Nor was she, but he hoped she would – it wasn't prurience on his part, he wanted, *needed* to understand the forces governing their triangle.

'Yes, I have met her,' she said at last, 'but not since it started.'

'Did you like her?'

'Yes...'

'How did it start?'

Her tongue touched her lips. 'We were at a conference together. It surprised us both, we were neither of us planning it.'

'How did Dr Medlar feel about Dr Goring?'

'How d'you mean?' She knew perfectly well.

'Did he like him?'

'I don't think he did, no.'

'He hated him, then?'

'Oh no, it wasn't as strong as that.'

'Why didn't he like him?'

'They'd worked together in the past. They just didn't get on with each other.'

'Did Dr Goring know about your relationship with Dr Medlar?'

'I – I'm sure he didn't... How could he have done?'

How indeed?

'When you left Dr Medlar on Friday, did you see anyone else?'

'No.'

'Not even the orderly?'

'I went out through reception especially to avoid the orderly.'

'Did you hear anything?'

She shook her head. 'No.'

'So what did you do then?'

She'd walked over to the car-park and driven home. No, she hadn't gone out much over the weekend, because she was on call; and no, Dr Medlar hadn't contacted her at all. Yes, she'd been called in on Sunday at around 4 p.m. to do a cross match.

'How long were you here?'

'Two, two and a half hours. Maybe longer.'

'Rather a long time for a cross match.'

Her eyes flicked up for a moment, questioning how he knew. 'It was a particularly difficult one. The patient had antibodies and I had to repeat everything.'

Tom's antennae twitched. Something wasn't quite right here...

'Did you see anyone else while you were here?'

'Other than the lab orderly, no. But I was in my lab most of the time, so I wouldn't have done.'

'Which lab orderly was it?'

'Craig. Craig Scratchley.'

'Was he aware that you were taking longer than usual?'

'It wouldn't have been any of his business how long I was taking. Besides–' again the

185

half-smile, although not quite so convincing – 'Craig isn't a very aware person.'

'But you'd been called in urgently and you were taking a long time – wasn't the ward screaming for the blood?'

'They don't scream, they niggle. First the sister phones, then the staff nurse, then perhaps the doctor...'

'Were they niggling at you?'

'Yes.'

'When you left, did Craig see you leave?'

'Yes, I told him when I was going.'

'What was he doing at the time?'

'What he usually does – watching television in the Issue Room.'

He'd have to see Craig, he thought. Meanwhile, there wasn't much else he could usefully ask her at the moment, so he thanked her and told her she could go. Then he rang Dominic and asked whether Verity was back yet. Dominic said he'd check and send her along if she was.

While he was waiting, Tom compared Maria's answers with Medlar's, and also those she'd given Bennett. They were all in accord, other than the discrepancy over the time she'd been in on Sunday – according to Bennett, it had been well over three hours. Whichever, it was a long time for a cross match. He'd check with Holly–

There was a cursory knock, the door flung open and a tall, elegant woman with long honey-coloured hair pushed her way in.

'You wanted to see me.'

He half rose. 'Miss Blane?'

'Ms Blane.' The skin over her high cheekbones was flushed, heightening her beauty. 'Friend of Ms Pengellis.'

'Have a seat.'

'I prefer to stand.'

'OK.' He sat down himself.

She moved closer, stood over him. 'I've just been to see Jessie – Ms Pengellis. She's very upset. She says you were asking questions about our love life. Perhaps this'll satisfy your curiosity.' She dropped something on the desk in front of him. It bounced, quivered a moment before settling. It was a large latex phallus, off-white, glistening, truly revolting in its detail.

Tom looked up at her. 'Is this for me? To keep?'

She was disconcerted, but only for an instant. 'Sure. You might find it comes in useful.'

'Thank you.' He picked it up, admired it for a moment, then dropped it into the out-tray. 'Now I need to ask you some questions.'

Her mouth tightened, her eyes flared and he knew he was almost certainly wasting his time. He leaned back in his chair to look up at her more easily.

'I'm here primarily because of the allegations Jessie made about Dr Goring on TV. Are they true, d'you think?'

'Ms Pengellis says so and that's good enough for me.'

'She also says that Dr Goring had some sort of spy here, who photocopied all her notes and gave them to him.'

'She's probably right.'

'Who do you think it was?'

She hesitated. 'I don't see the relevance.'

'As her friend, wouldn't you like to know?'

She stared back without replying, expressionless.

'You must have given it some thought.'

'I have.'

'And?'

'It's none of your business,' she said.

She knows, he thought. *She knows who it was, or at least, she thinks she does.* 'It might help clarify things.'

'I can't see how.'

'That Friday evening, Friday the seventh, you asked Jessie back to your house at about five o'clock and she stayed there all night?'

'Are you asking me or telling me?'

'Asking.'

'Then yes.'

'Did either of you leave the house at any time?'

'No.'

'So who do *you* think killed Dr Goring?'

'Isn't that the job of the police? I've already been through all this with them.'

'I'm asking you.'

'Then I don't know.'

'It might help Jessie if you had some idea.'

No answer.

'Don't you *want* to help Jessie?'

'Don't you *dare* speak to me about *helping Jessie*,' she blazed. Then, without warning, she put her hands under the front of the desk and heaved... It came up, toppling Tom backwards in his chair, then fell on top of him. His arms took some of the force, but he still let out a yell as it crashed into his ribs and the trays and pens and desk tidy scattered on the floor around him. She turned and walked out, slamming the door behind her.

He got his hands under the edge and pushed upwards, trying to lift the weight from his ribs. It went up about a foot, but he couldn't wriggle free because his legs were trapped by the chair. He was about to put his dignity to one side and call for help when the door opened and Medlar hurried in, followed by his secretary.

He didn't waste time asking questions. 'Take the other side, Judy,' he said, and together they lifted the desk back into position.

'Are you all right, Mr Jones?' He helped him to his feet.

'Not entirely sure,' Tom gasped.

'Sit down a minute.' He picked up the chair. 'Ye gods! What's *that?*' He was gazing down at the phallus.

'Present from Miss Blane,' Tom managed.

'Did she do this?' He gestured round at the mess and Tom nodded.

'But why?'

'Don't think she liked the questions I asked.'

'Well, neither did I for that matter, but... You may as well get back, Judy,' he said to the secretary. 'I'll see to Mr Jones.'

Judy walked out, suppressing a smile.

'Did it fall on your chest?' he asked Tom, who nodded again.

'Any pains?'

'A bit.'

'Better let me take a look. Sit down...'

Tom took off his jacket, undid his shirt and winced as Medlar prodded his rib cage.

'Well, I don't think you've broken anything,' he said at last, 'but you'd better have an X-ray to be on the safe side. Can you walk?'

'Yeah...'

Medlar picked up the phone and directory from the floor, looked up a number and keyed it in.

'They'll see you now,' he told Tom as he put the phone down. 'But I want you to come and tell me what happened here when they've finished with you so that I can get to the bottom of it. And I think we'll get rid of this.' He picked up the phallus with a paper towel and dropped it into the bin.

16

Medlar summoned Verity as soon as he got back to his office.

'I've just sent Mr Jones down to X-ray,' he told her. 'He may have cracked a rib. That's assault and I'd be within my rights to ask for your dismissal.'

'I'm sorry, Dr Medlar,' she said.

'Whatever possessed you?'

She told him that Tom had upset Jessie enough with his questioning to make her cry. 'And then he had the – the *temerity* to tell me, *me* – to help her.' She shrugged helplessly. 'I'd tipped the desk over before I knew what I was doing. I didn't realise it would hurt him like that.'

He returned her gaze in silence a moment, then said, 'Well, I know what he's like, so I can sympathise – to an extent. But if he makes a formal complaint, I'll have to do something about it. I think the best thing might be for you to apologise to him before he can–'

'No,' she said flatly.

'I beg your pardon?'

'I'm sorry, George, but there's no way I'm apologising to him.' She stared back at him, daring him to make the next move. She held the scourge and he knew it.

His eyes dropped. 'I'll tell him I've admonished you and hope he's satisfied with that,' he said at last.

Nearly an hour had passed by the time X-ray finished with Tom and he got back to his office. Someone had been in and cleared up the mess. His wallet, which he hadn't realised had been missing, was lying on the desk.

He went round to the director's office.

'Sit down, please,' Medlar said, and it was the 'please' more than anything that told Tom he was angry. 'Nothing broken, then?'

'No. Thank you.'

'Good.' Medlar paused before continuing. 'I've spoken to Verity and heard her version of events. She told me that you reduced Jessie to tears with your aggressive and intimate personal questions, which is why she presented you with the – er – trophy and pushed the desk over.' He regarded Tom without favour. 'I have to say that I have some sympathy with her.'

'I'm afraid that such questions are sometimes unavoidable,' Tom said, looking steadily back at him.

'Really? I'd be interested to hear why in this case.'

After a pause, Tom said, 'Jessie's alibi for the time Dr Goring was killed relies heavily on her claim to being a born-again lesbian. My questions were to test that claim.'

'And your conclusion?'

'That I'm not going to say.'

'The police didn't find such questions necessary.'

'I'm not the police.'

'Indeed you're not,' Medlar said pointedly. After another pause, he continued, 'Verity shouldn't have behaved as she did and I've admonished her.'

'Good.'

'But I would ask you to treat my staff with a little more sensitivity in future.'

I wonder if Maria's been chewing his ear...

'I'll do that,' he said, 'in as much as I'm able.'

Medlar looked at him with open dislike. 'Good,' he said.

'Paul,' Dominic said close to his ear and was rewarded with a startled yelp.

'Don't creep up on me like that, Dom.'

'Sorry.' The word was completely devoid of regret. 'His lordship down the corridor wants to see you.'

'What, the boss?'

'No, our very own private dickhead.'

Paul stared back at him. 'Eh?'

'Jones. He from the Department who's asking questions about Goring.'

'What's he want me for?'

'There's only one way you're going to find out.'

Having sent him on his way, Dominic went to look for Verity. He found her at her desk. She pointedly ignored him and continued filling in the form she was working on until it was clear that he was neither going to go away nor come to the point.

'Can I help you in any way?' she asked.

'I've just sent Paul down to Jones.'

Verity grunted. 'They deserve each other.'

'The boss told me about what happened between you and Jones.'

'Really.'

'Did he give you a bollocking?'

'Nothing I can't handle. Besides, I don't see that it's any concern of yours.'

He pulled a chair over to her desk, sat down and said quietly, 'Verity, if ever there was a time to forget past differences, it's now. D'you think I've enjoyed answering Jones's questions, fetching and carrying for him?'

She looked at him thoughtfully. 'No, I don't suppose you have much.'

'Is it true you threw a rubber willie at him?'

'More or less.' She told him what she'd done and why.

Dominic grinned. 'I've been referring to him as Our Very Own Private Dickhead without realising how appropriate it was.' He started laughing, and after a moment, she reluctantly joined in.

'He's a cool bastard though,' she said as they subsided. 'Asked me if he could keep it, then fired a load of questions at me.'

'Present for his wife, I expect. What sort of questions?'

'Oh, what time did Jessie come to my house, could she have slipped out during the night? What about you?'

'How well had I known Goring, was what Jessie said about him on the telly true – how the hell should I know that? Did I think Jessie killed him, and if not, who?'

'I got all that as well.'

Dominic paused, then said, 'He did say one strange thing – apparently Goring told the boss that he had a spy here, who photo-copied Jessie's files and gave them to him.' He watched Verity's face as he spoke. 'Jessie told me she suspected it, but I never really believed it. Did she say anything to you?'

'Yes,' Verity said coolly, 'she did, as a matter of fact. Perhaps you should have listened to her more carefully.' And with a thump, their relationship dropped back to its former level.

Tom leaned forward and said softly, 'You can pay a prostitute for more than just her body.'

'She wouldn't lie about a thing like that, would she?' Paul protested, 'Not to the police.'

Possibly not, Tom conceded to himself. He didn't like Paul any more than he had Dominic, although Paul's fundamental self-deceit made it easier to say why.

'She told the police you were with her for an hour, until eight-thirty, and yet you didn't get home until after ten. What were you doing after you left her?'

'I went for a drink.'

'Oh yes, on your own, at the King's Head, where no one can remember seeing you.'

'It was crowded. I felt ashamed if you must know, I wanted to be on my own. Besides, I'd told my wife I was going to a pub.'

'With Adrian Hodges, in fact?'

'Yes.'

'You've told her that before, have you?'

'*Yes!*'

Tom sighed inwardly; there was no easy way of either proving or disproving where he'd been...

The interview had started easily enough, with Tom asking him how well he'd known Goring.

'It was Dr Goring who employed me here, to take over Grouping after Pete Coleton became lab manager.'

He'd got on well with him, then? – Reasonably well, yes.

Had he still been on good terms with him when he'd come down this time? – They'd said hello, but that was about all.

Had he approved of Goring's reorganisation of the service?– Of course not, it was going to cost him his job.

Then Tom had moved on to Friday evening...

He said now, 'D'you like Jessie?'

Paul hesitated. 'Not much.'

'Why not?'

'She wore her stripes too heavily. She was too young for the job and it went to her head.' The past tense, Tom noted. 'It needs someone with more experience.'

'Someone like you, perhaps?'

Paul's eyes flicked up. 'I'd make a better job of it than her,' he said defiantly.

'In what way?'

'I know more than she did and I'd be a better manager. She had favourites, she set people against each other.'

'Divide and rule, perhaps?'

'Call it what you like – I happen to believe that you get the best out of people by treating them fairly.'

He was tacky, he was shifty and his pride was

197

inordinate, Tom thought, paraphrasing Kipling. 'D'you think she could have killed Dr Goring?'

Paul looked away, apparently giving the matter serious thought. 'She might have,' he said at last, 'after he sacked her. She's got an evil temper.'

'She says that someone photocopied all her notes and gave them to Dr Goring before the TV interview – that was you, wasn't it?'

'She would say something like that, wouldn't she?' He didn't seem to have noticed the accusation.

'You didn't answer me. It was *you*, wasn't it?'

'It wasn't *any* of us – she imagined it because he got the better of her.'

'But Dr Goring admitted to Dr Medlar that someone had kept him informed.'

'Did he?' For a moment, Paul looked genuinely surprised. *But about what?* Tom wondered. *The fact that Goring'd had a spy, or the fact he'd admitted it?*

'Well, it wasn't me,' he said.

'Did you see the interview?'

He nodded. 'Yes.'

'So what do you think about the accusation she made at the end of it?'

'Palpable bullshit. She did it in desperation because she'd lost the argument.'

'How can you possibly know that?'

198

'I've got eyes and ears,' he said. 'It was obvious Goring knew what he was talking about. What she said was a lie and she deserved to be sacked for it.'

'Did you know that the door handle of the freezing-room was broken?'

He blinked at the change of direction. 'Er – not at the time, no.'

'But you were at the meeting Jessie called, weren't you? When Steve Tanner came in to tell Dominic about it?'

'I left early.'

'Didn't you see the notice on the door?'

'Not then, no.'

'When?'

'Later. Someone told me about it.'

'When did they tell you?'

'I can't remember. Sometime Friday, I think.'

Tom switched the questioning back to his relationship with Goring, hoping to show it had more substance than he'd previously admitted, but Paul retreated behind a wall of monosyllables and Tom, realising he wasn't getting anywhere, let him go.

Was he really as obtuse as he seemed, Tom wondered as he washed his hands in the gents, or was it deliberate? Did he really think he could run the place better than Jessie? Tom knew from his own past experience, as well as from Holly, what a poisoned chalice it was.

As he went back up the corridor, a couple of girls glanced at him curiously and he heard them giggling after they'd passed him. He checked his fly as soon as he was back in the office, but nothing was adrift, nor had he dribbled, so he phoned Dominic and asked for Ashley to be sent along.

While he was waiting, he picked up the phone again and dialled the number Personnel had given him for Craig. After several rings, it was answered by a woman with a strong Devonian accent.

'Warm Welcome Farm.'

So someone there had a sense of humour, Tom thought as he explained that he wanted to come and talk to Craig. There was a tap on the door and a fresh-faced man of about thirty with a humorous face put his head round. Tom beckoned him in and pointed to the seat.

''Es, that's all right,' the woman on the phone said, and then told him how to find the farm. 'Y' can't miss it,' she added, which should have warned him.

He glanced at his watch as he put the phone down – getting on for five, so this would have to be the last interview today.

'Mr Jones, I presume?' the fresh-faced man said.

'And you're Mr Miles?'

'So you're going to beard Craig in his lair? Sorry, I couldn't help overhearing, but rather you than me.'

'Is he really that bad?'

'Depends on your point of view, I suppose.' He made a face. 'Jessie didn't think so.'

'Jealous?'

'Me? I'm a respectable married man.'

Tom said, 'And as such, do you believe in this affair of hers with Verity?'

Ashley hesitated, obviously taken by surprise. 'I really can't say.'

'So you don't believe in it?'

'As I said, I can't comment on it.'

Tom realised he wasn't going to get any further. 'How long have you been here?'

About four years, Ashley told him. No, he hadn't known Goring previously and he had no idea whether there was any truth in Jessie's allegation. He spoke easily, openly, and Tom found himself liking him.

'Where did you come from?' he asked him. 'Before you came here.'

'London.'

'I thought so. D'you miss it?'

'Yeah – about as much as I do Craig, come to think of it.'

Yes, he'd known about the faulty freezer door, it had been reported at the meeting Jessie had called. Who was there? He reeled off the same list as Jessie and Maria. No, none of them had left early so far as he could remember.

He became thoughtful when Tom told him about Jessie's theory of the rotten apple. 'You know, I thought when I watched the interview that he had everything off remarkably pat. It seemed too good – or bad, rather – to be true, so she could be right.'

'So, who?'

He took a breath. 'There are one or two here who don't like her, but as to whether they'd go that far ... I don't know.'

'But you do think that *someone* did?'

'I said she could be right, which isn't the same thing, is it? And I've no idea.'

'She was right, as it happens,' Tom said, and explained how he knew.

'Didn't Dr Goring say who it was?' Ashley asked after a pause.

'Apparently not.'

Ashley's expression didn't change. 'Well, I still don't have any idea who it was.'

'Did you like Jessie?'

He nodded, his frank blue eyes meeting Tom's. 'Yes, I did. Still do.'

'D'you think she could have killed Dr Goring?'

He gave a half-laugh. 'That's certainly putting it on the line.' He paused. 'I really don't think so.'

'Why not?'

'Because ... she just wouldn't. She isn't that nasty.'

'So, who?'

'Pass,' he said deliberately.

'That Friday night, what time did you meet Dominic?'

'About eight.' He didn't have to ask which Friday night.

'About?'

'It was just before or just after ... just after, I think.'

'What time did you leave home?'

Ashley regarded him with a lazy smile. 'About seven thirty, as I'm sure you already know. And yes, my only witness is my wife, and yes, I suppose I would have had just about enough time to dash in here, slam poor old Goring into the freezer and still meet Dom.'

'Did you?'

'Don't be stupid.'

So there was steel beneath all the good cheer... 'Why is it stupid?'

Ashley paused before answering, his eyes meeting Tom's again. 'Because I've got no motive and anyway–' another smile – 'I'm not that nasty either.'

Tom thought this as good a place to stop as any, so he thanked him and told him he could go. At the door, he turned.

'Is it true Verity chucked a dildo at you?'

'Where d'you hear that?'

'It's doing the rounds. One story has you catching it in your teeth and doing a belly dance.'

Tom smiled. 'So that explains it.'

'Explains what?'

'The funny looks I've been getting.'

'So she *did* do it...'

'She dropped it on the desk in front of me hoping to shock me, so I asked her if I could keep it.'

Ashley laughed. 'Hoping to shock her back, I suppose – no chance! Where is it now?'

'In the bin.'

Ashley laughed again and left.

17

'Come on in, Ash, take the weight off your feet.'

Ashley gently closed the door and did as he was bid, noting a trifle sourly how snug was the fit of Jessie's mantle on Dominic's shoulders.

'I'm on call tonight,' he said. 'I need the bleep.'

'Sure.' Dominic opened a drawer and handed it to him. 'Dickhead finished with you, has he?'

'He has.'

'How'd it go?'

'Well, Verity's right about one thing, he's a

cool sod. Asked me outright if I'd killed Goring.'

'What did you say?'

'Told him not to be stupid.' He paused. 'Did he ask you that?'

'Not in so many words, no. He wanted chapter and verse on exactly what I was doing before I met you, though.'

'What's his game, Dom? We've already been through all that with the police.' He glanced over Dominic's shoulder. 'Talk of the devil...'

Dominic glanced round in time to see a panda car passing the window, then turned back to Ashley. 'I think he's telling the truth – about one thing, anyway. Mad Maggie's shitting herself at the possibility that Goering was closing Tamar in order to give his son-in-law a leg-up.'

'Was he, d'you think?'

Dominic shrugged. 'I don't know and I don't really care any more.'

Ashley studied him closely. 'Seems pretty incredible, though. What d'you think about the other business, that Goring had a spy here?'

'I would have said it was a load of bollocks, a symptom of the stress Jessie was under, but Dickhead says that Goering confirmed it to the boss.'

'Any ideas?'

A tap on the door prevented Dominic

from answering.

'Evenin' all.' It was Verity, in cockney mode. 'Ain't cha got no 'omes to go to, then?'

'We were talking about Dickhead,' Dominic said.

She smiled faintly. 'Put you through the mill, did he?' she said to Ashley.

'Sort of.' He gave her the gist of the interview.

'Sounds as though you got off lightly.' She looked from one to the other of them. 'Has he seen all of us now?'

'All except Adrian,' Dominic replied. 'Said he'd see him first thing tomorrow.'

'He won't get much out of him,' Verity said.

'So then it'll be back to the beginning and third degrees all round,' Ashley said morosely.

'Let me put it this way,' said Verity, 'I shan't be responsible for my actions if he does...'

Dominic was looking past her to the open door, where Arthur the orderly was standing with a uniformed policeman. 'Can I help you?' he said.

'I'm looking for Miss Verity Blane,' the policeman said.

'That's me,' Verity told him, 'and it's *Ms*.'

'Ah. Well, I'd be grateful if you'd accompany me to the station to help with our enquiries, Ms Blane.'

'Surely,' she said easily.

'Verity, wait a minute.' Dominic got up and went to the door. 'D'you need any help, can I phone anyone for you...?'

'It's all right, it's all been arranged,' she said to no one in particular.

He watched them go, then slowly came back in and sat down. Ashley got up and gently pushed the door shut. 'What the hell are we supposed to make of that?'

'I don't know,' Dominic said slowly.

Tom, meanwhile, was lost. The instructions he'd been given were easy enough to follow on the main road, but then he'd turned off, and once past the village of Catspaw, where he was supposed to find the farm signposted on the right, he'd instead dropped into a valley and come to a ford surrounded by tall trees. The sign said 'Deep Ford', and by the look of the dark water swirling past his headlamps, it wasn't kidding. There was no room to turn round, and the packhorse bridge beside it was too narrow even for the Cooper.

He pulled out the map and trained the light on it, but found himself glancing up again at the surrounding trees. For all his city breeding, Tom wasn't normally bothered by the countryside, but there was something about the way the gibbous moon filtered through the network of bare branches above...

He told himself not to be a fool, then locked all the doors and tried to concentrate on the map. Yes, he'd taken the wrong bloody turning after Catspaw. He put the map down, slewed himself round in the seat and started reversing back, looking for a place to turn. His neck had a crick before he found one, a gateway silhouetted by the moon. He turned into it, felt the back wheels sinking into mud... *Sod it!* He spun the steering wheel, found first and gingerly let in the clutch ... and the front wheels span for sickening moments before gripping and pulling the little car away. Five minutes later he was in Catspaw, and five minutes after that, he'd found the track to the farm.

He'd seriously considered giving up after leaving the ford, but supposed that since he'd told them he was coming, he ought to carry on... Now, as the Cooper grounded in a rut for the second time, he wished he hadn't. He gritted his teeth, lurched on and a few minutes later, beneath another clump of trees, he reached the farm.

He parked beside what he thought must be the farmhouse and climbed out. Dim light squeezed past a drawn curtain. He found the door. There was no bell, so he brought down the ancient knocker. A few moments later, the door creaked open to reveal a woman whose face was as shapeless as her clothes.

''Es, m'dear?'

'Mrs Scratchley? I've come to see Craig. I spoke to you on the phone.'

'So 'e did. 'E's down in the cowshed, milkin'.' Her accent was as ripe as the smells escaping past her. 'Jus' past the 'ouse, on yer right. Can't miss it.'

'Thanks.'

The door crunched shut behind him as he gloomily followed instructions.

It wasn't quite so bad as he'd thought. He came round the side of the house and saw a light above a doorway across the farmyard. He could hear the hum of an electric motor inside.

He picked his way across and pushed the door open. The hum became louder and a long line of cows gently steamed in the dim light

'Aye?'

He jumped as a sinewy man in overalls emerged from between two of them.

'I'm looking for Craig Scratchley.'

'Oh aye... *Craig...*' he bellowed, and another figure appeared.

'My name's Jones–' Tom began.

'I know,' Craig cut him off. 'Down here.'

He led Tom along the row of dangling tails to a small room with a wooden table and broken-backed chair that seemed to be some kind of office.

Does the stuff I put in my coffee really come from a place like this? Tom wondered as Craig said:

'So what d'you wanna know, then?'

'Only to confirm what Jessie Pengellis told me this morning,' Tom said, keen to get the visit over.

'Depends on what she told you, dunnit?' He was putting on the yokel aggro for Tom's benefit, although his accent wasn't naturally as strong as his parents'.

'That on Friday the seventh, you had – er – a disagreement with her, she told you to pack and leave her house, and then left you to do that.'

'Well, that's the truth,' he said, then added deliberately, 'The truth as far as it goes, like.'

Tom looked up at him. 'What d'you mean, as far as it goes?'

'I mean jus' that, as far as it goes.'

'Is there any more?'

Craig shrugged. 'Might be. Depends, dunnit?'

'Depends on what?'

'On what you think it's worth.'

Tom said, 'How about it's worth me not telling the police that you've been messing them about?'

'Then I dunno what you're talkin' about, do I, mister.'

Tom sighed as he pulled out his wallet and extracted a ten pound note.

Craig peered at it. 'Godda be worth more'n a tenner.'

'Why don't you try me and we'll see, eh?' Tom said, wondering what could have possessed Jessie to have allowed him into her house, let alone her bed. *Ah, the ways of a man with a maid...*

Craig took the note. 'Well, I did what she said and left after a couple of hours. After I got back here, I remembered somethin' I forgot, so I went back again ... and what d'you think I saw?'

'Well, what?'

'Jessie,' he said. 'I saw Jessie.'

'What time was this?' Tom asked after a pause.

''Bout nine. Half-past, maybe.'

'What was she doing?'

Craig shrugged. 'She got out of her car an' went inside.'

'Then what?'

'Then nothin'. I weren't goin' in there with her there, was I?'

Not after you'd done the place over, no. 'So why didn't you tell the police this?'

He shrugged again. 'Didn' ask me, did they?'

Tom could think of a better reason. 'Does Jessie know you saw her?'

''Course not.'

Bloody liar... He was about to leave it there when he thought of something else. 'The last weekend you worked at the centre, the Sunday, Maria was called in, wasn't she?'

Craig looked meaningfully back at him and Tom reluctantly found another note. 'This is the lot,' he said. 'OK?'

'OK,' Craig said, taking it. 'Yeah, Maria was called in Sunday, for an urgent cross match.'

'How long was she there?'

Well, she'd come in about four, left about seven. Yes, he supposed it was a long time for a cross match, but she'd stayed behind tidying up for a bit.

'Was she in her lab the whole time?'

He shook his head. 'No...' The ward had rung at about half-five asking where the blood was, he'd gone looking for her but couldn't find her at first, then he'd found her in the drivers' room looking through the key box. No, he didn't know why. She'd issued the blood at about six and left at just before seven.

'And between six and seven she was tidying up?'

That was what she'd said. No, he hadn't seen her, why should he have?

Tom paused, but couldn't think of anything else to ask. 'OK, thanks for your help, Craig.' He made to go past him but Craig moved in the way.

'You said more after I told you, mister.'

Tom shook his head. 'No, I didn't, I said that that was the lot.' He allowed his voice to harden. 'So if you'd be so kind...'

As though on signal, two figures loomed in the doorway – the sinewy man and another, younger one, Craig's big brother, Tom assumed. He was holding a pitchfork.

'You heard him, didn' you, Dad? He said more after I told him.'

'I 'eard un,' said the sinewy one. 'Pay up, mister.'

Tom knew he'd have to part with something, but didn't want his wallet completely emptied. He looked Dad in the eye.

'I've already given him twenty, which is more than what he's told me's worth. I'll give him another five, but that's it.'

'Ten,' said Craig.

'Five,' said Tom.

'Ten,' said Big Brother. The prongs of the pitchfork had somehow aligned themselves with Tom's belly.

Tom pretended to consider, then shrugged. 'All right, ten,' he said to Dad, 'but that's an end to it, OK?'

Dad gave a curt nod.

Tom pushed the money at Craig, then, not hesitating, pushed his way through them to the cow stall. He heard one of them mutter something, followed by laughter. He walked steadily past the cows and out. He knew he daren't hurry. He crossed the yard in measured paces, feeling eyes on his back for every one of them...

Round the side of the house and there was the Cooper facing him. He wished he'd turned it round now– *Oh, shit!* One of the front tyres was flat...

Not a coincidence.

He opened the door. felt under the steering wheel, brought out his gun and slipped it into his pocket. *Not that it'll be much good against a twelve bore...*

He unlocked the boot, pulled out the jack and torch and unscrewed the spare wheel ... took them to the front of the car, peering into the darkness ahead – nothing... *Maybe they did it as insurance in case I wouldn't pay up – maybe...*

Forcing himself to be methodical, he prised off the hub cap and loosened the wheel nuts before jacking up the car. Spun off the nuts and dropped them into the hub cap with a muted clang. Dragged the wheel off.

He aligned the spare in the weak light of the torch, then his head snapped up as he thought he heard a noise... Nothing, just the cows in the yard.

He lifted the wheel again. One bolt scraped through ... but not the others. He twisted the wheel a little and tried again ... and again, but they wouldn't go through.

He reached behind, felt for the bolt and tried to guide it through... *Ah, got it!*

More noise: he looked up as a cow materialised, floating through the gloom towards him, followed by another, then another...

He snatched up two of the nuts, fitted one and spun it as the cows parted in bovine streams around the front of the car, their hooves gently knocking the ground, their breath heavy on his neck, then a hoof sent the hub cap flying with its remaining nuts. He fitted the second and spun it, thinking, *Two'll have to do...* A flank nudged his shoulder and there was a thin pattering among the hooves...

Oh no! He tried to shrink into his coat and squeeze himself against the car but felt his head and shoulders being gently spattered...

He released the jack, snatched up the wheel brace and tightened the nuts so savagely they squealed, then opened the door, threw wheel, jack, torch and brace on to the passenger seat...

As suddenly as it had begun, the bovine flood subsided and a voice, Big Brother's he thought, said, 'Got a problem then, mate?'

'Nothing I can't handle,' Tom said between his teeth, realising at that moment that he'd panicked for nothing.

With a low chuckle, BB followed the cows into the darkness. Tom glared after him, then, seeing a glint on the ground, picked up his hub cap and threw it after the wheel and jack.

He got in, turned the car, and as he headed for the track his headlights picked out the last of the cows turning into a gateway. BB was nowhere in sight.

He negotiated the track and, once on the road, drove back to Sticklepath, composing a letter in his head to Brussels arguing that British farmers were being treated far too leniently and should have all their subsidies withdrawn.

18

At Tamar gaol, Prisoner 017984 Bailey had become increasingly pissed off with Prisoner 013257 Harding's attitude, and during the evening recreation period his limited patience had finally snapped. He attacked Harding with the dinner knife he'd especially sharpened for the purpose and, in doing so, managed to slice through his liver.

Ashley was called back to the centre not long after he arrived home. When he got there and realised the patient was a prisoner, he rang Dominic.

'He's in a bad way and they want five units

of red label now,' he said. 'Should I do the group in your lab?'

'No,' said Dominic. 'Get some disposable gowns and do it in Maria's lab. I'll be along in ten minutes.' He phoned Medlar to let him know what was happening, then set off for the centre himself.

Prisoners are susceptible to both hepatitis and HIV, and work on their blood was usually carried out in the Category 3 Containment lab in Microbiology. Harding, however, was in imminent danger of bleeding to death. He'd been given haemocell, a volume expander, to keep his blood pressure up, but he needed more red cells – urgently; thus five units of 'red label' (blood of Harding's group, but not specifically cross matched for him) had been ordered, to be followed by a further ten units of cross matched blood. Grouping his sample would take only a few minutes, whereas cross matching takes an hour.

'A Positive,' Ashley told Dominic when he arrived.

'I'll issue the red label,' Dominic said. 'You get the cross match started.'

He'd just issued it when Medlar arrived.

'Thought I'd better come in for this one,' he said. 'How's it going?'

'OK,' said Dominic, surprised to see him.

'Can I do anything?'

'I don't think so, thanks, doctor – although

you could let the ward know we're going as fast as we can.'

'Been on at you, have they?'

'You could say that. I'll go and set up the hepatitis and HIV tests.'

'Won't the hospital lab be doing that?'

'They might,' Dominic said, 'but we do need to know, and it's frankly easier doing it ourselves than chasing after them.'

'Fair enough,' Medlar said, smiling.

Meanwhile, further indignities awaited the manure-speckled Tom when he arrived back at Sticklepath.

'Oh, the Scratchleys,' Henry said, laughing. 'You shouldn't pay any heed to them. Bit rough and ready maybe, but they wouldn't do you any harm. Not *real* harm,' he added, looking Tom over.

Ha bloody ha, Tom thought. 'How did the place get its name?' he asked. 'I can't believe any of them have ever heard of *Cold Comfort Farm,* let alone read it.'

'Oh, one of the other farmers hereabouts called it Warm Welcome years ago as a joke, and it stuck. The Scratchleys went along with it without really understanding it.'

Tom then phoned Bennett to tell him about Jessie's fibs, only to learn that she'd gone to the police station that afternoon to admit them herself and make a statement. Craig had been blackmailing her, she'd said.

They'd also brought in Verity for questioning.

'So she could have saved me the trip,' Tom said grimly. *Not to mention thirty quid and a dry cleaning bill...*

'I don't think either of them are in the business of saving you anything, Mr Jones,' said Bennett. 'They've both complained about your aggressive questioning, as has Dr Medlar.'

Tom groaned and said he'd come and see him first thing, then went to sulk in the bath.

'Has it occurred to you,' he asked Bennett at nine the next morning, 'that those who complain so loudly about me might have motives other than outraged modesty?'

Bennett snorted. 'Of course it's bloody occurred to me. Has it occurred to *you* that we've been looking at the whole thing the wrong way round?' He leaned forward. 'You asked me on Sunday how Pengellis could've persuaded Goring into the centre that night – the answer is, she didn't. Blane did, by telling him she'd got something on Pengellis. We know he was looking for evidence against her.'

'And that evidence, of course, would've been in the freezer,' said Tom, forbearing to mention that he'd already suggested something of the kind on Sunday.

'Exactly.'

'Well, it fits ... except that why did Jessie go back to her own house that night?'

Bennett shrugged. 'One of those things we'll never know. It probably never occurred to her she'd been seen.'

'And why did they later move the body?'

'To confuse us over the place of death, make it look as though he'd drowned.'

'But why take the risk?' persisted Tom. 'That body would not have been easy to move frozen, and they could so easily have been caught.'

'But they weren't, were they?' Bennett said impatiently. 'Maybe when Pengellis realised on Saturday that it hadn't been found, she thought it was worth the risk.'

'If you're that sure, why didn't you hang on to them?'

'Because Stephanie Heath, their solicitor, is too bloody fly by half.' Bennett snarled, realising he'd sworn twice in the last few minutes. 'She's made trouble for us before.'

'What exactly happened?' Tom asked.

Bennett showed him their statements and, at Tom's request, played him some of the taped interviews. Hearing Jessie's voice was like having her in the room with him...

'I was troubled about what had happened between us and couldn't sleep. I got up, at around nine, I think, and slipped out of the house without waking her. I drove home, only to find it wrecked – by Craig, I assumed.'

'Did you see him?' (Bennett)

'No, I didn't. I cleared up as much of the mess as I could, then had a large whisky and went to bed.'

'What time would that have been?'

'Ten thirty, eleven – I'm not sure'

Yes, it was true she'd been forced into admitting this because Craig was black-mailing her – first for the money she'd with-held because of the damage, and then for more – but she was now telling the truth...

'I'd been put in a very difficult position, inspector.'

'In what way?'

'Verity phoned me at home on Tuesday. She told me what had happened, and that she'd told you I'd spent all Friday night with her. Just after that, the police car came to pick me up. I was confused, disorientated – at the time, it seemed easier to simply go along with it. I wish I hadn't, now.'

Tom said to Bennett, 'It could be the truth.'

Bennett snorted again.

'Put it another way,' said Tom, 'it'll be next to impossible to disprove it.'

Verity, after she'd been picked up at the centre, had confirmed all this. When first questioned by the police on Monday, she'd told them that Jessie had been with her all night without realising its importance.

Why had she done this? Bennett wanted to know.

'Partly out of pride, inspector–'

'How d'you mean, *pride?*'

'I didn't want to admit that she'd sneaked off like a thief in the night. Also...' she hesitated. 'I did it partly to put pressure on her, to make her admit her true sexual orientation.'

She'd then phoned Jessie and they'd agreed they'd better stick to it.

Stephanie Heath had forcibly pointed out that the case against them was as weak and circumstantial as ever, and that they would have told the truth earlier had it not been for the sexual harassment to which they'd been subjected. Bennett had reluctantly let them both go, Verity a short while after Jessie.

'Harassment, always harassment,' he said now, wearily. 'I'd be interested to meet *anybody* who could sexually harass Blane.'

'D'you still think they're lying?' Tom asked.

''Course I do.' He didn't sound quite so sure, though.

Tom leaned forward. 'It comes down to this – if Verity was at the centre shutting Goring in the freezer, why did Jessie go home and risk their alibi? Why didn't she stay at Verity's?'

'I don't bloody know,' said Bennett.

The first thing Tom saw when he got back to his temporary office in the centre was an envelope with his name on it on the desk. He opened it and extracted a single sheet of paper. The message on it was typed in capitals:

ASK DOMINIC TUDOR WHO HAD THE BEST OPPORTUNITY TO SHIT ON JESSIE. ASK HIM HOW HE LIKED THE SMELL OF GORING'S BUM.

He thought about it for a few minutes, then put it into a transparent plastic envelope to preserve any fingerprints. Then he asked Dominic to come down.

As soon as he'd sat, Tom handed him the message. His eyes widened as he read it.

'Where did this come from?' he said, looking up. He hadn't coloured or shown any sign of embarrassment.

'I found it here on the desk when I arrived. The point is, is it true?'

'It's absolutely ridiculous,' Dominic said after a moment's hesitation.

'Is it, though? You see, it does make rather a good point about who had the best opportunity to pass Jessie's thoughts on to Goring–'

'That's rubbish,' Dominic protested. 'We

223

all had exactly the same opportunity to photocopy those files she left on her desk.'

'You know, I never really believed in that,' Tom said conversationally. 'It was too short a time for Goring to prepare himself so thoroughly. No, it needed someone with access to her thoughts as well as her files, someone she trusted, someone who–'

'That could be Verity as much as me.'

'Someone who knew Goring from the past,' Tom continued, 'someone with–'

'All right, all *right*,' Dominic capitulated suddenly. 'It was me.'

'Why?'

After a pause, not looking at Tom, he began haltingly, 'I – I came to realise about three months ago that Jessie couldn't possibly win, that the centre was going to close come what may – and that she was ruining all our chances of finding work elsewhere. She was dragging us down with her. I did my best to persuade her–'

'Did you go to Goring, or did he come to you?'

'Neither, really.' He swallowed, still not looking at Tom. 'You were right, I did get to know him when he was interim director here. We always got on. Then I met him at a one-day conference a couple of months or so ago and we got talking. He was interested in my research, said it was a shame if it was wasted. Then he invited me up to London for a chat about it. I went, and that's how it started.'

'Do any of the others here know?'

'Well, one of them does, obviously.' He sighed. 'I've no idea who, though.'

'Didn't you ever find it difficult, maintaining the role of friend and adviser while kebabbing her at the same time? I'm just curious...'

'Yes, yes, *yes*. I hated it, I – I hated myself sometimes.' His eyes flickered up again. 'But I really thought it was for the best, and I continually tried to persuade her to give it up and settle for what she could.'

'Big of you.'

Dominic looked up, met his eyes, said defiantly, 'Yes, it would have been big of me, if I'd succeeded. I'd have been doing her the best favour ever.'

'I take it you didn't realise she was going to accuse Goring of nepotism in the interview?'

'I had no idea. I'd have warned him if I had.'

'Didn't he blame you, for not warning him?'

'Probably, although I never got to find out. I kept out of his way after the interview.'

'He didn't try to contact you?'

'No, although I'm sure he'd have got round to it.' He continued: 'Do the others have to know about–'

'You were saying just now about your research,' Tom interrupted, 'that Goring said it would be a shame if it was wasted. Was that by way of a bribe?'

He hesitated again, said, 'I suppose it was. He told me he'd find me a job in another centre where I could go on with it.' Another pause, then: 'They say every man has his price, and that was mine.' He sighed. 'Not that it'll do me any good now.' He looked up. 'Do the others have to know about this?'

Tom didn't say anything and Dominic continued: 'Does Dr Medlar have to know? You see, I'm dependent on him now for a reference.'

Tom felt no obligation whatever to protect him– *Treacherous little turd* – but couldn't see any direct need to expose him ... and a hold on him might come in useful later...

'I'll have to think about that,' he said at last, not minding at all if Dominic squirmed on a skewer himself for a while.

Dominic compressed his lips, then said, 'Could you let me know tomorrow? The thing is–'

'Can't, I'm afraid. I'm off to Poole for the day.'

'Thursday, then? I'm applying for a job...'

'All right. And now, you can trot off and find Adrian Hodges and send him along to me.'

19

It was a deeply preoccupied Dominic who walked slowly back up the corridor from Tom's office.

How had it degenerated into this? he wondered. *Will he go and tell Medlar anyway, just out of spite?*

Oh well, he told himself, he'd got out of scrapes before, hadn't he? And he would again...

He went into Blood Issue where he found Adrian light-penning some units of blood into a box.

'Jones wants to see you,' he said without preamble. 'Now.'

'Tell him I'm busy,' Adrian said without bothering to look up.

Dominic grabbed his shoulder and swung him round: 'I don't care what you do when you get there,' he said through clenched teeth, 'you can kick his face in with my blessing, but I'm telling you to get down there – *now.*'

'Oh, so this urgent order can wait, can it?' Adrian said, calmly removing his hand.

Resisting with great difficulty the urge to strangle Adrian on the spot, Dominic said,

'All right, finish the order, then get down there.' He turned to go.

Adrian said, 'Actually, the thing to do if you really wanted to get to him would be to chuck some blood over him.'

Dominic, who was half-way to the door, stopped and looked back. 'What d'you mean?'

'He's scared of blood – at least, he was a few years ago. Something to do with his brother being a haemophiliac and getting AIDS.'

'How d'you know that?'

'I was here when he came down before. You know, the plasma scam, just before you came.'

'That was him, was it...?'

Adrian was the person Tom had least looked forward to interviewing, which was perhaps why he'd left him till last. Adrian had had 'a thing' about Holly during Tom's visit eight years earlier and hadn't been best gruntled when she'd preferred Tom. He'd eventually made such a nuisance of himself that Tom had nutmegged him at a hospital disco, pretending afterwards (as Adrian writhed on the floor) that it was an accident. It was a memory that would tend to linger, Tom reflected now.

Adrian wasn't exactly rushing to join him, so he turned his thoughts to the anonymous note and who might have sent it. He read it through again. Two sentences: both instructions that were really facts, both mildly obscene.

Something about that, about its whole tone, persuaded Tom that it was Verity. Maybe Jessie had worked it out and told her ... was it worth challenging Verity with it now? Probably not...

His reverie was interrupted by a single knock. 'Come in,' he called, and there was Adrian.

'Hello,' Tom said. 'Come and have a seat.'

Adrian did so without speaking. He hadn't changed much. The same thickset, powerful body with face to match, the same resentful expression.

'It's been a long time,' Tom observed. Inane, but whatever he said would have sounded wrong.

'Yeah,' said Adrian.

Well, enough reminiscing... 'I'm sure you already know why I'm here?'

'Yeah.'

'I'm trying to find out as much as I can about Dr Goring's visit, and his death, of course. Did you know him at all?'

No, not beyond a nodding acquaintance, either during his time as interim director or later. No, he hadn't liked him – he was responsible for them losing their jobs, wasn't he? And no, he had no idea whether

Jessie's allegation was true or not – how could he have?

'Did you often cover for Paul Bannister?'

'How d'you mean, cover for him?' He knew very well.

'Did he often say he was out with you when he was doing something else?'

After a pause, Adrian said, 'Not often, no.'

'How often?'

He shrugged. 'Twice, maybe three times.'

'That Friday, did he ask you to tell the police he'd been out with you?'

'No. I wouldn't have lied to the police anyway.' He paused again. 'I didn't like lying to his wife, but his marriage is his own business, I suppose...' he looked as though he was going to say more, then changed his mind.

It fitted with Adrian's own bitterness, Tom thought. Holly had heard, through her old colleagues, that he'd married after she'd left, but it hadn't worked out and he'd gone back to live with his parents.

'So other than to come back here at around seven to fetch something, you didn't go out that night?'

'No.'

'What was it you came back to fetch?'

'A book. I can read, believe it or not.'

'I believe it. What was the book?'

'*Tarka the Otter*, if you must know.'

'Appropriate, for this area.'

After another pause, Adrian said, 'I'd never realised how good it was before. They made us read it at school and it put me off.'

Tom smiled. 'You and me both,' he said.

'You've never read it?' Tom shook his head and Adrian said, 'You should – it's good.'

'I'll do that.'

Adrian said slowly, 'I don't know what's happened to us here ... this place, it's gone right down the toilet since we were told it was closing.'

'In what way?'

'Nobody cares about anything any more – except bitching, bad-mouthing, back-stabbing ... and jumping in and out of bed with each other...' He tailed off.

'I've seen it for myself,' Tom said. After a moment, he said, 'So other than for Arthur Selwick, you didn't see anyone or hear anything while you were here?'

'No.'

'How long were you here?'

'Five minutes, if that. Arthur's already told all this to the police, hasn't he?'

He had, and there didn't seem much point in keeping Adrian any longer. 'How far away d'you live?'

'About a mile.'

'See anyone on the way?'

'Only Maria, at the bottom of the road here.'

Tom said casually. 'You didn't mention that to the police?'

'They didn't ask me that. They asked me if I'd seen anyone here.'

'You're sure it was Maria?'

'Yes. Her face was lit by a street lamp.'

'Did she see you?'

'I don't think so. Is it important?'

'I don't know. Probably not. Just after seven, you said?'

'Yes.'

After a pause, Tom said, 'Adrian, I'm honestly not sure whether it's important or not, but I'd like you to keep it to yourself for the moment – please.'

'From Maria, you mean?'

'From Maria, from everyone. OK?'

'All right,' he said. 'Is that all?'

Tom nodded. 'Yes, it is. Thanks.'

He got up, hesitated. 'How is Holly?' he said at last.

'She's very well.'

'I'm glad. Would you give her my regards?'

'Yes, I'll do that,' said Tom.

Adrian nodded and left.

Tom sat back, smiled wryly to himself. If it hadn't been for that most casually put of questions, and Adrian's concept of literal truth ... and he *had* been telling the truth, there was no reason for him not to. Maria had been driving away from the centre at seven when she'd sworn she was with

Medlar until eight, which made them both liars. He could challenge Medlar with it now, or he could challenge Maria ... who was probably the weaker link...

He knew he ought to tell Bennett about it, but if he could break Maria now, and he knew he could do that better than Bennett, then maybe he could break the case as well.

Jessie slammed the door of her car hard enough to make the neighbour digging his garden look up, then went to the door of Verity's house and rang the bell. The pressure building behind her left eye wasn't quite a pain – yet, but she knew that within an hour or so it would evolve into a full-blown migraine.

She rang the bell again. She shouldn't have come, she wouldn't have had to if Verity hadn't been so persistent...

After being released the night before, Jessie had gone home and had been flopped on the sofa with a large whisky when the phone rang.

'It's me, flower,' Verity said. 'They let you go, then?'

'Sounds like it, doesn't it?' Jessie said, immediately regretting her churlishness.

'He still doesn't believe us. Bennett, I mean.'

'I know.'

'Can you come round? We need to talk about it.'

'Better not, I've just drunk enough whisky to tip me over the breathalyser.' She hadn't, not yet, she just didn't want to see Verity.

'I'll come round to you, then.'

'Verity, I can't take any more tonight – can't it wait till tomorrow, please?'

'It's important.'

'Tell me now, then.'

'I can't, not over the phone.' She hesitated, said, 'I know who shat on you with Goring.'

After another pause, Jessie said, 'Well, who?'

'I'm not telling you over the phone.'

Jessie had done her best to persuade her, but Verity refused and Jessie had eventually slammed the phone down in frustration.

Did it matter? she'd wondered. Did it have any bearing? It might, but what could she do about it now...?

She had needed more than the whisky in her glass before she'd been able to sleep that night.

Now, she knelt, pushed open the letter flap and shouted loudly, 'Verity, it's me, Jessie.'

The door gave slightly under her fingers ... she pushed it open, stood up and went a little way into the hall.

'Verity?' she called.

She looked into the living-room, saw the foot protruding from behind the arm of the sofa. She knew perfectly well what it meant, but still had to look.

Verity was lying on her back, her eyes wide open as though in astonishment, staring up at the ceiling...

The astonishment was appropriate, Jessie reflected as she picked up the phone, since a large latex phallus had been thrust crudely into her mouth.

Tom listened patiently while Maria recited once again how she'd stayed with Medlar in his office on Friday evening until eight. She didn't show anything like so much embarrassment this time round, he thought, perhaps because he hadn't dwelled on the sexual aspect.

'So you left him at just before eight and he left five minutes later?'

'Yes.'

'How d'you know he left five minutes later?'

She made a mouth. 'I suppose I don't, strictly speaking–' she'd gained in confidence now – 'but the police are satisfied he did, aren't they? Didn't he arrive home shortly after that?'

'But nobody saw *you* arrive home, did they?'

'They wouldn't, I live alone.'

'Did anyone see you leave the centre?'

'I told you before, I left by the back corridor so that nobody would see me.'

'As it happens, Maria, somebody did see you leaving.'

She stiffened.

'It was when you were driving away.'

She regarded him warily, not speaking.

'The problem being that it was just after seven when they saw you.'

Her tongue touched her lips. 'Then they're mistaken. It *was* dark...' She gave her characteristic half-smile. 'And so am I.'

Tom smiled back. 'There was no mistake, you were going under a street lamp. And it was your car.'

'Who was it?'

'I don't think that really matters at this stage, do you?'

'Well, whoever it was, it's their word against mine. And Dr Medlar's.'

'I'd like to turn now to the following Sunday,' Tom continued smoothly. 'You were called in to do a cross match, you were telling me yesterday.'

'Yes...?'

'A cross match takes an hour at the most. You were here for over three hours.'

Maria swallowed nervously. 'I thought I told you, it was a very difficult cross match and I had to repeat all the tests.'

'Because the patient had antibodies, I

think you said?'

'Er – yes, that's right.'

'So you would have put up a panel to identify it, wouldn't you?'

'Yes...'

'And the results of that would be in the computer?'

She nodded slowly, her eyes on his face.

'Perhaps you'd like to show me? We can go along to your lab, if you like.'

She closed her eyes for a moment. 'I wasn't telling you the truth yesterday,' she said, opening them again. 'I didn't put up a panel. I got the patient's blood group wrong – that's why I had to repeat everything. I didn't tell you before because I was so embarrassed about it.'

'How did such an experienced operator as you come to make such a fundamental error?'

'I don't know. It was just one of those things.'

'But that's why the blood was delayed and the ward had to telephone and ask where it was?'

'Yes.'

'While you were in your lab working against the clock trying to rectify your mistake?'

'Yes,' she said faintly.

'Craig Scratchley, who you told me is not an aware person, took the call and says that he couldn't find you in your lab.'

Her tongue touched her lips. 'That would have been during one of the incubation periods, I expect.'

'So where were you?'

'In the loo, I imagine. I do have to use the loo occasionally like anyone else.' Her voice was ragged now, bordering on hysteria.

'The unaware Craig also told me that he found you in the drivers' room, going through the keys to all the vehicles.'

'I – I was checking which driver was on, what van he would use...'

'Why? That's not your job, surely?'

'I just wanted to be sure.'

'Craig also told me that he thought you'd gone home after you'd issued the blood at six, but that then you reappeared an hour later.'

'I – I was putting the results into the computer, tidying everything away...'

'Indeed you were. You were tidying away Dr Goring's body, weren't you? Dumping it in the Tamar.'

'*No!*' She half rose from her seat. 'No – I've never heard anything so...'

'Ridiculous? So it may be, but that's what you were doing.'

She was shaking her head. 'No...'

'The time, the opportunity, it has to be you, Maria. I don't have absolute proof, not yet, but we're having forensic tests done on all the vans, which should tie it up.' This really was stretching the truth, but Tom knew that if she didn't break now, she might not at all.

She was sitting upright, very still, her eyes and lips clenched tight and tears following each other down her face ... and to his astonishment, he suddenly realised that she was beautiful. He said, 'I don't know how you managed it, but I do know that it was you who moved him. Did you kill him, Maria?'

'Yes,' she whispered.

'When?'

She opened her eyes. 'Do you have a handkerchief, please?'

He handed her one and she carefully wiped her face.

'It was Friday night,' she said at last. 'You were right, I did leave at seven, but I came back half an hour later. I'd arranged to meet him – Dr Goring – in the underground park. Nobody saw us, we came up in the lift. I told him there was something he should see in the freezer and shut him in while he was looking.'

'What did you do then?'

'I left him there and went home. Nobody saw me.'

'What did you tell him he should see?'

'Something he could use to sack Jessie.'

'What was it?'

'I didn't tell him what. There wasn't anything.'

'Why did you do it, Maria?'

'Because of what he was doing to the centre and everyone in it, because he was trying to ruin Jessie ... making misery for everyone.'

'How did you manage to get the body out of the centre?'

'I'm stronger than I look. You know: "Lift that bale, tote that barge..."' She gave a twisted smile, continued: 'When I was called in and realised that no one had found the body, I decided to put it in the river to confuse the police...'

She'd positioned one of the centre's vans by the lift, she told him, then lifted the body on to a trolley with the hand-operated fork-lift from the stores. 'That was the hardest part,' she said, 'but luckily, he was hunched up, except for one arm.'

There was no other way she could have known about *that*...

She'd covered it with a large dust sheet, pushed it through Plasma to the reception lift, then manoeuvred it into the van. Then she'd driven to a disused wharf and pushed it in the river before returning to the centre. Listening to her, Tom had no doubt that she was telling the truth.

'Well, we'd better get you down to the police station,' he said.

He rang Bennett and told him he was bringing someone to see him. Bennett seemed to hesitate, then told Tom that something had come up and he'd already sent a car to collect him.

20

Tom didn't have long to wonder why because the car arrived almost straight away. When they got to the station, Maria was taken to an interview room while Bennett took Tom up to his own office.

'So what does she have to say that's so important, Mr Jones?'

'Only that she killed Dr Goring.'

Bennett goggled. *'What?'*

'Although I'm not–'

'How come she told you?' he demanded.

As Tom explained, Bennett's mouth tightened and his eyes glittered.

'You should have brought that information to *us*, not questioned her about it yourself.'

'I'm sorry, inspector, but I thought it best to hit her with what I had straight away.'

'So that's what you thought, is it?' Bennett said between his teeth.

'Yes, because I'm the one who knows how long it takes to do a cross match, to–'

'Your brief was to assist us, sir. Now, there are some questions I want to ask you.'

Tom didn't much like the way he was looking at him. 'Aren't you going to take Miss N'Kanu's statement before she changes her mind about it?'

'All in good time.' He opened a drawer and brought out a sealed plastic bag. 'Would this be your identity card, by any chance, sir? It has your name on it.'

Tom took the bag. 'Yes, it is. Where did you find it?'

'It would be true to say, would it not, that you had a quarrel with Miss Verity Blane yesterday afternoon during which she pushed a desk on to you, necessitating your having an X-ray?'

'You already know that. Where did you find my card?'

'Underneath the body, the dead body, of Miss Blane.'

'*What?*' It was Tom's turn to goggle.

'She's been found murdered, strangled, and I'd like to know how come your ID card was under her body, sir.'

'So would I, inspector,' Tom said weakly. 'Where was she found?'

'In her home.'

'Well, I've never been there, I don't even know where it is.'

'You're telling me you know nothing about her death?'

242

'Of course not, I–'

'In which case you won't mind letting us take your fingerprints. For elimination purposes.'

Tom thought quickly. He knew he'd never been to Verity's house, so where was the harm? 'All right,' he said.

Bennett picked up his phone and pushed a button. 'Sergeant – send Bendle along with his kit, please.'

He put the phone down. There was a silence which Tom, broke by saying, 'Who found her?'

'Miss Pengellis.'

'When?'

'This morning. She phoned us from Miss Blane's house not long after you left the station.'

After another short silence, Tom said, 'I really think you ought to take Miss N'Kanu's statement, I'm afraid she might change–'

Bennett's fist crashed down on to his desk. '*Don't* tell me how to do my job, sir.'

There was a knock on the door and a man came in with the fingerprinting kit. Tom had had it done before, although not quite under these circumstances.

When it was finished, Bennett said, 'And now if you'd like to wait while we check them, I'll go and see Miss N'Kanu.'

Tom was escorted to a small room and left there.

Verity murdered and they wanted to check his prints? Check them against what...? He took out a cheroot, then noticed a No Smoking sign on the table. He put his head round the door to find the uniformed constable sitting on a chair outside. The sight infuriated him beyond measure.

'Can I help you, sir?'

'Yes, you can, constable. I've been put in a No Smoking room and I wish to smoke.'

'I don't think I can help there, sir.'

'Either you find me a room where I can smoke, *now*, or I light up in here. OK?'

They found him one. He lit up. What the *hell* was it all about...

A few minutes later, he found out. Two men in plain clothes came in with recording equipment and shut the door.

'I'm Detective Sergeant Mulholland and this is Detective Constable Marsh. We'd like to go over a couple of things with you, sir.'

'OK,' said Tom, holding his temper in check.

Marsh deftly set up the equipment, tested it, then they all identified themselves.

Mulholland opened the questioning. 'Did you interview Miss Verity Blane at the Transfusion Centre yesterday, sir?'

'I did.'

Had she assaulted him there, necessitating a visit to X-ray? – She had.

This must have annoyed him? – No, it had

shocked rather than annoyed him...

'Did you meet with Miss Blane subsequent to that incident?'

'I did not.'

'Are you sure about that, sir? Not at any time or at any place yesterday evening?'

'Yes, I am sure.'

'Then perhaps you'd like to tell us where you were yesterday evening, sir?'

He told them about Warm Welcome Farm, how he'd driven back to Sticklepath and later gone to the local pub.

'So you were in the White Hart public house from about nine till ten?'

'That's what I said.'

'Did anybody see you?'

'Of course they did. I expect they'd remember me, too.'

'We'll be checking on that, sir–'

'Sergeant, what's going on here? Are you seriously trying to suggest I'm a suspect? I am supposed to be working here myself – with Inspector Bennett.'

Mulholland looked at him a moment before replying.

'I'll tell you what's going on, sir. We've found your fingerprints in Miss Blane's house.'

'That's impossible,' Tom said, trying to speak calmly as a prickle ran over the top of his head. 'I've never been there. Exactly *where* did you find these prints?'

Mulholland pursed his lips, then said, 'On a rubber penis that had been pushed into Miss Blane's mouth... You find that amusing, do you, sir?'

'No, I don't find it amusing, sergeant, it's just that I can explain now how they got there.' He told him what had happened before Verity had pushed the desk on to him.

After another pause Mulholland said, 'Were there any witnesses to this, sir?'

'Not as such, no, although Dr Medlar came in shortly afterwards.' He explained how Medlar had thrown the phallus into the bin.

'So who else would have known that, sir?'

'The only person *I* told was Ashley Miles, although he'll probably tell you that *he* told plenty of others.'

Mulholland made a couple of notes on his pad. 'But nobody actually witnessed the incident?'

'No, sergeant,' Tom said. Then, 'How much longer do you intend holding me here?'

Mulholland considered him a moment before saying, 'We'll need to take your photo and check your story with the landlord–'

'No,' Tom said, his patience evaporated. 'I've given you an explanation and enough's enough. I want a phone – now, please.'

'Just as soon as we've–'

'I want a phone – *now*, please.'

They found him one. In a few succinct sentences, he told Marcus what had happened. Twenty minutes later, he was taken up to Bennett's office.

'I'm sorry about the misunderstanding, Mr Jones,' Bennett said carefully. He was red in the face and uncomfortable. 'But what with your ID card and the finger-prints, you'll understand that we had to thoroughly check it out.'

Tom looked at him without replying. He'd been over-zealous, maybe even a little vindictive, and they both knew it, but perhaps the blow torch he'd undoubtedly just had applied to him was sufficient unto the day...

Bennett wriggled slightly and continued, 'So now we're left with the problem of who did kill Miss Blane, and why.'

'And also whether the two killings are connected, inspector.'

'D'you think they are?'

'I'd say so, wouldn't you?'

Bennett said, 'Well, Miss N'Kanu has confessed to killing Dr Goring, as you said she would.'

'D'you believe her?'

'I see no reason not to. We're checking out her story, having Forensic go over the van. Are you suggesting that she killed Miss

Blane as well?'

'I'm not convinced she killed either of them.'

Bennett hesitated. 'Shall we stick with Miss Blane's killing for the moment? If it were an isolated case, I'd have said it had the hallmarks of a sex crime. Wouldn't you?'

'The penis, you mean?'

'Yes.' He grimaced with distaste. 'The fact that it had been put into her mouth.'

'But this isn't an isolated case, is it, inspector? The penis was put there with the sole purpose of incriminating me.' *And you fell for it ...* he didn't add. He took out his cheroots. 'D'you have an ashtray?'

Bennett looked at the No Smoking sign on his door, then resignedly opened a drawer and handed him one. 'I believe you told Sergeant Mulholland that it was Miss Blane who – er – presented it to you.'

'That's right.' He lit his cheroot.

'And that Dr Medlar deposited it in the rubbish bin?'

'Yes.'

'So what we have to work out now is how it got from there to Miss Blane's house. The only person you told was Ashley Miles?'

'Yes, but I'm sure he'd have told some of the others. The story was doing the rounds anyway.'

'One person he'd have certainly told would have been his friend Mr Tudor,'

Bennett mused.

'Ye-es,' said Tom. 'There's something you should know about Dominic Tudor, inspector...' He told him about the anonymous note he'd found and how Dominic had admitted to being Goring's earpiece and betraying Jessie.

'I can't say I'm altogether surprised,' said Bennett. 'Any ideas who wrote it?'

'I'd say Verity, although it's only a gut feeling. But it does mean that Dominic had no motive for killing Goring, since he was more use to him alive.'

Bennett thought about this, then said, 'That may be so in Dr Goring's case, but not in Blane's.'

'How d'you mean?'

'Well, you just said that you think Blane left the note about Tudor betraying Pengellis – what if he knew she suspected him and killed her to keep her quiet?'

'Is that really a strong enough motive for murder?'

'Didn't you tell me that if it came out, it would destroy his prospects for getting another job? Isn't that motive enough?'

'I suppose it could be,' Tom said doubtfully. 'But surely, a much more likely motive for someone would be if she'd known they killed Goring.'

'Also true,' agreed Bennett. 'But you're presupposing a link between the killings, and I'm not yet convinced there is one.'

'You really fancy Dominic for it, then?'

Bennett sighed. 'Probably just wishful thinking.' He looked away for a moment, then back at Tom. 'There is another possibility we haven't considered, and that is that Blane herself might have taken your ID card and the – er – object back to her house.'

'But why would she do that?'

'Bear with me a moment. If she was the one who put the note on your desk, then she could well have found your ID then and taken it and the – er … home.'

'But *why?*'

'Well, we know she'd didn't like you, maybe she thought she could do you some harm with them. But the point I'm making is that whoever killed her might have found the – er – penis–' he'd said it at last – 'and your ID already there.'

Tom thought about this, then said, 'That would certainly throw the field open, wouldn't it?'

'I'd say so. And we were talking of a sex crime...'

Tom grinned at him. 'It's a neat theory, inspector. We'll keep it in mind, shall we?' He paused. 'I have an alternative if you're interested, although no proof.'

'I'm listening.'

Tom told him.

21

The tape was running and the occupants of the room had identified themselves. Maria had refused a solicitor, although a WPC was present.

'Miss N'Kanu,' Bennett said, 'you told us in your statement how you shut Dr Goring in the freezer and later removed his body. I'd like to touch on one or two points again...'

Touching on one or two points meant Maria reiterating everything at length while Bennett probed for inconsistencies. There weren't any, she simply repeated the story as though by heart in a flat, almost bored voice.

'What were you doing last night?' Bennett said, changing direction.

'Last night?' For the first time, she looked surprised.

'Yes, say from about seven.'

'I was at home in my flat...' She'd had a meal, tidied the place up, phoned her parents, read for a while and then gone to bed.

Had she gone out at all? – No.

'You see Miss N'Kanu, sometime yesterday evening, Verity Blane was strangled in her home.'

Maria went very still, her face a mask.

'You've just told us you were in all night, so it couldn't have been you. And yet we're sure she was murdered by the same person who murdered Dr Goring.' Bennett wasn't sure yet, although he carried it off convincingly enough.

Still Maria didn't say anything. She just stared over his shoulder at the wall behind him, her lips slightly apart.

'Do you still maintain that you murdered Dr Goring?'

No answer.

'You see, Miss N'Kanu, we don't think you did murder Dr Goring. We think you're trying to protect someone.'

'What I've told you is the truth.'

'I know it is, in part. I believe you moved Dr Goring's body, all our checks bear that out, but you did that to protect the same person, didn't you?'

No response.

'You found the body when you went to the freezer for something, and it was the shock of *that* that caused you to misgroup the patient's blood, wasn't it?'

No response.

'Now, are you going to claim Miss Blane's murder as well, or are you going to consider whether or not it's wise to go on protecting a murderer who may kill again?'

'I ... I need time to think.'

And that was all they could get out of her.

Mulholland and Marsh, meanwhile, drove Tom back to the centre, then commandeered his room and started questioning staff. Verity's death hadn't been announced.

Adrian confirmed he'd seen Maria leaving the centre, but had no idea whether she might have returned. He also confirmed that he knew about Tom, Verity and the phallus – he'd overheard Ashley telling Dominic and asked about it.

Ashley confirmed that he'd told several people about Tom's version of events.

'Why did you find it necessary to tell so many people, sir?'

'Because I thought it was funny and wanted to share it. God knows, we've little enough to laugh about here at the moment...'

So who had he told? Well ... there was Mark, his deputy, Dominic, Paul, Adrian ... maybe others, he couldn't remember.

'Did you come into this room at all after Mr Jones left, sir?'

'What, *this* room? No.'

'Not at all during the afternoon or evening?'

'No.'

'Are you telling us you didn't remove the rubber penis from the rubbish bin, sir?'

Ashley stared at him. 'Why on earth

should I do that?'

'Answer the question, please, sir.'

'No, I didn't.'

'Did you see anyone else come into this room?'

'No.'

He told them how he'd been called back to the centre and how Dominic and Dr Medlar had joined him... Yes, he'd been the last to leave, at around ten... Dr Medlar had left at around eight-fifteen and Dominic at around nine.

Yes, he'd gone straight home – his wife could confirm the approximate time... Yes, Verity's house was on his way, and no, he hadn't stopped there.

Dominic told a similar story. He'd known about the phallus – from Dr Medlar, from Verity herself, and then from Ashley... No, he hadn't told anyone else.

'Did you come into this room yesterday afternoon or evening, sir?'

Dominic thought, then said, 'Not yesterday, no. Mr Jones did ask me some questions, but that was in the manager's room.'

'Did you see anyone else coming in here?'

'No. Although...' He hesitated.

'Yes, sir?'

'I think I may have seen someone coming out.'

'How d'you mean, sir, think?'

'I came round the corner from the corridor and saw Verity walking away.'

The two detectives looked at each other, then Mulholland said, 'What time would this have been, sir?'

'About half-past three.'

'Did she see you?'

'I don't think so.'

Marsh noted it down, then Mulholland asked him about the previous evening. He told them how he'd been called by Ashley and how in turn he'd informed Dr Medlar, who'd also come in. 'I was a bit surprised about that, to tell you the truth.'

'Why was that, sir?'

'He usually only comes in if there's a specific medical problem.'

He'd left the centre at about a quarter past nine, he thought... Yes, his route home went near to Verity's house but not past it, and no, he hadn't stopped there. His wife would confirm that he was home at about nine thirty.

After he'd gone, Mulholland turned to March. 'Well, what d'you think, Dave?'

Marsh took a breath. 'Either of them *could* have been lying, but I think they were telling the truth.'

Mulholland nodded slowly. 'I think so, too. Best tell the guv'nor, I suppose.'

The tape was running and the occupants of

the room had identified themselves. Mulholland had replaced the WPC.

'Dr Medlar,' Bennett began, 'I'd like to go through with you again the events of Friday evening, Friday the seventh of January, that is.'

'We've already been through that in great detail,' Medlar observed. 'More than once.'

'And now I'd like to go through it again, doctor.'

'If I didn't know otherwise, inspector, I'd suspect you of prurience.'

Bennett didn't reply, partly because he wasn't sure what prurience was.

'Very well,' Medlar said. 'But before I do, there's an inaccuracy in my previous statement that I should perhaps put right.' Bennett still didn't say anything, so he went on, 'I stated earlier that Miss N'Kanu left me at eight o'clock that evening, just before. The truth is that it was nearer seven than eight.'

'So what you said in your earlier statement was a lie?'

Medlar flinched slightly at the word 'lie'. 'I suppose I panicked. I thought it would look bad if I said I stayed there alone.'

'Look bad? How do you mean, look bad?'

Medlar drew a breath. 'Just that. In the circumstances of Adam's death, I felt it would seem ... tidier if we'd left at the same time.'

'That's very candid of you, if I may say so, doctor. So you lied because you thought it would otherwise look bad in the circumstances of Dr Goring's death?' Medlar didn't reply, so Bennett said, 'Is that what you mean, doctor?' He'd been irritated by Medlar's avoidance of his trap and wanted to inflict some damage for the tape. 'Well, doctor?'

'In essence, yes,' Medlar said at last.

'So now we come to the question of what you were doing after Miss N'Kanu left you.'

After another pause, Medlar said, 'I sat in my office for a while smoking my pipe.' As though reminded of it, he pulled it out of his pocket and lit it now. 'I wasn't proud of what had happened and wanted to think things over.'

'How long would you say this thinking took you?'

'Not very long, ten or fifteen minutes perhaps.'

'What did you do then?'

'I had a shower.'

'A *shower?*'

'Yes, inspector, a shower.'

'Why?'

Medlar answered as though to a backward child. 'Because I didn't want my wife to detect any lingering traces of my lovemaking, inspector, that's why.'

'Whereabouts did you take this shower?'

Medlar sighed and told him there was a loo with a shower room just along the corridor from his office... How long had it taken? About twenty minutes, he thought – the clock in his car had said ten to eight when he left.

Bennett said, 'You're obviously concerned to keep your affair with Miss N'Kanu from your wife?'

Medlar looked guarded. 'Yes. She has enough to put up with as it is.'

'So you'd go to considerable lengths to avoid hurting your wife?'

'I'd certainly go to the lengths of having a shower, inspector.' He tapped out the dottle from his pipe and began refilling it.

'And also of lying about what you were doing, doctor.' Statement, not question.

'Lying is unavoidable in an illicit relationship.'

'What about yesterday evening? What were you doing from about seven, let's say?'

Medlar explained how he'd been called into the centre by Dominic.

Mulholland said, 'According to Mr Tudor, he phoned you just to let you know what was going on. Why was it necessary for you to go in, sir?'

Medlar turned to answer him. 'Involving a prisoner as it did, it was an unusual situation which might call for a medical judgement.'

'Couldn't you have delivered that from home, sir?'

Medlar hesitated, then said, 'Yes, I suppose I could have.'

'Then why didn't you?'

'Have you ever lived with a chronically sick person, sergeant?'

'No, sir.'

'It's emotionally draining and there are times when, no matter how much you love them, you have to get out for a while. That's why I went to the centre when Dominic called.'

'I see, sir,' said Mulholland sceptically.

So what time had he left the centre? – About eight thirty.

What time had he got home? – Around nine, the nine o'clock news had been on.

Bennett said, 'I believe you pass Verity Blane's house on your way home?'

'I believe I do.'

'Did you stop there?'

A faint smile. 'Are you accusing me of having an affair with her as well, inspector? I assure you I haven't the stamina.'

Too bloody glib by far... 'Answer the question, would you, doctor.'

'No, I didn't stop there.'

'Yesterday, when you complained to me about Mr Jones and told me about the scene with Miss Blane, you didn't tell me she'd presented him with a rubber penis.'

'I didn't see the relevance of that particular morsel, inspector.'

'The relevance is that Miss Blane was clearly looking for trouble, which is not the way you told it.'

'Then I'm sorry, inspector. I told it the way I saw it.'

'Mr Jones says that you discarded the rubber penis into the bin.'

'In that instance, Mr Jones was telling the truth.'

'Was it you who tidied the room after you'd sent him to X-ray?'

'It was.'

'Why? I mean, why not get a cleaner to do it?'

'For one thing, our cleaners have been contracted, from outside and have very specific job descriptions, and for another, it was only a matter of picking up a few things from the floor and replacing them on the desk.'

'Did you notice Mr Jones's wallet?'

'Yes, I put it back on the desk along with everything else.'

'Except for his ID card, which you kept.'

'I did no such thing.'

'And the rubber penis, which you recovered from the bin.'

Medlar regarded him with something between amusement and contempt. 'You seem to have an unhealthy fascination with that particular object, inspector.'

Bennett didn't appear to notice. 'You told us just now that you didn't call at Miss Blane's house last night, doctor?'

'That's right.'

'Your fingerprints have been found in the house.'

'I have called there on previous occasions.'

'When was the last occasion?'

'A few days ago, I can't remember the date.'

'Why did you ... what was the purpose of your visit?'

'She had a magazine article about multiple sclerosis she thought might interest me.'

'Couldn't she have brought it into work?'

'I wanted it urgently. Inspector, why d'you keep asking me about Verity? Is something the matter with her?'

'You could say that, doctor,' Bennett said, watching him closely. 'She was found strangled this morning.'

'Good *God*...' So far as Bennett could tell, the reaction could have been genuine. 'Are you trying to tell me she's dead?'

'She is, yes.'

'But how?'

'As I said, she was strangled, we think sometime yesterday evening. She was found with the rubber penis in her mouth.'

'And you think I did it? What possible motive could I have had for that?'

'Her silence, doctor. You've already told us that you would go to some lengths to prevent your wife finding out about Miss N'Kanu.'

'If you regard having a shower and telling a few porkies as "some lengths", then yes. You're being over-imaginative again, inspector.'

'I don't think so, doctor.'

Light seemed to dawn on Medlar. 'You think I killed Adam as well, don't you? My God, what kind of person d'you think I am?'

'Perhaps a desperate one?'

Medlar said, 'I don't think I'm going to say any more without a solicitor.'

22

After Mulholland and Marsh had driven Tom to the centre, he collected his case and left them to it. As he walked back along the corridor, he thought, *If I'm right, this'll be the last time...*

He wasn't sorry about that. Although his haemophobia hadn't bothered him as much as he'd feared, the centre was a sad, sad place. If the atmosphere had been subdued before, it was sepulchral now: the staff walked around like automata and spoke in low, almost conspiratorial voices. Verity's death hadn't been announced yet, nor any reason for Maria's disappearance, but it was as though they all knew. The whole place had the surreality of an edifice about to collapse on itself and Tom wondered whether it could last the six months left to it. He went down to his car and drove thoughtfully back to Sticklepath.

Although he'd been the one who'd set it up, he knew he wouldn't be entirely happy until Medlar actually confessed. Why this should be, he wasn't sure. It all fitted: after bidding Maria fond farewell, he'd have waited for Goring, perhaps in the underground park, perhaps by the lift...

'I think I've found what you wanted, Adam. We'll go through here, shall we? I'd rather the orderly didn't see us...'

Then slam bam and home to his wife. Simple.

Maria had found the body and moved it because she'd known at once who'd killed him. Had she told Medlar what she'd done? Tom somehow doubted it, so he must have been puzzled when it wasn't discovered, even more so when it turned up in the river, but he'd carried it off with aplomb.

But unfortunately for him, Verity had somehow worked it out and put the squeeze on him. It certainly explained why Medlar let her get away with her behaviour, why he'd complained about him to Bennett on her behalf... Had she tried to squeeze him too hard, or had he removed her anyway simply because she knew? Probably something they'd never know.

Holly was there on her own when he got back to Sticklepath, her parents having taken Hal to the marine aquarium in Tamar for the afternoon.

Tom hadn't eaten since breakfast, so he hacked some bread from the loaf and devoured it, telling her between mouthfuls what had happened.

'His poor wife,' Holly said.

'Yes...'

It was still light and Tom, his immediate hunger slaked, said on impulse, 'I need some air, let's take the dog out.'

'All right, so long as we're not too long. I said I'd get dinner ready.'

They donned coats, walked down the lane, clambered over a stile and started up the hill that was Sticklepath's backdrop. The dog ran round them in circles. The sun had just set but a golden glow persisted on the horizon, giving the illusion of a light that would never fade. The higher they climbed, the richer it became. They stopped at the summit beside a gnarled hawthorn that still held clumps of red berries and stared deep into the light. Serried ranks of hilltops ran away from them and dissolved into the flux on the horizon. There was no wind.

Holly said, 'Light like that makes me think of ... oh, I don't know, magicians...'

He glanced at her and she continued, 'It's as though any minute it'll coalesce into something that'll come galloping out at us...'

'A knight in white armour perhaps – 'course, you've already got one of those.'

'Really?' She sniffed. 'I was thinking more of an angel...'

'On horseback?'

'Why not?'

She was right, Tom thought, there was something tangible in there and it just needed a magician to unlock it – rather like life, really...

He looked at her again. Her face reflected the glow so that it seemed to be coming from within her, and for a moment, he was taken back to the time when they'd first met. She'd glowed like candlewax then. He smiled at the memory and put an arm round her. He gently kissed her cheek, and then her mouth. Her lips were powder dry, then soft, then yielding and suddenly, he knew he had to have her; whether for some noble purpose such as affirming life or just because he had to have her, he wasn't sure...

'I know that look,' she said, 'and there isn't time.'

'They won't be back for an hour.'

'They might...'

'Well, it's either there or here,' he said.

She giggled. 'Don't you mean, it's neither here nor there?'

'No, I don't,' he growled.

They woke to the sound of the front door slamming and Hal shouting. 'Mummeee...!'

'Oh my God,' Holly said, jumping out of bed. 'The dinner...'

Dinner was late. The phone rang while they were finishing it and Henry went to answer it.

'It's for you,' he said to Tom as he came back.

'Hello?' Tom said into the receiver.

'Mr Jones? It's Sarah Medlar here – George Medlar's wife.'

'Yes, Mrs Medlar?'

'I'd like to talk to you. Could you come over, d'you think? Please.'

'When?'

'Tonight, if you wouldn't mind, please.'

He did mind. 'I don't think I can really be of any help to you, Mrs Medlar.'

'I want you to tell the police something for me. I think you owe me that at least.'

Tom hesitated. It would serve no purpose and probably be unpleasant, but he'd already hesitated too long. 'All right,' he said. 'Where do you live?'

She told him and he said he'd be with her in an hour.

'It can't hurt just to listen to her,' Holly said.

Tom grunted.

He set off, driving slowly through the lanes. The moon was down, but the night was alive with stars that faded as he approached Tamar. He found the address easily enough, turned into the drive as she'd suggested and parked beside a white Escort that seemed vaguely familiar.

An efficient-looking woman in nurse's uniform opened the door and took him through to the living-room. A fire burned in the grate, a Mozart piano concerto was playing and there was an aroma in the air that he couldn't place. The figure in the wheelchair was obviously Sarah Medlar, but it was the other figure opposite her on the sofa that made him jump slightly.

'You already know Jessie, of course,' Sarah said to him. 'I'm Sarah Medlar.' She lifted her right hand, which he took.

'Hello, Mrs Medlar.'

'Do sit down. Would you like some tea or coffee?'

'No thanks, I've only just had one.'

'It was good of you to come at such short notice.'

Tom didn't reply and Jessie said, 'I'm going in a moment, Mr Jones. I wonder if I could

267

talk to you tomorrow? I'll be back working at the centre – Dr Medlar arranged it.'

Makes sense, I suppose. 'I'm not here during the day, it'll have to be in the evening.'

'Yes, that's all right. You know where my house is, don't you?'

'Yes.'

She stood up. 'I'll be going then, Sarah. You'll let me know if you need anything, won't you?'

'Of course I will. Thank you for coming, my dear.'

Jessie quickly kissed her cheek, said goodbye again and turned to Tom. 'Tomorrow evening then, Mr Jones,' she said and left.

'A dear girl,' Sarah said as the front door closed. 'A real friend.'

The concerto tinkled. Tom said, 'How can I help you, Mrs Medlar?'

Her eyes came back to him, reproachfully he thought, and he said, 'I'm sorry, I didn't mean to sound so abrupt.' He was feeling acutely self-conscious.

'The police are still holding my husband. He told me over the phone that it was you who pointed them in his direction.'

So it was going to be as bad as he'd thought... 'What makes him think that?'

'He's not a complete fool. I asked you here tonight because I'm hoping you will help me unpoint them.'

He said, 'I'll listen to what you have to

say, of course.'

'The police seem to think he killed Adam in order to prevent him telling me about his relationship with Maria N'Kanu.'

'You know about that?' Tom said after a pause.

'I've known for some time – I'm not a complete fool either, Mr Jones, however I may look.'

'I'm aware of that.'

'George is human and male, but he's also honourable. He wouldn't leave me in this state for another woman. I've always known that. Adam's silence is simply not reason enough for George to have killed him.'

'Forgive me, Mrs Medlar, but did *he* know that? Know that you knew he wouldn't leave you, if you see what I mean.'

'Yes.'

'But when I spoke to him yesterday, he made it very plain that he didn't want you to know about Maria.'

'Because he didn't want to hurt me.'

'*Were* you hurt?' he asked. 'When you realised he was having an affair?'

She hesitated. 'I was, a little, but I'm also a pragmatist. Mr Jones,' she said quickly, trying to regain the initiative, 'the point is, whatever else George may be, he's not a killer.'

'Nor are any of us, until the circumstances arise.'

'Are the police assuming that the same person killed both Adam and Verity?'

'They think it's likely.'

She said, 'It *may* be conceivable – barely *just* conceivable that George would kill Adam...' Her grey eyes seemed to grow in size, be almost hypnotic. 'But not poor Verity. Never. I want you to tell the police that.'

'But what if Verity had somehow found out that he'd killed Dr–'

'He had a particular reason for wanting Verity alive,' she interrupted.

Tom waited.

'I have multiple sclerosis, as you can see. It doesn't only look unpleasant, it feels unpleasant as well. There are various palliatives, but I have found only one to be of any help, and that's marijuana.'

The smell...

'Unfortunately, it's an illegal substance and MS sufferers have been prosecuted for using it. A medical trial is due to take place to determine its efficacy, but it'll probably take five years, which is of no use to me. Verity was our supplier, which is why George's fingerprints were found in her home. Will you tell the police that for me, Mr Jones?'

'Yes, if that's what you want.'

She closed her eyes, opened them again. 'This has been quite a strain.' She fumbled in the pocket of the wheelchair, brought out a tin. 'Perhaps you'd light another ... one of these for me?'

He took the tin and opened it. There were perhaps half a dozen reefers inside. He put one between her lips and lit it for her. She gratefully drew and inhaled, taking it out of her mouth with her good hand. The bitter-sweet smell filled his nostrils.

'You realise that if I do as you ask, the police may well confiscate your supply and prosecute you?'

'I'll take that risk.'

'You may find it difficult to get any more.'

'I know that.'

He said, 'I'll try and persuade them to leave you alone, but I'm not sure that I'm your best advocate. Couldn't your doctor put in a word for you?'

'It's possible.'

'Does he know?'

She exhaled smoke. 'Probably, although I've never actually told him. I didn't want him to be an accessory after the fact.'

He said, 'It's a mess, isn't it?'

'Yes,' she said simply.

He'd expected her to blame him for it and when she didn't, he said, 'And I'm sorry about it.'

'In that case, perhaps you'd do something else for me.'

He waited.

'Roll me some ... more of these. You'll find the materials in the top drawer over there.'

He went over, found tobacco, papers and another tin containing the dried leaves.

'What proportion should I use?'

'Half and half.'

Strong. He began rolling. 'How will you light them?'

'I can usually manage so long as they're within reach.'

'What about the police?'

'I'm hoping they won't search my wheelchair.'

Tom wouldn't have bet on that, but didn't say so. 'Does your nurse know?'

'I think so, although neither of us have said anything.'

His fingers began to ache from the unaccustomed exercise and he vaguely wondered why she hadn't asked Jessie.

'If the police do come,' he said, 'it might be better if you could hide the tin somewhere around your body. They might not search you personally.'

'Thank you. I'll do that.'

He'd rolled about two dozen reefers before the marijuana ran out. He packed them into her tin with the others. She thanked him again and he left.

It had begun drizzling and the streets gleamed dully as he drove over to the police station. Bennett was still there.

'Any developments?' Tom asked.

Bennett shook his head. 'Dr Medlar won't change his story, and Miss N'Kanu still refuses to say anything. We're holding them tonight and I'll go on questioning them tomorrow.'

He listened without expression as Tom told him about Medlar's relationship with Verity.

'We found the plants in her house,' he said. 'Dr Medlar didn't say a word to us about it.' He thought for a moment. 'If Blane knew he'd killed Goring and was putting the black on him in some way, that's still a strong enough motive for him to kill her.'

Tom slowly nodded, then said, 'D'you have to do anything about Mrs Medlar? I'm sure the stuff does help her and that her doctor would–'

'You know the answer to that, Mr Jones. If I don't do anything, I'm breaking the law myself.'

'I accept that,' Tom said, 'but does the law demand that you act immediately? In view of your other, surely more important duties.'

'No, Mr Jones,' he said after a moment. 'On reflection, I don't believe the law does demand that I act immediately.'

23

Tom had already set off for Poole the next morning when the phone in his car went. He flipped the switch:

'Hello.'

'Is that Mr Jones?'

'Speaking.'

'It's Dr Goldman here, East Dorset Transfusion Centre.'

Tom asked him to hold on and found a gateway in the narrow lane where he could stop.

'Yes, Dr Goldman?'

'I'm afraid something's come up and I'm going to have to reschedule our appointment.'

'Later today, perhaps?'

'I'm afraid not. I'm going to be tied up all day.'

Tom tried to swallow his irritation. 'Tomorrow, then?'

'I think tomorrow should be all right – let me just cheek my diary a moment... Yes, shall we say twelve?'

Tom agreed and rang off, and then sat awhile thinking about it. Did it have any bearing? Goldman hadn't made any attempt to say *why* he was cancelling, or indeed to apologise, just that he couldn't make it.

Should he press on to Poole and see Dr Derby anyway? No, he couldn't face the double trip. He rang him from where he was and explained what had happened. Derby agreed readily enough to see him the following day, but said that the only really convenient time was at eleven. He had a stutter, Tom noticed.

He drove slowly back to Sticklepath, looking for different angles – did Goldman suspect Diana Small of passing information on to Jessie, had he changed the appointment for a time she'd be absent? If she *was* absent tomorrow, it would be suspicious...

'Hello,' said Holly in surprise when he got back. 'Problems?'

He explained.

'What a pain,' she said. Then, 'Want some coffee? I was just having one.'

'Tom,' she said as they were drinking it, 'you know I was going to go and see Debbie today ... well, Mum and Dad have had to go into town, so I'll take the Mini if you don't need it.' She always referred to the Cooper as the Mini.

'Sure,' Tom said. Then, as an afterthought: 'You'll be taking Hal as well?'

'Well, Debbie's house isn't particularly child-friendly, nor Debbie for that matter, so if you wouldn't mind...'

275

He had been thinking of going for a walk. 'All right,' he said.

A little while after she'd gone, Hal climbed into his lap, grinned up at him and said, 'Wham,' pointing to the door. After the third time, Tom realised he didn't mean the pop group, but the male sheep. He found wellies for them both and they spent a not unpleasant hour wandering round the smallholding.

They went back in when they saw Henry and Kath return and explained where Holly was.

'There's been an accident on the bypass,' Kath said. 'Terrible tail-back, I hope she hasn't been caught up in it.'

The phone rang and Henry answered it.

'How long ago did she leave?' he asked Tom.

'Well over an hour,' Tom said. 'Why?'

'It's Debbie – she says Holly hasn't arrived yet...'

They all looked at each other. 'I expect she's been held up in the tail-back,' Kath said at last.

It happened in no time at all, or with agonising slowness, depending on your point of view. She'd just penetrated the clouds of spray thrown up by the tanker and was pulling in front of it when, with a clatter, a black screen sprang up in front of her. She braked instinctively, realising at the same time that the Cooper's bonnet had released ... then a horn like a ship's hooter blasted at her an instant before the tanker hit the Cooper. Her head struck the back rest as the little car shot forward and spun round. The tanker had swerved to the left to try and avoid her and now jack-knifed, sweeping a Transit aside as a broom would a match box, then went through a 300-degree turn before shuddering to a stop across the carriageway... About a dozen cars slammed into it...

For Holly, the world and her life revolved slowly in front of her until the Transit hit her and they ended locked together against the central barrier.

Several people saw the crash and phoned the emergency services, but a patrol car going the other way saw it happen and pulled into the verge.

'Oh, shit...' said the driver, then, 'I'll radio and get some signs up – you see to it here.'

'Thanks,' said the other drily as he grabbed the first aid kit. He jumped out and, judging his moment, ran across the carriageway.

About twenty cars and vans were piled against the tanker (not petrol, thank God) and perhaps another thirty at various angles around it. A strange silence seemed to hang over everything, broken only by the occasional shout. People wandered about, lost. The tanker driver, apparently unhurt, was staring at the Cooper.

'It was 'er,' he said to the patrolman, whose name was Wilson. 'It was, she jus' slammed on 'er anchors in front of me...'

'All right, sir,' Wilson said, his voice sounding even stranger than the silence. 'I'll see to it. Would you help me by getting these people off the road, please, sir?' He knew he was taking a risk asking for even that much help – Health and Safety rules laid down that anyone assisting at a traffic accident wore prescribed clothing and Wilson could be held responsible if anything happened to the driver.

Holly and the van driver were both unconscious but didn't seem to be hurt badly, so he ran back to the pile-up. He smelt petrol and it suddenly occurred to him that the man with the lighted cigarette might be a fire risk...

He sprinted over, snatched it from him and pinched it out between his fingers. 'Would you get off the road, sir, and *don't* smoke, please.'

He ran over to another man who was trying to pull a car door open. 'Would you please get off the road, sir.'

'It's my daughter, she's in there...'

Wilson wrenched open the door and was nearly sick – a girl of about fourteen looked at him dully, then down at her wrist. Her hand was attached to it by a piece of gristle and blood was pumping from the mess.

Wilson swallowed. 'All right, miss,' he said crouching down beside her. He opened the kit ...

Tourniquet, where's the fucking tourniquet? He wished fervently that he'd paid more attention to the first aid lectures... He couldn't find it, so in desperation, he pulled out his bootlace, gently rolled up her sleeve and tied it round–

It was at this point she started screaming, again and again and–

'What the hell are you doing?' yelled the father.

'Trying to stop the bleeding, sir,' Wilson replied stoically. 'It's all right, miss, there's an ambulance on its way and we'll soon have you in hospital...' Never had words sounded so inadequate. He found a bandage and wrapped it crudely round her wrist ... to get her off the road or not? Probably not – if there was going to be a fire, it would have happened by now, wouldn't it? And moving her might make things worse...

'Could you stay with her, sir? The ambulance'll be here soon.' *I fuckin' 'ope...*

As soon as he stood up, someone shouted, 'Over here, officer.'

He climbed his way over. *Oh Christ...*

This time it was a driver and his foot had

been completely severed. He pulled out his other bootlace...

A few minutes later, the other patrolman found him. 'They're on their way,' he said, 'the lot.'

'Chopper?'

'Yeah. Is it bad?'

'Fuckin' terrible. Gimme a hand with this bloke...'

Bennett and Mulholland had resumed questioning Medlar when news of the crash came through. The desk sergeant beckoned them out and told them what had happened. 'I've got the lab manager of the Transfusion Centre on the phone, sir. She says they urgently need Dr Medlar back there.'

Bennett took the phone and spoke to Jessie. 'Don't you have any other doctors there?'

'None that can do Dr Medlar's job, no – the deputy left a month ago. We must have him for the medical decisions, *now...*'

It was a situation Bennett had never come across before, releasing a suspected murderer for humanitarian purposes. Still, he hadn't been actually charged yet, had he?

'I'll have to take advice on that,' he told Jessie.

'Well, please hurry ... and inspector, we could do with Miss N'Kanu as well.'

He phoned the superintendent. 'I don't think we've got much choice, sir. We'd be crucified if anyone died because we wouldn't release him.'

'All right, Vic, but he's still in custody, so he stays handcuffed to you every second. Yes, the woman too, so long as she doesn't have any contact with Medlar.'

Bennett explained the situation to Medlar and they were on their way inside two minutes. Maria went in a separate car with WPC Collins.

'How bad it is?' Medlar asked Bennett.

'Pretty bad, at least twenty casualties.'

He phoned the Donor Organiser.

'I'm calling in all the emergency panel,' she told him. 'We ought to get around fifty. Will that be enough?'

'I don't think so – better get local radio and telly to put out a general call for donors and then make sure the bleed ward's ready for them – oh, and get John to arrange a shuttle for getting blood back from the sessions.'

The first person he saw when he arrived was Jessie.

'What are the stocks like?' he asked.

'Not bad,' she said, trying to tear her eyes away from the handcuffs. 'The Flying Squad blood's already gone.'

'How many units?'

She made a face. 'Four.'

'Nothing like enough,' Medlar agreed. 'But they might save someone's life.'

In fact, they saved two lives: the girl with the almost severed hand, and the man with the completely severed foot. Both had lost a lot more than two pints, but the Flying Squad blood was enough to keep them alive until the helicopter got them to hospital.

Jessie was with Maria (and WPC Collins) in her lab when Adrian bustled in. 'I've just had a call from the chopper – they want twenty units of O neg as soon as they land.'

Maria looked at Jessie. 'We can't, can we?'

Jessie turned to Adrian. 'How many in stock at the moment?'

'About thirty, we've had a run on them.'

'Are they still on the phone?'

'Yes,' Adrian nodded.

She rang Medlar, who was in his office handcuffed to Bennett, and explained, then Adrian put him through to the helicopter.

'Dr Medlar here.'

'This is Dr Scott.' Medlar could hear the rotors in the background. 'I've got two patients bleeding to death here. They need blood the moment we get in, which is why I must have the O neg.'

'Have they had any blood?'

'Two units each, but they've lost a hell of a lot.'

'I'm sorry, but we can't give you O neg. It'll clear us out and we have other patients who–'

'And these two may die if they don't get it,' Scott shouted.

'D'you have haemocell?' Medlar asked.

'Of course we do, but they need *blood*, man.'

'Give them haemocell now, take samples and get them to us the moment you land and we'll give you group specific blood within five minutes.'

'That's not good en–'

'I'm sorry, but I can't let you have our O negs.'

'Then if they die, it'll be on your hands,' Scott snapped, and broke the connection.

If he could see me now, Medlar thought. He put the phone down and it immediately rang again...

Tom tried the Cooper's phone and got the unobtainable signal. He then tried the police station and was told that those unharmed would have had the opportunity to phone their worried relatives by now and that the casualties were all being taken to hospital. They didn't know whether or not anyone had been killed...

He relayed the news to Henry and Kath. 'I'm getting over to the hospital now,' he said.

His parents-in-law looked at each other.

'I'll stay with Hal,' Henry said, 'if you promise you'll ring me as soon as you know anything...'

Like a purposeful insect, the helicopter homed on to the hospital and landed, and the waiting paramedics hustled the stretchers to Accident and Emergency. A lone figure ran to the centre clutching the blood samples.

Maria inspected the tubes to make sure the blood was clotted before centrifuging them quickly and dropping cells and serum from them into the racked test tubes she'd set up. Then, after a fifteen-second spin, she took them back into the racks before inspecting them...

'O pos for Simon Collins... B pos for Emma Graythorpe. Could you check them for me, please, Ashley?'

Ashley, who'd been drafted into her lab, did so, then Maria rang Adrian and asked him to get the blood. He was with them in less than half a minute.

'That was quick,' said Maria.

'I got ten of every group ready and issued them as soon as I heard the chopper,' he said.

Ashley attached the red labels and as soon as he'd finished, they loaded them into a cool box and the waiting paramedic took them to A & E.

The helicopter returned with two more victims, one of them a woman with a ruptured spleen whose group really was O negative. The centre's entire stock was used on her before the night was over. Jessie and Medlar exchanged wry smiles when they heard.

For the first time in a long time, and also for the last time, Tamar Transfusion Centre worked as a team, a unit.

Maria and Ashley cross matched into the evening, taking the centre's stock of blood to its lowest level ever.

Paul grouped the emergency bleed and the day's sessions as they came in, while Dominic tested them for hepatitis and AIDS; by midnight, they had brought the stock back up to something workable.

Holly's eyes opened and she frowned in concentration as they focused on him. ''Lo, Tom.'

He silently sighed with relief. The doctor had told him she was only concussed, but... But.

'Hello, Holly. How're you feeling?'

Her face twitched. 'I've got a terrible headache.'

'I'll ask them if they can give you something for it.'

'Where am I?'

'Hospital.'

'Where's Hal?'

'With your father. Would you like to see him?'

'Yes, I would.' Her brow furrowed. 'I was in a crash, wasn't I?'

'Yes. You're going to be all right, though.'

'Is the Mini badly damaged?'

He smiled. 'I've no idea – it hasn't exactly been the top of my priorities.'

She swallowed. 'Was anybody hurt?'

'Some, but no one was killed.' *So far as I know...*

'It was my fault, Tom...' Her face crumpled and she began to cry.

He squeezed her hand. 'No, it wasn't.'

'It *was*, the bonnet came up and I lost control.'

'How d'you mean, the bonnet came up?'

'It just did, in front of my face. I'd just overtaken the lorry and it came up.'

The sister came over. 'Are you all right, Mrs Jones?'

'She's just come round,' Tom said unnecessarily.

'I can see that. How are you feeling?' she asked Holly.

'Terrible headache.'

'I'll get you something for it.' To Tom she said, 'Please try not to excite or upset her.'

'It wasn't your fault,' Tom repeated after the sister had gone. 'Tell me what happened...'

They gave her a sedative and some painkillers. When she'd calmed down, Tom left her with Kath and phoned Henry to give him the news. He drove back to Sticklepath to bring them in, then hired a Vauxhall Vectra and went to look at the Cooper for himself.

'Well, there she is.'

'Is it a write-off?'

The police vehicle examiner tilted his hand from side to side. 'Depends how much you love her, I suppose.'

At that moment, the Cooper was looking more pathetic than lovable and Tom realised how lucky Holly had been.

'I'll just collect a couple of things, then,' he said.

'It's your car.'

He wrenched the door open, found his gun under the dash and slipped it into his pocket – Holly didn't have a licence, so he could have been in trouble if the police had found it first. Then he went to the front and prised up the bonnet.

It had been twisted out of shape by its impact with the central barrier, which might have explained the broken safety catch. It didn't, however, explain why the main catch had been screwed down so that it couldn't engage with the bonnet, or the three lumps of Blu-Tack stuck at intervals along the sill.

He called the vehicle examiner over.

He looked at them, said, 'This being a Mini, the bonnet would have come unstuck at about sixty, I should think.'

'She'd just overtaken a lorry.'

'That would be about right, then. Have you made any enemies lately, sir?'

'Looks that way, doesn't it?'

He drove to the police station and told Bennett.

'Was it meant to kill you, d'you think?' Bennett asked. 'Plenty of people have survived loose bonnets before.'

'My wife nearly didn't.'

'No.'

Tom said, 'I had been wondering whether it was meant to delay...' He told him about his planned trip to Poole.

'How many people knew about that?'

'Quite a few, I didn't make a secret of it.'

They tossed around a few ideas before Tom went back to the hospital.

Holly was looking much better, but they were going to keep her in overnight for observation. Tom took Henry to one side and told him he was going to Poole in the morning.

'I'd have thought you'd have wanted to stay with your wife,' Henry said.

Tom told him about the Cooper. 'I want to catch the – the *person* who did it. They didn't want me to go to Poole for some reason, so the best way of catching them is to find out why not.'

Henry thought about it, then nodded. 'I take your point,' he said. 'But when you do find out, you'll leave the rough stuff to the police, won't you? One casualty in the family's enough for now.'

24

Tom left for Poole at eight the next morning. The hospital had told him that Holly had had a good night and would probably be discharged later in the day.

He had plenty of time for thinking during the three-hour journey. He thought he knew who'd booby-trapped the Cooper but didn't yet understand why they didn't want him to go to Poole.

He arrived at just before eleven and found the General Hospital, which was on the same site as the Transfusion Centre. He'd subconsciously expected Dr Mike Derby to be as brash and confident as his father-in-law had been, so he was surprised to be faced with a slight, bespectacled figure with a diffident manner.

'So you m-made it, Mr Jones.' He held out his hand. 'C-come along to my office...

Now, how c-can I help you?' The stutter hadn't been quite so apparent on the phone.

Tom commiserated with him for his loss of his father-in-law before coming to the point.

'Were you aware of the rumour that Dr Goring was keeping East Dorset open so that you could become its new research director?'

Derby gave an ironic chuckle. 'I c-could hardly *not* be aware of it. I was watching the TV interview myself, with one of my c-colleagues ... it was ac-cutely emb-barrass-ing.'

Tom didn't say anything and after a pause, Derby continued: 'I won't deny that I'd have l-liked the job, but I'm sure the decision to keep East Dorset open was nothing to do with my amb-bitions.'

'Why are you so sure?'

'B-because I only heard about the post three months ago. The decision to keep the centre open was taken six months ago.'

Which was fair enough, Tom thought – assuming Derby was telling the truth about his ignorance. 'You said just now that you would have liked the job – aren't you still applying for it?'

'N-no.' He sighed. 'I've withdrawn. Had to really, after the TV interview. N-no one would've believed I'd got it on my own m-merits.'

'Is that really still the case, now that your

father-in-law's dead?'

'It w-wouldn't be in g-good taste now, anyway.'

He had a point there, Tom thought. They talked for a little about the progress of the police enquiry, then shook hands again before he left.

Dr Goldman was a different matter altogether. He began by telling Tom how lucky he was to be seen at all that week, then, although he obviously knew why Tom was there, visibly fluffed out his feathers when he told him.

'It's a tissue of lies,' he said as though Tom had been personally responsible for it, 'an insult to the memory of a decent man.' He himself was a small man, white of hair and face, with lines around a rather pinched mouth.

'Are you saying that Dr Goring never discussed the closure with you?'

'The only time was when he told me that East Dorset was to remain open. Not otherwise.'

'Did he ever discuss the research director post with you?'

'No. I informed the directorate that I wanted to create the post, but I never at any time discussed the matter directly with Adam.'

'Is it possible that, knowing about the post, he kept the centre open on the assumption that Dr Derby would get the job?'

'That would have been quite an assumption – there's been a great deal of interest expressed in the post from some very strong candidates.'

Tom kept silent, and after a moment Goldman continued: 'Besides, the decision to keep the centre open was made long before the post was actually announced – that wasn't until October. I can show you the paperwork with the dates if you like.'

'No, that won't be necessary. But you have become aware of Dr Derby's interest in the post since the centre's future was secured?'

'I was aware of his interest, yes, but I do take exception to the word "secured".'

'I'm sorry?' Tom feigned surprised. 'What's wrong with it?'

'It smacks of collusion, of deals – as I'm sure you're well aware.'

Your words, doctor... Tom thought. 'Did you know that Dr Derby has withdrawn his application?'

'Yes, I do. Just as well, really – he wouldn't have got the job.'

'Why d'you say that?'

'I thought you said just now that you'd met him. I can assure you there are many other candidates more prepossessing.' After a pause, he continued: 'Forgive *me*, Mr Jones, but why are you hounding Dr

Goring's memory in this way?' His voice had gained in confidence now.

'I'm not hounding him or his memory, but this rumour does have to be investigated.'

Goldman said, 'Well, I hope I've convinced you that it's absolutely baseless.'

Like hell, Tom thought, but realised that to push him any further would be almost certainly counter-productive. 'You've been very helpful, Dr Goldman,' he said truthfully.

Goldman grunted his satisfaction. 'My pleasure.' He stirred. 'And now, if there's nothing further...'

Tom had already thought out his next move. 'Nothing I need bother you with, although I would like a word with one of your staff before I go.'

'Oh?' Suspicion flooded back. 'Who, may I ask?'

'Only the lab manager.'

'Why?'

'To pass on regards from his opposite number.'

'Oh, I see. Very well, I'll take you along to him.'

As they walked in silence along the corridor, Tom reflected that if there was any truth in Jessie's story, *if*, then Goldman must suspect that someone in East Dorset had been talking to her. They reached an office and Goldman tapped on the open door.

'Tony, this is Mr Jones from the Department of Health. He wanted a word with you. Mr Jones, Tony Chase.'

Chase stood up and shook hands with Tom. 'Hello.' Goldman watched them.

Tom said, 'It's only that I've been working in Tamar this week and Jessie Pengellis asked me to pass on her regards to you.'

'Did she? Oh right.' Confusion crossed his face as Goldman watched. 'Nice of her. Do reciprocate them.'

'I'll do that.'

'Er – didn't I hear that she'd been suspended?'

'Yes, pending an enquiry into the TV interview she gave.' He decided not to mention yesterday's emergency.

'That was an unfortunate business... I wish...' Whatever it was he wished, he suddenly thought better of it and said, 'Who's been acting up for her?'

'Dominic Tudor.'

'Well, he's an ambitious lad, so it'll be good experience for him. Not that I imagine it's a particularly onerous job at this stage.' Still Goldman watched and listened.

Tom said, 'Actually, he's got quite a lot on his plate at the moment, what with his own department and his CJD research.' He was marking time now, filling the air with talk to confuse Goldman and make sure he had no reason to suspect Diana Small.

294

'What CJD research is that?' Chase asked.

'He's screening donor blood for antibodies to some bacterium or other...' Tom searched for the word...

'*Acinetobacter?*' said Chase.

'That's the one.'

'So he's doing it too, is he?' Chase grinned. 'Must be catching.'

'You're doing the same thing here?'

'Yes,' said Chase. He looked at Goldman. 'It was Dr Goring's idea, wasn't it?'

'Professor Blom's originally,' said Goldman. 'Adam's idea was that we could back him up by looking for antibodies in donor blood.'

Chase's phone went. 'Excuse me,' he said.

'Time I was going anyway,' Tom said, glad of an excuse to break off.

'Give Dominic my regards as well while you're about it,' Chase said as he reached for his phone.

As Goldman saw him off the premises, Tom hoped that he hadn't just blighted Chase's relationship with his boss, especially since he hadn't learnt anything from him. Interesting though, the way Goldman had stuck to them, watching and listening to every word...

He made his way back to the General Hospital and found a phone booth, from where he rang the centre and asked to be put through to Diana Small.

'Hello?'

'Miss Small, my name's Jones. I'm from the Department of Health and I need to talk to you.'

'What about, Mr Jones? It's Mrs, by the way, Mrs Small.'

How much should he tell her over the phone? He had to get her away from the centre... 'I've been talking to Jessie Pengellis at the Tamar centre and–'

'I've nothing to say about that,' she said quickly, 'I don't wish to discuss it.'

Tom said, 'Don't hang up... I've rung you like this so that no one *would* know about it, and no one will if you just give me a few minutes.'

'I don't wish to discuss it,' she repeated, her voice sibilated as though she was whispering. 'Please leave me alone.'

'You may *have* to discuss it one way or another. My way prevents it becoming official.'

Silence.

'Talk to me now and no one need ever know of your involvement.'

'Where are you?' she said at last.

'At the main hospital entrance.'

Another silence, then: 'I'll be with you in five minutes. How will I know you?'

'I'll be by the phone booth–' he spotted a flower vendor – 'with a bunch of flowers.'

'All right.'

He bought the flowers. After a few minutes, the realisation came over him that he needed the loo rather urgently, but that would have to wait...

After nearly fifteen minutes, he was debating whether to ring her again when a short, rather dumpy figure with permed brown hair came in. She spotted him immediately and came over.

'Mr Jones?'

He handed her his card.

She said, 'I'm sorry I'm late but I didn't want to leave my lab too obviously after your call.'

'That's all right,' Tom said, wondering what kind of place East Dorset centre was. 'Shall we sit down?'

She looked round nervously before speaking. 'You can tell Jessie I'll never forgive her for the way she let me down. I'll never trust her again.'

Tom nodded, thought it better to let her get it off her chest.

'I've got two children, my husband is out of work and if I lose my job, we lose our home – d'you understand that?'

'Yes, I do, which is why I approached you the way I did.' He thought it best not to tell her he'd already seen Goldman.

'What do you want to know?'

Her lips pursed as he quickly explained.

'D'you swear to me that it won't ever

come out that I told you?'

'Yes,' said Tom, hoping it was true.

'It was a coincidence,' she began at last, 'the purest coincidence...'

She'd been working late and had remembered some photocopies she'd left in the secretary's office. No one was there, the director's door was shut and there was a low murmur of voices from behind it. As she'd picked up the photocopies, she'd knocked a bottle of Tippex on to the floor and it had rolled under the desk. She'd had to crawl underneath to retrieve it and Goring's voice had hit her as though from a radio:

'...asking for, Charles, is that you give Mike the chance.'

'And you'll fund the creation of the post and ensure that East Dorset doesn't close?'

'Yes.'

There was a grille beside her head and some trick of the acoustics was funnelling the voices through.

Goldman said, 'I have to say that Mike wouldn't be my first choice. He doesn't exactly inspire confidence.'

She knew she should go but was welded to the spot by what she was hearing.

'And I'm telling you, Charles, that he's made for the job. Haven't you read his research in *BMJ* on the structure and function of complement?'

'No, I don't think I have.'

'Well, do read it, and you'll see what I mean. He's no extrovert, I'll agree, but he's brilliant, capable of the very best research. He won't disappoint you.'

There was a brief pause, then Goldman said, 'Adam, forgive me for being so cynical, but it does occur to me that it's a foregone conclusion anyway that East Dorset stays open rather than Tamar.'

Goring said softly, 'Well, of course, there's nothing to stop you gambling on that, Charles. Calling my bluff.'

'Oh, I hope that won't be necessary,' Goldman said quickly, then, 'It's just that it's often occurred to me that we in the Transfusion Centre get so little recognition for what we do...'

Goring gave a chuckle. 'I think I see what you're getting at. Would Charles Goldman MBE go some way to redressing your concerns? It would seem to have a certain ring to it.'

'Mm. It would seem that we both have something to think about.'

'Indeed we have.' A chair scraped. 'Read his research, Charles, and I'll come and see you again tomorrow.'

It was too late for her to move now, the door opened and Goring's immaculately polished shoes appeared beside her. 'Please don't trouble, Charles, I'll see myself out.'

She froze, terrified he would notice the

white of her lab coat under the desk.

'Until tomorrow then, Adam.'

Goring's footsteps faded down the corridor and Goldman withdrew into his room, shutting the door behind him.

She'd waited for several moments while she drew in some deep breaths, then eased herself out and made for the door. Without warning, Goldman's door had opened again.

'Diana – what are you doing here?'

'I just came to collect these, doctor.' She held up the photocopies.

'All right,' he'd said. 'I just wondered.'

She'd gone back to her lab and sat down for a few minutes trying to look normal before taking off her lab coat and going home. The Tippex had still been in her pocket...

'And this was six months ago?' Tom asked her now.

'Yes, last July.'

'I realise you didn't hear all they said, but was it your impression that the research director post was Dr Goring's idea?'

'No. I think it was something Dr Goldman had applied to do anyway.'

'From what you told me earlier,' Tom said after a pause, 'it's very much to your advantage that your centre stays open.' His bladder was screaming at him, but he had to assure himself she was telling the truth.

'So it may be,' she said primly, 'but that doesn't alter the fact that corruption is wrong.'

Prim she may have been, but Tom believed her. She was, he reflected, the honest salt on which the NHS depends, and the asset it's most prone to abuse.

'Whatever persuaded you to tell Jessie, knowing the situation Tamar was in?'

She shrugged helplessly. 'Wine, Mr Jones, wine persuaded me...' They'd been to a symposium and she'd had some wine with her lunch. 'Always a mistake with a head like mine.' She sighed. 'And I felt so sorry for her, knowing the pickle she was in. Never again,' she added darkly.

'You know she's been suspended, pending enquiry?'

Diana sighed. 'Yes ... I wouldn't have wished that on her.'

Tom quickly went through it again with her, then asked if anything she'd heard had suggested that Dr Derby had known about it. No, it hadn't, she said. He thanked her and let her go, and she disappeared as discreetly as she'd arrived.

He almost ran to the loo, then had a sandwich for lunch in the League of Friends bar before starting back to Tamar.

So what did it all mean?

The most likely scenario was that Goring, knowing that Goldman wanted to set up a research post, had used his knowledge and position to try and influence him ... although Goldman had probably been correct in thinking the decision to close Tamar had already been taken. So where did corruption begin? he wondered. And had Derby known about it?

Something we'll never know for sure, he thought, although he tended to think not. The whole thing was academic anyway. Even if poor Diana was forced to make a statement, it would be her word against Goldman's.

Did anything he'd learned indicate who'd trepanned his car? To whose advantage was it if he hadn't made it to Poole?

Goldman? *Can't see how.* Medlar? Jessie?

Jessie – it always came back to Jessie, even though he still couldn't understand why she didn't want him to get to Poole. To help Medlar in some way?

What was it Bennett had said? If Verity was the one who'd left the note about Dominic on his desk, then she could have taken his ID card and the phallus home with her then ... to be found later by her killer...

Jessie ... who'd found Verity's body ... who could have sabotaged his car while Sarah Medlar kept him busy ... but why?

Had Diana said anything which might have incriminated her?

He systematically cast his mind back over

everything he'd heard that day...

It was dark by the time he reached the outskirts of Tamar. He'd intended finding Jessie, to have it out with her, but now he headed for the city centre and the public library. It was still open. After half an hour there, he drove to the Transfusion Centre.

25

He roused Arthur and told him he'd come to check on something. Then, leaving him to his TV, he went into the manager's office to look for the key to Microbiology – alone of the labs, Micro was kept locked because of the hepatitis and HIV material stored there. It was, as he'd half expected, hanging in the open key box on the wall. He'd often wondered why people bothered with key boxes when they were nearly always left open.

He walked softly down the corridor stippled with shadows, round to the Micro Lab and unlocked it, unaware that Arthur had forsaken his telly for a moment to watch him.

Darkness, and a loud whispering noise... He found the light switch and blinked in the sudden brightness. A large room with benches all around its perimeter and more forming an island in the middle; the whispering came from the air-conditioning vent in the ceiling and he remembered that Microbiology was always kept under negative pressure because of the hazardous material.

He looked round. Where were the record books most likely to be kept?

A small office with glass walls separated this room from the next. He went in, glanced over the ledgers and folders on the shelves, then sat down to go through them.

Nothing.

He went back into the main lab again. Heavy dispensing equipment lined the central benches. There was no sign of any record books that he could see. A large rack of glass tubes filled with blood had been left on the bench – someone had been careless... He shied away from them, pulled open a drawer and took out a book. It was marked 'TPHA' – that was something to do with syphilis, wasn't it?

He tried all the other drawers in the island, then walked slowly round the perimeter of the room. There were centrifuges, mixers, fridges, and in one corner a shower cubicle. He started going through all the drawers until, in another corner, he found a book marked '*Acinetobactor* antibodies'.

He took it out and opened it – lists of donation numbers with results beside them.

He turned to the beginning and found a date... May, more than six months ago!

He *had* to make sure. He took the book with him into the office, found an outside line and phoned the East Dorset centre. An orderly there gave him Goldman's number. He dialled.

'Can I speak to Dr Goldman, please?'

'Speaking.'

'It's Tom Jones from the Department of Health here. I called on you at the centre earlier today.'

'I remember. I hope you've got a good reason for ringing me at home.'

'I have, doctor. D'you remember telling me today that Dr Goring had suggested to you that you do some research looking for *Acinetobacter* antibodies?'

'I do, yes.'

'Can you remember exactly when Dr Goring made the suggestion?'

'Couldn't this have waited?' His voice crackled with irritation.

'It's difficult to explain over the phone, doctor, but it really is important. Please.'

'I think it was last November.'

'November ... are you sure of that?'

'Yes, Mr Jones, I am sure. Was there anything else?'

'One more thing – did Dr Goring mention that the same work was already being done in Tamar?'

'Yes. His idea was to amalgamate the work in the new research department. Anything else? No? Then goodbye.'

There was a heavy clunk in his ear. He slowly put his own phone down, reflecting that Goldman had just unwittingly given himself away, by admitting that he had discussed the research department with Goring when he'd said earlier that he hadn't–

A feeling made him turn quickly to see Dominic at the other end of the room, staring at him ... the whisper of the air-conditioning had covered his entry.

How long had he been there, how much had he heard?

'Can I help you at all, Mr Jones?'

Tom stood up, moved to the door of the office. 'Not really, thanks. I just needed to check something.'

'If you'd asked me, I might have been able to help you,' Dominic said, walking towards him. 'Apart from the small matter of good manners.'

Tom forced a smile. 'I'm sorry, but you weren't around to ask.'

'I'm only a phone call away – that sounds a bit like a BT advert, doesn't it?' He stepped past Tom into the office and picked up the book. '*Acinetobacter* – and it was Dr Goldman you were talking to just now, wasn't it?'

'Yes.' Tom took a pace backwards and slipped his hand into his pocket. 'Thanks to your results, I've just caught him out in a direct lie. He was planning to rig that research job—'

'Oh, stop trying to bullshit me, Jones. You *know*, don't you?'

An electric tremor ran from Tom's temples down the back of his neck as he thought: *That's what you must have said to Verity...*

'Oh, don't worry, I'm not going to *do* anything,' Dominic said wearily as he put the book back on the desk. 'That is a gun in your pocket, I presume?'

Well, I'm as sure as hell not pleased to see you, Tom thought, but didn't say anything.

Dominic continued: 'It's a fair cop, guv, *force majeure* and all that, but I would quite like to know how you found out. Morbid curiosity. Wouldn't you like to tell me how clever you've been, where I went wrong?'

'Not particularly, no. I think it's probably best if we—'

'Indulge me – please?' He stepped back out of the office.

Tom thought for a moment, then shrugged. He had the gun, didn't he?

'All right. It *was* you who left me the note about your selling Jessie out to Goring, wasn't it?'

A single nod.

'That was a mistake.'

'Why?'

'Well, at first it had the intended effect, made it seem as though you had no motive for killing Goring, that he was of more use to you alive because he was going to find you another job where you could continue your research. But as soon as I found out that he'd apparently sold out on *you*, then you did have a motive, and a strong one.'

'How *did* you find out?'

'The manager at Poole told me yesterday, purely by chance. Which is, I presume, why you tried to stop me getting there?'

Another nod.

'But that wasn't all your note did. By telling me you were Goring's snout, it also told me who was in the best position to persuade him to come into the centre that night and into the freezer – yourself.' He paused. 'How did you persuade him?'

Dominic pursed his lips, then shrugged his shoulders himself. 'I told him I'd found some evidence he could use against Jessie, but that he should come and see it for himself.'

'So it was premeditated.'

'No, I had actually found something, some high risk CJD material in the freezer that shouldn't have been there. But I'd also heard from a company rep who'd taken me out to lunch that East Dorset were doing the same work as me and I wanted to have it out with him.' He gave a half-chuckle.

'You know, I couldn't believe that he'd actually do that to me...' For the first time, his face fleetingly showed some emotion. 'I challenged him with it after I'd shown him the CJD stuff. He didn't deny it, he gave me some horseshit about finding me a job at East Dorset, that the more studies there were the better, but I knew from his expression he was shafting me, that he'd make sure that *he* got the credit for *my* research...'

His eyes became faraway for a moment and he said slowly, *'And there was absolutely nothing I could do about it.* I didn't think. I just pushed him over and slammed the door. I knew he couldn't open it from inside, so I switched the light off and pulled the fuse out of the alarm. No one heard us. No one knew we were there.'

After a short silence, Tom said, 'And then you dashed over to the library, pulled some books from the Returned shelf and had them stamped before going to meet Ashley?'

'How did you know that?'

'I went to the library and had them check their computer. Those books had all been returned five minutes before you took them out.' He paused, then said, 'As a matter of fact, I'm as certain as I can be that he *was* going to find you a job – at East Dorset.'

'Working for his precious son-in-law, I suppose,' Dominic spat. 'It was *my* idea, *my* research, *I* should have been...' He tailed off as though aware of how he sounded.

My God, Tom thought. 'I believe you when you say you did it spontaneously, but you could have gone back at that stage and let him out. He couldn't have proved anything, it'd have been your word against his.'

'Oh, come on! Who d'you think would have been believed?' He sighed. 'You don't understand what he was like. Anyone who crossed him, *anyone,* got squashed sooner or later. He'd have destroyed me – that's why I didn't let him out.'

There was plenty more Tom could have said about that, but there was no point at this stage. He said, 'You must have been surprised when the body wasn't discovered.'

Dominic smiled, moved over to the bench. 'I was at first, but I resisted the mistake of going to the freezer and making the "discovery" myself.' Even now, Tom thought he could hear a self-congratulatory note in his voice. 'I worked out that Maria was the most likely person to have moved him, then realised she must have thought Medlar had done it.'

'You knew about them, then?'

'Of course I did, we all did. It was obvious whenever they were together.'

'Were you going to let him take the rap for it?'

Dominic said, 'Oh, he'd have got off in the

end, I expect. As far as I was concerned, the more confused things were, the better.'

'Which is why you planted my ID on Verity, I suppose?'

'Yes, but looking back, I think that might have been a mistake as well.'

'It was, it narrowed the probability down to Medlar, Ashley or you.' He didn't tell him that he'd wondered earlier whether it was Jessie. 'Why did you kill her? Had she found out?'

Something that might have been remorse touched his face. 'I realised she knew something because she kept dropping little hints, but I didn't know whether it was the fact that I'd been Goring's snout, as you so picaresquely describe it, or that I'd actually killed him. When the police came for her on Monday, I thought she was going to tell them, that they'd be coming for me at any moment...'

He seemed to shudder at the thought, then moistened his lips and continued: 'I *had* to find out what her game was, what she knew. I found your ID card on the floor when I left the note for you and took the rubber willie as an afterthought.' He smiled without humour. 'Then I called at her house on the way home.' The faraway look came over him again. 'She didn't want to let me in, but I crowded her, said I had something important to tell her. I could see she was uneasy, so I said, "You know, don't you?" to see what she *did* know. If it was only that I'd sold out Jessie, she'd have come out with it, sneered at me, but she didn't do that ... she just stared at me and said, "You killed him..." After that, I had to kill her as well.'

'So in fact she *hadn't* known, you killed her for nothing.'

'She'd have worked it out. She was jealous of me, she hated me...'

He blinked as though coming out of a trance, peered at Tom. 'You don't seem very shocked.'

'I'd already worked most of it out myself.'

'I mean, shocked by me, by the fact that I was able to do it so easily, by my very awfulness.'

'It's easier the second time, so I'm told.' What had really shocked Tom was that Dominic had been able to sit in a pub, chatting with Ashley while knowing that Goring was battering at the freezer door...

It was time to go. 'I see you as pathetic as much as anything. Did you really think Goring was going to put you in charge–'

He didn't get any further because Dominic had snatched up the rack of tubes from the bench and thrown them at him, keeping hold of the rack so that the tubes struck him in a shower. The blood spurted out as they hit him, covering him in globs of it...

He screamed, forgetting all about his gun as he jerked his hand from his pocket, to try and brush the blood away from his face and hair... Then Dominic was on him. He tried to throw a punch at him, but it was too little, too late. Dominic's fist sank into his belly, he doubled over, then a knee crunched into his face and he collapsed on to the floor.

Dominic hauled him over, took the gun and key from his pocket and stood, looking down at him.

Tom's eyes opened...

'Pathetic, am I?' Dominic sneered. He pointed the gun at Tom's head, his finger tightening on the trigger, then he changed his mind and kicked him in the face instead.

Tom groaned and lay still.

Dominic ran quickly over to the fridge, took out more racks and upended them over Tom's head. Tom gave another scream, held his hands over his face as glass shattered and tinkled and the blood splattered around him.

Dominic said, 'That's blood from over two hundred people, untested blood. Think about it – you might be in the AIDS club already.'

He kicked him again, then went quickly into the office and yanked out the phone lead. Then he went out, pulling the door shut and locking it behind him.

He checked himself over, then walked up the corridor to Blood Issue.

'Thanks, Arthur,' he said, going over to the orderly. 'I've sent him on his way with a flea in his ear.'

'Any time, Dom,' the orderly said.

''Night, Arthur,' Dominic said, and left the centre for the last time.

Tom lay shaking, whimpering, unable to move... *Is this really me?* a voice deep inside his head asked. He could taste the blood in his mouth but didn't know whether it was his own or from one of the tubes. *Does it matter?* the voice asked. *Yes, yes!*

He said aloud, 'I will not get AIDS, I will not get AIDS...'

But why shouldn't he get AIDS? Frank had, and Tom had watched him die.

'But Frank was a haemophiliac,' he said aloud.

But he'd just had blood from over two hundred people poured over him, hadn't he? And some of it would have worked into his system by now.

Immunoglobulin – they do it for hepatitis, don't they, maybe they do one for AIDS...?

He pushed himself up, yelped as a broken tube cut into his palm, then staggered over to the door and pulled at it for a few moments before he realised it was locked.

He battered at it, yelled 'Help!' over and

314

over before remembering how far he was from the issue office and that Arthur was deaf.

He ran over to Dominic's office and snatched up the phone, then saw the ripped-out cable at the same time he heard the silence in the earpiece.

Then he remembered something Holly had told him... *The sooner you can wash off contaminated blood, the less chance there is it will infect you.* He half ran, half scuttled over to the shower, tore off his clothes and stood under it, not caring that the water was cold, stayed there until the water stopped running red before turning it off. He stepped out of the cubicle, shivering violently in the air-stream ... couldn't see a towel, couldn't put his clothes back on, couldn't get out, couldn't even walk over the glassstrewn floor ... he'd die of cold before anything else...

Then the door opened and Jessie came in.

26

She had pulled up next to Dominic's car wondering what he was doing there. She didn't recognise the Vectra next to it.

As she got out of her own car, Dominic

himself emerged from the centre, then stopped dead when he saw her.

'Hi, Dommo, what's on?'

'Hello, Jessie,' he said. 'I just came to pick up something...'

'Same here,' she said, thinking that his voice sounded strange.

He stared at her as though unsure what to say or do next, then said, 'Well, see you tomorrow, then,' and went over to his car.

She watched as he drove off, then used her card key to get in. She hadn't left anything behind, she'd been trying to contact Tom all day and had come to the centre on the off-chance he was here.

She walked into Blood Issue and Arthur nearly levitated.

'What's going on, Arthur?'

'Nothin' ... nothin's goin' on.'

'Dominic looks at me like a ghost and you jump like a scalded kangaroo... 'What was he doing here, anyway?'

Arthur didn't reply and she said, 'Well, Arthur?'

'I called 'im in,' he said at last.

'Why?'

''Cos that government bloke was sniffin' round 'is lab.'

'What government bloke – d'you mean Mr Jones?'

'Yeah...'

'Is he here now?'

'Dominic said 'e sent 'im away with a flea in his ear.'

That didn't sound much like the Jones Jessie knew and loved... She went quickly to her office to get the key to the Micro Lab – it wasn't in the key box, nor the master key she normally kept there.

She ran down to Medlar's office, found his, then ran to Microbiology...

Her eyes widened as she opened the door and took in the scene. The floor was covered in blood and glass, behind which stood Tom Jones, naked, dripping, his hair plastered to his scalp.

'What on earth are you doing?' she heard herself say.

Tom tried to cover himself with his hands. 'For G-God's sake f-find me a t-towel,' he chattered, and she realised he was shivering uncontrollably.

She stepped round the mess on the floor, opened a cupboard next to the cubicle and pulled several out. He snatched one and wrapped it round his midriff while she draped another over his shoulders.

'What's going on?' she tried again. She looked round. 'What's this mess, was it Dominic...?'

'He-he-he chucked b-blood over me...'

'Why?'

''Cos I'm scared of it...' His eyes rolled round at her and she realised that he wasn't

317

joking, that he was terrified.

'But why? I mean why did he do it?' she added, seeing the ambiguity of the question.

'P-please, c-can I have some immuno-globulin for AIDS?'

'You're not going to get AIDS from this.'

'M-my brother did...'

She stared at him.

'He-he was haemophiliac and he died of AIDS.'

She said, 'If he was haemophiliac, he'd have had blood from thousands of different people...' He was looking so utterly wretched that, without thinking, she put her arm round him. 'There're only a hundred or so here. We'll test them all, but I promise you won't get AIDS.'

He didn't say anything and she said, 'Why did Dominic do this to you?'

'He-he killed Goring, and Verity... I must tell Bennett.'

Jessie's mouth hung open and she shook her head from side to side. 'Dominic? I don't believe you. *Why...?*'

'T-take too long now... Please, f-find me some clothes.'

She saw that his own were covered in blood. 'I think there're some in the drivers' room.' She found another towel and draped it over him. 'You get yourself dry while I look.' Was this really the same Jones that had terrorised her in her house?

After she'd gone, Tom stared at his clothes – his underpants wouldn't have blood on them, would they?

He finished drying himself and pulled them on. He couldn't stop shaking.

She came back in with a dark jacket and trousers and a pullover. 'Are you dry yet?'

'Think so. Ha-has my shirt got blood on it?'

She turned it over. 'Yes.'

He pulled on the clothes she'd brought, which were all a size too large, then his own socks and shoes. She helped him up. They skirted the mess on the floor, then Jessie locked the door and they started back up the corridor.

'But *why?*' Jessie burst out, unable to restrain herself. 'Why did Dominic kill them?'

Tom tried to drag his thoughts together. 'He-he was the one who shat on you, he-he was Goring's spy.'

They reached her office and he slumped on to her chair. 'He thought Goring was pinching his research, so he got him in here and shut him in the freezer.'

Her mouth moved as she tried to work it all out. 'But why Verity?'

'He thought she knew and he killed her to keep her quiet.' He picked up the phone and keyed in Bennett's number.

'It seems like your instincts were right,' he

told him when he answered. 'It was Tudor all along.' He explained briefly what had happened. 'And I'm afraid he's got my gun,' he added.

Jessie could hear the explosion at the other end.

'I'm sorry...' Tom said humbly. He listened some more, then turned to Jessie. 'D'you know the make and number of his car?'

She found it and he relayed it back.

'Any idea of where he might go?'

'France,' she said without hesitation.

'Why?'

'He's part French. He's bilingual and got family over there.'

Tom passed the information over and Bennett swore again. 'So that's a dozen different ports he could be making for – not to mention the Tunnel. How long's he been gone?'

Tom looked at his watch. 'Half an hour, maybe three-quarters.'

'So if there's a ferry going from here, he could already be on it.' He paused. 'I'll get on to them now. You and Miss Pengellis had better come down to the station.'

'He's mad at you,' Jessie said as he put down the phone.

'You could say that.' He told her what they were supposed to do. 'But I'm not going anywhere till I've had a coffee and a smoke.'

She took him to the drivers' room and put on the kettle.

'Not that I'm ungrateful,' Tom said, 'but is there a shirt here? This jersey's itching me like hell.'

She rummaged around till she'd found him one, then made coffee.

'Milk and no sugar, isn't it?'

'You've got a good memory.'

'There are some things you don't forget,' she said drily.

Tom smiled sheepishly, then said, 'Do me another favour? Get me my cheroots...'

He put the shirt on while she was gone, then cupped his hands round the hot coffee mug until she came back.

'Recovered?' She handed him his cheroots.

He nodded as he lit one.

'How did you find out it was Dominic?'

He told her about his trip to Poole, but again leaving out that he'd suspected her. Instead he said, 'I'm sorry I was a bit rough when we met.'

She stubbed out the cigarette she'd been smoking. 'D'you want another coffee?'

'Please.'

She got up to make it. 'That night,' she began with her back to him, 'that Friday...' she told him about the state she'd been in and the hashish Verity had given her. 'When it wore off and I realised what had happened, I just had to get out ... but then, after she told the police I'd been with her all night, I had to pretend to go along with her.'

'Which is what she intended.'

She turned, put the coffee down in front of him and took another cigarette. 'You say that, but I still feel guilty – as though I'm part responsible for her death.'

'Well, don't,' said Tom. 'She didn't deserve to be killed the way she was, but she did take advantage of you when you were vulnerable.'

She smiled at him wanly. 'As you said yourself, she seduced me.'

Her face dimpled as she smiled, her dark eyes grew huge and he felt himself drawn into them again. When she'd found him naked, he'd thought she was the most wondrous thing he'd ever seen, and when she'd put her arm round him, he'd felt like crying...

He smiled back at her now. 'I'm not sure whether doping comes under the heading of seduction.' He found himself wishing he had longer to get to know her, realised it was probably as well that he didn't.

He tried to fill in a few more gaps for her as they finished their coffee, then said, 'I suppose we'd better go and report to His Nibs.'

As they drove away from the centre in the Vectra, a Mondeo with a blue lamp emerged from the underground park about fifty yards ahead of them and started down the hill.

'One of ours,' Jessie said. Then, 'I didn't see any driver come in, did you?'

Tom said slowly, 'But you saw Dominic driving away in his car?'

'Yes...'

'What's to have stopped him driving down there and swapping cars?' The Mondeo went under a street lamp. 'Is it him? Can you recognise him?'

'I think so...'

'I'll get a bit closer.'

'He'll see us... It's him, I'm sure it is. What are we going to do?'

'I don't want to lose him. Are there any phone boxes around?'

'Why?'

'I'll drop you off and you can phone the police.'

'But you said you didn't want to lose him.'

'I'll leave you and follow him.'

'He'll notice.'

'Not necessarily.'

He slowed down, allowing a couple of cars to get between them at the roundabout at the bottom of the hill.

She said, 'You're going to try and stop him on your own, aren't you?'

He didn't reply and she said, 'It's not worth it, Tom.' It was the first time she'd used his Christian name.

'Look for a phone box.'

But like policemen when you really need them, there weren't any.

Dominic turned right while the other cars went straight on, so they were directly behind him again. Tom hung back, allowed another car to filter in from the right, then Dominic turned right again. They followed ... he turned left...

'I think he's seen us,' Tom said.

'No, I think he's going to the marina,' Jessie said.

They glanced at each other.

'He hasn't got a boat, has he?'

'I don't think so.'

'He hasn't had the time to arrange a pick-up or anything like that.'

'But he must have known the risk when you went to East Dorset.'

'But he can't have actually *known*...'

'He might ... what if Tony Chase rang him?'

Myriad thoughts flashed and flickered through Tom's mind. *He'll see us any minute if he hasn't already ... but he can't get away if we give the police his number ... or can he? What if he is meeting a boat here? He's armed, with my gun... I can't risk Jessie... But if he is meeting a boat, he could get away... My responsibility to stop him... He nearly killed Holly, could've been Hal as well...*

The lights ahead changed and Dominic

slowed down. Tom said, 'I'll drop you here.'

'What are you going to do?'

'Just get out of the car.'

'No...'

There might not be another chance... 'Hang on then,' he said, and put his foot down. *Hit him hard enough to stun him but not shove him out into the traffic...*

The Vectra leapt forward. *Hit him at an angle, spin him...* The Mondeo expanded, filled their screen ... at the last moment, he twitched the wheel, ploughed into the Mondeo's nearside lights. They were catapulted forward, then the bag ballooned, forced the air from Tom's lungs. *Not hard enough...* 'Stay here,' he shouted as the bag collapsed. *I didn't hit him hard enough...* He felt for the door handle, stumbled out and ran at the Mondeo ... but Dominic had already tumbled out, Tom's gun in his hand. He fired, missed... Tom was moving, thinking in slow motion... *I'm not going to make it...*

'*Dommo!*' Jessie shouted.

Dominic swivelled round, fired again. Tom leapt at him, scythed the edge of his hand into his wrist – *God, don't let me be too late.* The gun dropped on to the road and skittered under the car.

The lights changed – red, red-amber, green – as Dominic turned and lashed at Tom in a blind fury. He knew he wasn't going to get away now, but he wanted to hurt him, smash him, kill him if he could...

A car behind hooted as Jessie reached under the Mondeo for the gun and ran round to them.

Tom felt himself weakening as he warded off the blows. The kicks Dominic had landed earlier had taken their toll and Jessie could see that he was losing, that Dominic would overpower him any moment – then what? The gun weighed heavy in her hands ... *I can't, I can't...*

The lights changed again – green, amber, red. Tom knew he'd have Dominic's hands round his throat any second. He took a deliberate step back, then lunged forward with all his strength as Dominic came for him. His right fist caught him on the point of the jaw with both their weights behind it, and Dominic crumpled into the road.

'Shee-it...!' Tom staggered back against the Mondeo, gasping, shaking and nursing his hand.

'Are you all right?'

He heaved in a breath. 'Never felt better.'

After a moment, he looked up at her. 'Thanks, Jessie ... if you hadn't yelled when you did...'

'That was a hell of a risk you took.'

'Yeah. We got him though, didn't we?'

Two or three people had got out of their cars and were hovering nervously around.

Tom said wearily to none of them in particular, 'If any of you have got a mobile phone, call the police, would you?'

'I already have,' said one of them.

27

'I suppose,' Lady Margaret said after a pause, 'that it comes down to how, exactly, one defines corruption.'

Tom and Marcus waited.

She continued, 'If Adam Goring had kept East Dorset open instead of Tamar solely to provide his son-in-law with the research post, then his actions would have been corrupt. But the fact is, he would have made the same decision anyway.'

'It could be argued,' Marcus said, 'that it made him ... less amenable to discussion.'

'Yes, but with no difference to the eventual outcome. The corruption was theoretical.'

'Theoretical corruption,' Marcus mused. 'An interesting concept. But what about his conversation with Dr Goldman, the one overheard by the Scientific Officer? He was making – if not a virtue out of a necessity, then an uncertainty out of a certainty, for the purpose of putting pressure on Goldman to support his son-in-law. Which is corruption by any definition. Not to mention the matter of the MBE...'

'Well, Dr Goldman certainly won't be getting *that*,' said Lady Margaret. 'The question is whether Dr Derby knew about it.'

Marcus turned to Tom. 'You spoke to him, Tom – what do you think?'

'It can only be an opinion, but no, I don't think he did.'

'How certain are you about that?' Lady Margaret asked.

'As certain as I can be,' Tom said. 'For what it's worth, I was rather impressed by Dr Derby... I think that Dr Goring was probably right about his qualities.'

'I think I may have a word with Dr Goldman myself,' Lady Margaret said ominously. 'The matter of the research post could be held in abeyance for a few months, and afterwards, Dr Derby could be encouraged to apply.'

Tom said, 'If you speak to Dr Goldman, isn't there a risk that he might guess where the information came from and ... take it out on the person involved?'

'That will not happen,' said Lady Margaret firmly. 'I suppose,' she continued after another pause, 'that it could have been worse. Adam doesn't exactly come out smelling of violets, but he was clearly nothing like so corrupt as that woman,

Pengellis, implied.'

Which doesn't sound so good for Jessie, Tom thought. 'But given the information she had, it wasn't an unreasonable conclusion to reach.'

'I'm afraid we must differ there, Mr Jones – she should have checked her facts.'

'Difficult to see how–'

'Besides which, it was quite unforgivable for her to go public in that way... Adam was certainly right about the Tamar centre itself being a nest of corruption. One way and another, this has been a deeply depressing and unedifying business.'

'Yes,' agreed Marcus, 'it has...'

'But,' prompted Lady M. 'Your tone suggests a "but", Mr Evans.'

'It was an "and" actually,' Marcus said. 'And unnecessary, I was going to say.'

'Explain,' she said, her own tone ominously tinged once more.

Marcus seemed to come to a decision. 'As I understand it, the purpose of this reorganisation is to save ten million a year. I would suggest that this affair alone has cost a significant chunk of that.'

She reflected, then said, 'Your sums may well be right, but the purpose of the reorganisation is *not* just to save ten million a year. It's to create a more efficient service with year on year savings. A different matter altogether.'

You're on a minefield, Tom thought. *Let her have the last word...* but Marcus for once had abandoned his usual emollience.

'I'm sure you're right in that the closures will provide savings, but we do come down to the old chestnut of how much a person's life is worth. If Tamar Transfusion Centre hadn't been there, at least four people involved in that car crash would have died.'

'That also has to be a matter of opinion,' she said. 'Tamar will continue to have a blood bank in the hospital, and any extra blood needed can be flown from East Dorset or Bristol.'

'Which takes time.'

She said deliberately, 'I had hoped it wouldn't be necessary to remind you of this, but the police feel that it was Mr Jones's impetuosity in taking on Tudor instead of going to them, as well as his carelessness with his gun, that very nearly *did* lead to fatalities.'

So they *had* complained to her, Marcus thought. He'd tried to persuade them not to.

'That is a gross distortion of the facts,' he said evenly. 'Mr Jones didn't "take on" Tudor, he went to the centre to find the evidence he needed against him, evidence he was going to present to the police. Unfortunately, the lab orderly telephoned Tudor, who came in and found him looking for it.'

'You and the police will have to agree to differ on that,' Lady M. said with an air of finality. 'And now, fascinating though this discussion has been, I really must ask you to excuse me.'

She saw them to her door, thanked them again for their help and said goodbye.

When they were outside, Tom said, 'What on earth made you take *her* on like that? I've never thought of you as the *hara-kiri* type.'

'I suppose not.' Marcus sighed. 'It's just that I think that those in their isolated power towers should be told about the consequences of their actions occasionally.'

'You'll never change their minds.'

'I know that.'

'And they do tend to remember the names of those who did the telling.'

'Yes. They should still be told, though.'

After the car crash, the centre's staff were fêted by the media as heroes and heroines for two days, and then it was all forgotten. The centre closed six months later.

Most of the staff were found jobs in other parts of the country. Some, like Paul and Ashley and Maria, accepted them, while others, like Adrian, preferred to stay and take their chances in Tamar. Medlar took early retirement. Bennett forgot about the marijuana and Sarah found another supplier. She is aware that Medlar and Maria

331

maintain an occasional relationship, but doesn't think too much about it.

Jessie, as Dominic had predicted, found herself unemployable in the Health Service. She went home to Cornwall to help her parents run their antiques business. She is already something of an expert.

The publishers hope that this book has given you enjoyable reading. Large Print Books are especially designed to be as easy to see and hold as possible. If you wish a complete list of our books please ask at your local library or write directly to:

Magna Large Print Books
Magna House, Long Preston,
Skipton, North Yorkshire.
BD23 4ND

This Large Print Book for the partially sighted, who cannot read normal print, is published under the auspices of

THE ULVERSCROFT FOUNDATION

THE ULVERSCROFT FOUNDATION

... we hope that you have enjoyed this Large Print Book. Please think for a moment about those people who have worse eyesight problems than you ... and are unable to even read or enjoy Large Print, without great difficulty.

You can help them by sending a donation, large or small to:

**The Ulverscroft Foundation,
1, The Green, Bradgate Road,
Anstey, Leicestershire, LE7 7FU,
England.**
or request a copy of our brochure for more details.

The Foundation will use all your help to assist those people who are handicapped by various sight problems and need special attention.

Thank you very much for your help.